# MR. HAT TRICK

AINSLEY BOOTH

SADIE HALLER

BOOTH HALLER BOOKS

# DEDICATION

*For our Frisky Beavers*

## ABOUT THIS BOOK

Sasha:
He's a player. End of story.
I'm not interested.

Tate:
Something about her lights me up inside. Makes me reckless.
So what if she doesn't like me?
I like her—a lot.
And once I turn on the charm, she doesn't stand a chance.

Sasha:
Fine. Maybe we can use each other for sex.
And the occasional late night conversation that nobody else will
understand. That doesn't mean anything…

THE PLAY-BY-PLAY:

- They don't like each other, but they both like sex—and
  watching

- They have more in common with each other than they want to admit
- Sometimes the best fuck buddies are friends, too



- This is a hockey romance heavy on body-checking and double entendres, and light on ice-time. Let's call it hockey-adjacent. We make up for that with angsty fighting, happy screwing, and a love story so secret even the main characters don't see it coming.

1

SASHA

*end of August*
*Ottawa*

A STICKY, oppressive heat wave has taken hold of the city. Being outside for any length of time is cruel, and I've just been dumped two blocks from my apartment by a cabbie who definitely did not get a tip.

There's a very real chance I might wilt before I get home. I set my sights on the coffee shop ahead, because an iced latte just my might save my life.

At least I'm done people-ing for the day. I've just come from the hospital where all of my friends had gathered to welcome into the world a brand-new baby boy.

All of my friends except one, not that Tate Nilsson is my friend. But he's been a pretty constant part of our social circle for the last year, and yet when the telephone tree spread the news that Violet was in labour, he was nowhere to be found.

So when I pull open the door to the coffee shop and find him taking a selfie with two teenage girls—gross—I'm totally ready to lay a strip into him. Who the hell does he think he is?

An NHL All-Star, the captain of the Ottawa Senators, and unrepentant, self-described manwhore, that's who.

But when he follows me outside, he says the one thing that could soften my heart towards him.

"I was traded an hour ago to the Vancouver Lumberjacks."

There aren't many excuses that would have me feeling sorry for him, but no wonder he's trying to assuage his stupid male ego by taking pictures with fans—he's just been dealt a career gut punch.

This is not a conversation to be had in public.

*You don't need to have it at all.* Except I do. I'm not going to leave him to his own devices to deal with this. If I do that, he'll probably wind up sleeping with someone who's bad news, or worse.

I grab his hand—ignoring how good it feels, because gross—and drag him around the corner to my apartment building.

He blessedly stays quiet. He's not normally a private person, but I guess making a scene on a day like today might not be great for his image.

And I'm *so* not down for being linked to his over-the-top public persona.

At all.

My kindness has limits, and they're bound by the gossip blogs on one side and sports talk radio on the other.

I curl up in my favourite chair and Tate takes the couch.

When he doesn't say anything, I decide to storm ahead. That's kind of my thing in general. "The Lumberjacks?" We were literally just with the owner of the Lumberjacks at my best friend Ellie's wedding in June. I know business is a whole separate thing, but that feels kind of weird. "That's Jack Benton's team. Did you know this was coming at the wedding?"

He shakes his head. "No clue. And he'd already sold the team. This decision was made quite recently, too. It's a long, complicated, stupid story."

"When do you go?"

"Soon. I need to find a place to stay, because I won't like whatever hotel the team has arranged. I have a month before training starts, but I want to find a house."

"Do you need help with that? Maybe you could stay at Gavin's place." I snap my fingers together. "No, you'll want to be closer to the arena, right?"

"Sasha."

"Of course, you won't want to buy right away, so maybe we can find you a sublet."

"Sasha."

"And—"

"Hey, Hot Stuff, settle down for a second. I don't need you to play real estate agent for me, but I appreciate the offer of help."

My mouth drops open. *Hot Stuff?* And he's clearly not coping well with this, of course he needs my help.

"What I really needed was someone to hear it from me first. To say it out loud. I'm being traded. Now that I've done that, I can move forward. It'll be fine."

Oh, maybe he doesn't need my help. Damn it. I'm good at being helpful. I'm less good with sticky emotions. "Right."

After a long stretch of silence, he gives me a sideways glance. "Sorry for calling you Hot Stuff."

"It's better than calling me a bitch." Which he almost did when I snapped at him about hanging on the teenagers.

"I stopped myself."

"It was in your head, though."

"Not really. No, seriously, I don't think you're…Jesus, Sasha, I promise you I don't think you're a bitch, not in a bad way. I think you're made of steel and you fucking turn me on like crazy when you pop your claws out."

I open my mouth to snap at him again, then stop. Wait. What?

My eyes bug out of my head. I turn Tate on? Tate, who goes to sex clubs and lounges like a king. Tate, who probably picks up puck bunnies by the half-dozen for adorable bunny orgies. He thinks I'm made of steel?

I turn him on?

We exchange wordless looks, because seriously, what the fuck?

But he recovers sooner. "Ignore me. I tend to just say shit like that."

That's a lie. He's totally lying, I can see it on his face. And in that moment, a few things slam together.

The memory of sitting next to Tate on a couch in Max's basement for the kinky holiday play party. What that felt like, the sexuality that radiated off of him.

My general dislike of everything that he is, but my personal, grudging like for who he is. I've never had a hate fuck, because principles and all that, but...Tate could be that guy. Check off that fantasy.

Add in the fact that he's leaving the city, and I hear myself offer him a single night before I can stop the words from sliding out. "One night."

He does a double take, because really, who saw that coming? Not me. But his double take comes with a side of guarded interest. "Pardon?"

Oh yeah, hockey boy. I glance out the window and school my features. Can't be too excited about this. I'm a bitch, after all. And a whole night is excessive. "One afternoon."

"I don't follow."

If he's going to play hard to get, I'm out. "Never mind."

He grins. Right, he likes the claws. And he's not playing hard to get any longer. "You're talking about sex? I'm in."

I hold up my finger. "I want it officially noted that I still don't like you."

"Noted."

"And you're okay with that?"

"Hot Stuff, I'm more than okay with that. If you want to tell me that you hate me while I'm balls deep inside you, you'll feel just how much I don't mind that kind of smack talk."

"This is a terrible idea," I whisper.

He stands up and peels off his t-shirt.

Okay, no, it's a crazy good idea. I point toward my bedroom. "Just this one time, you understand?"

"Perfectly." He gives me a wicked, wolfish grin that lights up his eyes. We definitely don't need to exchange any lingering looks. I drop my gaze to his body instead. Good lord, he's unreal. His torso is all cut lines and hard ridges. When he turns around, his back is more of the same sculpted perfection, and my tongue slides out of my mouth all on its own.

I want to lick him.

I want to bite him.

I want to ride him hard and shake this secret crush I've been harbouring since Christmas, when all those muscles kept shifting next to me on a couch as we watched people get flogged at a kink party.

And more than anything, I want to get up close and personal with the hard, straining bulge I notice out of the corner of my eye.

"Where do you want me?" he drawls as he stops beside the bed. "And what do you want to do?"

"That's good," I say, my heart hammering in my throat. I stop a few feet back and look at him again. Tate is *not* my type. He's big and brawny and full of ego. I bet he doesn't have a sensitive bone in his entire body. "And I want to have sex."

"That's a big category of activity."

Right. He's into some kinky shit. "Uh, just sex. But nothing boring. I like…athletic sex."

His eyes darken. "Got it. Interesting, vigorous fucking."

That sounds perfect. I lick my lips, and he doesn't miss it.

"You want a taste of something, Sasha?"

Dirty, twisted heat blooms low in my belly. "Maybe."

I get another wolfish grin at that, and he unbuttons his cargo shorts. They drop to the floor, and he steps out of them. Long, solid legs. The muscles of his thighs are clearly defined even under a light, golden dusting of hair.

And as I drag my gaze up his body, there's that bulge again, obscenely stretching out the front of grey boxer briefs.

I lick my lips. Again.

He groans. "Do that again on your knees."

I'm not going to pretend I don't want that as much as he does. I drop in front of him, and he helps me tug his waistband down.

His cock is hard and heavy already, a straining weight in my hand as I give him a first squeeze. *What do you like, Tate?*

Luckily for me, he's not shy about vocalizing anything.

"Yeah, hold me nice and tight. Gah. Just like that. Fucking hell, Sasha. Stop licking your lips unless they're against my dick." He chuckles as I do it again, but seriously, I'm excited about tasting him.

That's kind of different.

I like sex as much as the next person, but I tend to be kind of bossy. The best sex I've ever had has been when I'm in charge and the person I'm with is a quick study.

I don't remember the last time I *wanted* like this. Wanted a cock in my mouth, hands in my hair. Maybe some thrusting I don't expect… And now my mouth is watering again.

I don't test his limits. I lean in and give him that lick instead, wide and wet, all the way around the head of his shaft. He tastes clean and masculine, and I breathe in the scent of his skin. It's always good when you like the smell of a person, and the faint edge of musk and heat rising from his body swirls into my brain in a yummy way.

I wrap my fist around his heavy length and stroke him against my parted lips. I bring him into my mouth, one slow jerk at a time, until I've enveloped the thick head of his dick with my lips.

Then I swallow.

He shouts in surprise, and his hands tangle in my hair.

I work my tongue against the underneath of his erection, tasting him as my hand moves faster, slicked now with my spit. I jack and suck him at the same time, bumping my lips into my fingers in a way that I know makes him feel like the king of the world.

It's almost predictable how he starts groaning the dirty talk to me. "Take it all. Yeah, just like that. Your mouth is so fucking hot. You're a good cocksucker, aren't you? Fucking full of surprises, Sasha. Love that. Ah, fuck yeah. Your tongue. So…good…" But then he surprises me. "Fuck. Slow down, tiger. Make this last. I gotta get my mouth on you. Fuck."

He hisses and fists his hand tight in the loose strands of my hair, then he growls an apology before gathering it up all up in a ponytail, which he uses to tug me back.

My lips slide off him with a wet pop, and I chase a bead of pre-come that forms at his slit as he holds me a few inches away from his cock. "Why'd you stop me?" I whisper playfully, batting my eyelashes up at him.

"You want my come in your mouth?"

Yes. "Sure."

He smirks down at me. "Maybe later. Up."

Oh, he's so bossy. I roll my eyes as I stand, and he lets go of my hair, only to pull me close. His mouth covers mine, going from zero to kisses-that-taste-like-cock-sixty in a heartbeat. He presses hard into my mouth, his tongue fucking against mine. Tasting me where I've just tasted him, where I've swallowed his pre-come. I can still feel where his cock bumped against the top of my mouth, against my tongue, and now he's there too, savagely marking those same spots with rough licks that make me squirm and want to climb up his body so he can fuck my pussy, too.

"Condoms," I breathe as I break away. "Bedside table."

"Excellent." He pushes me onto the bed and yanks the drawer

open. He grabs the box and rains a handful of condoms down on my belly. "That'll get us started."

He stands at the side of the bed for a moment, looking down at me with a fondly dirty smirk on his face. His cock is still hard, standing obscenely out from his body, and the whole scene makes me hot and achy. His eyes darken as he reaches for the button on my shorts. "Time for you to get naked."

I couldn't agree more. I shiver as he strips me. Panties go with the shorts, and his eyes hood as he leans in and presses a hot, wet kiss to the bare skin of my mound.

"You are so fucking hot," he whispers, his breath licking against my skin. "From the inside out, you're full of surprises."

He works his way up my torso, pushing up my shirt with each hungry, pulling kiss. He sucks at the skin on my belly until I arch beneath him, then he bares more and more of me until my shirt is gone and then his mouth is on my breasts, biting at my bra and sucking on my nipples through the silk.

"Rip the bra and I'll kill you," I whisper.

He chuckles. "Noted."

"I'm serious."

"I get that." Bracing one hand beside my head, he levers up with ease, and smiles down at me. "Like I said, you being a spitfire turns me on."

"Tate—" I cut myself off, and he makes an approving sound. He holds my gaze, and slowly I find myself melting for him. I don't want to be an ice queen today. Although spitfire has a nice ring to it. I give him a slow, real smile. "It's a front clasp. Just FYI."

"Excellent." Sliding my bra strap down, he leans down and kisses my shoulder. His nimble fingers pop the clasp on my bra and my breasts spring free.

He groans and cups my flesh, his touch surprisingly gentle. "Underneath it all, you're soft as can be, aren't you?"

I smile again. "Lies."

He circles my nipple with his finger, his expression lust-drunk and careless as he flicks a glance up at my face. "Nah. You're silk beneath steel. And if I'm the only one who can see that, then I'm fucking lucky."

"Enough," I whisper. Enough poetry, enough sweetness. I arch my back, desperate now for his mouth to replace his too-gentle touch. I need a hard suck, something—

He ducks his head and closes his teeth about my flesh.

"Ah!" I'm startled, that's all. As I gasp, I realize it doesn't hurt. But still... "You bit me. Hard."

"You liked it."

"We didn't discuss biting."

"Mmm. Right. We should. How do you feel about biting?"

"I like it."

He laughs. "Okay. Now can we discuss a ball gag?" He swings his head away from my swatting hand, then catches my wrist and pulls my fingers to his mouth. He bites them, too. Just enough snap to send shivers down my spine, but nothing else.

"Is sexy biting your superpower?"

He grins. "One of them."

"Show me the rest."

Returning to my breasts, he sucks on my nipples until they're swollen and hard, then he covers those peaks with his hands and rolls me over. Still squeezing them, he teases the nipples between his fingers as he bites and licks his way down my spine.

When he lets go of my breasts, it's only so he can squeeze my ass instead. The hard press of his fingers sends a hot, skittering tremble under my skin.

That's nothing compared to how I feel when he slides his tongue down the cleft between my cheeks. I groan and bury my face in the pillow as he eats me out. Definitely a superpower. His mouth is everywhere, his tongue firm and wide and hungry as he licks everywhere between my legs.

My thighs are shaking by the time he flips me over again, and

I scramble back up the bed so I can have something to lean against as he dips his head between my legs again.

His thick, wavy brown hair glints with natural highlights in the afternoon sun streaming in my window. I reach for him, and he lifts his face just enough to give me a sloppy, happy smile.

"Ready to get fucked, Sasha?"

So ready. "Bring it on."

He hauls me back down the bed, my legs splayed wide on either side of him. He stares my swollen, soaked pussy as he rolls on a condom, then he palms my hips and hitches my lower body up.

I secretly love how he can manhandle me with ease.

The head of his cock lands heavy against my clit, making me jerk because I'm sensitive now. Sensitive and ready and aching to be filled. "Now," I plead.

He grins and notches us together.

Time seems to pause as I follow his gaze to where we're connected now. The tip of his cock hidden inside my body, the thick, long stretch of his erection a promise of more to come. Athletic sex. Ha. I had no idea what I was asking for. Every muscle in his body is locked and flexed, ready to pump into me as soon as a starter's pistol fires, or I say the magic word, whatever that might be.

He pushes in another half inch, and I groan.

"You want this?" he purrs the question, his gaze hooded behind heavy eyelids as he looks down at me.

"Yes." I stretch my arms above my head. "I want you, Tate."

Those are the magic words. He thrusts hard, filling me in a single pump of his hips. He falls forward, covering me with his body, too, and then it's on. He's fluid and intense, a rolling thunder of sex and sensation. My legs crawl up his body, my thighs gripping his waist as he moves above me. Thighs, pelvis—cock, hard and deep, nailing every single pleasure point inside my body—abs, chest, arms. Over and over again, he moves his body in a wave that drives his cock into me, then out again, and it's all I can do to hold on.

I curve my hands over his shoulders, sinking my nails into his back. He grunts as I squeeze, and I make myself let go.

"Sorry," I gasp, and he bites my ear.

"Never be sorry about leaving your mark on me," he growls, his breath hot against my neck. "Claw me up all you want."

That's a hell of an offer. I clutch my arms around him again and do just that, and as he slams into me, I know he was right to grab a fistful of condoms.

I'm not going to be done with just one orgasm.

And since we can't do this again—ever, no matter what—I'm going to have to make sure we go through the entire pack before I kick his tight, perfect ass out the door at the end of the night.

2

———————

TATE

*beginning of October, two months later*
*Vancouver*

TONIGHT IS THE SEASON OPENER, my tenth in the NHL.

Game Day.

For more than twenty years, the fall has meant the start of a new season of hockey. For the last decade, that's been in the NHL, and for the last six years, I wore the C on my jersey as I skated onto the ice with the Ottawa Senators.

Not today, though.

My move out to the west coast has been quite the news story, despite my best efforts to be excited about it in public. Unfortunately, actions speak louder than words and I'm struggling on the ice. I've been here for eight weeks now, and the media is still all over the fact my adjustment has been rocky to say the least.

We've got an evening game against Calgary, so I sleep in a bit, then watch the news while I roll out my muscles and eat breakfast. I need to be at the Lumberjacks' arena, affectionately called The Pulpmill, by nine-thirty for our morning skate.

Back in Ottawa, I'd already be there by now, shooting the shit with my guys and watching tape in the viewing room. But here in Vancouver, the locker room doesn't have that same jovial vibe. Everyone is tense and I don't know why. I don't think it's me, but it will be if I don't get my game together soon.

I'm slowly packing up my bag to head to the rink when my phone lights up.

**Sasha: Kick some ass tonight.**

I stare at my phone. After eight weeks of silence, she's the last person I expected to hear from today. I scroll back in the message history. Six texts from me to her without any response. The first two are kind of cringe-worthy in hindsight.

How was I supposed to know she'd go radio-silent after we slept together?

*Because she has standards and you have, to put it mildly, a reputation she wants nothing to do with.*

Yeah, I should have seen it coming a mile away that fucking Sasha would be a disaster. After the fact, of course—the actual fucking was spectacular.

Hence my reaching out to her for a repeat, which she'd ignored.

She'd also dodged my text to say goodbye before I left Ottawa, and four more messages I'd sent her since I'd arrived here in Vancouver. Funny shit I knew she'd secretly find funny.

And now, out of the blue, she's sending me a good luck message?

Oh, it's fucking *on.*

**Tate: You want me to be thinking about you when I score my first goal?**
**Sasha: Your first goal? Of how many?**
**Tate: Two today. And I'll take that as a yes, you want me to think about you.**

**Sasha: This was a mistake.**
**Tate: Miss you too, tiger.**

She sends a picture of her middle finger. I want to lick it.

This is me in a nutshell—super serious about hockey, and a bit of a prick about everything else in my life. Especially Sasha Brewster.

I probably need to get laid. Two months is a long time in Tate Land to go without the sweet, tight welcome of a hot pussy.

But as long as I look at the texts to Sasha—and now the texts back from her—I won't be picking up anyone else. That's not how I roll.

So instead of thinking ahead to celebrating my first game as a Lumberjack with a random hottie, I have a quick wank in the shower as I remember Sasha crawling down my body, the tip of her tongue pressed to the corner of her mouth as her lips part.

Her mouth on my cock.

The low, hungry moans she made as she swallowed around my heavy length.

No, nothing Sasha's done with me has been a mistake. Not texting, and not our afternoon together in August.

I have to get to the rink. I can't think about that finger, or the blurry smile I could just catch the edge of in the background of the picture.

I can't think about Sasha right now.

But later?

I'll do a hell of a lot of thinking later. I turn off my phone and tuck it away.

It's a ten minute drive from my new condo to the Lumber-jacks arena.

Fifteen if there's traffic, which I don't mind. An extra five minutes to get my head in the game has never hurt. I had a longer drive in Ottawa.

I'll add that to the short list of things I like about having been traded to Vancouver.

Short commute.

Mountain views.

A young, hungry team eager to win the Cup.

That last point should be reason enough, but after being blindsided with this trade, from a team that went all the way to game seven of the division final last year…I feel the need to have some other advantages here, too.

Because if the Sens get there this year, and I'm left out in the cold, that's going to be a punch in the gut all over again.

That kind of negative talk is completely unhelpful, of course. I know that. I crank up the raggaeton on the stereo in my still-got-that-new-car-smell SUV. I got a Land Rover for out here. Back home I've got a pick up, but I wanted something different. I had them install the same audio deck and speaker system, though.

I like my music. Gets me in the zone for a game.

Gets me in the zone for kink, too.

*Stop thinking about Sasha.*

We hadn't even gone there, though. Our single afternoon had just been two people, two bodies, and a shit tonne of pleasure.

But we've got some shared experiences with kink, too. Last Christmas, she sat next to me on a couch at my friend Max's place during his holiday play party, and as she watched my buddy Brandon flog someone on the St. Andrew's Cross, I watched Sasha.

Wide eyes, swollen lips, chest rising and falling in shallow, horny breaths.

*Stop thinking—*

Thank Christ for short drives. I slide into the underground garage at the arena. As it is already, I'm going to need to compose myself so I don't stroll into the Lumberjacks locker room with a semi.

The cold trickle of doubt that slides down my spine at the

thought of dressing for this game does the trick. Arousal vanquished.

Despite my cocky promises to Sasha, I'm not as confident as I should be right now. It's been a long time since I've needed to admit that to myself.

A few other guys are arriving at the same time, and I give them silent nods as we head inside. Front office staff go out of their way to give us big smiles and high-fives—because for everyone else, today is like Christmas Eve. The start of something really special.

Out in the arena, every seat will be draped with a Lumber-jacks t-shirt. Every fan arriving will get an axe-shaped noise-maker to chop in the air as they cheer us on.

And in our dressing room, I'll find my uniform waiting for me, prepared with care by the equipment guys.

It's game day, and I'm not sure where my head is at. Something needs to change.

3

# SASHA

*Ottawa*

I WATCH the Lumberjacks season opener on my laptop, in bed. I cringe and wince and bite my fist, and when it ends, I pause the feed on a shot of Tate—head lowered, face twisted in anger.

I'm not sure if I want to yell at him or console him. Is it possible to do both at the same time? But I can't do either, because even though I subscribed to NHL TV so I could watch Tate's games from across the country, I'll never tell him—or anyone else—just how closely I'm following the former Senators captain with his new team.

I'm trying to avoid the press coverage, and just watch him. But it's hard to listen to the announcers talk about whether or not the critical reception he's received in the Vancouver papers is justified, given his wobbly performance in both the pre-season and tonight's game.

*Maybe if people gave him some space, he'd adjust faster.* But I know that's not how it works at his level. He's a pro. And not just a pro, but a top-earning star—so he's expected to be a top-producer of goals and assists, no matter the conditions.

There's no room for sentiment in the NHL. Loyalty is misplaced and when you least expect it, they'll blindside you with a cross-country move because of the almighty dollar.

I know all about ruthless business decisions.

I was practically raised in a boardroom. My father took my grandfather's tool-and-die operation and grew it into a multinational automotive parts manufacturing conglomerate. He owns a part of almost every pro sport team in Toronto, and he's as cold-hearted as they come.

I'm cut from exactly the same cloth, and I hate it.

I hate that my father can see those similarities, too. That he's picked me to be his successor, even though I want nothing to do with Brewster Industries.

Besides, I've found other outlets for my business instincts. I'm forging my own path, not that my father knows it. I've gone out of my way to make sure he doesn't. Michael Brewster isn't the only one in the family who knows how to play with numbered companies and shell corporations.

The last thing I do before bed is check my email. My meeting for the morning is still on. Then I click back to the screen shot of Tate's pissed-off mug, and shake my head.

He needs to sort himself out, and he knows it.

A pang of some soft feeling I don't like zips through me, and I squash it.

*That's what happens when you play with fire.* If fire was six-foot-three and two hundred pounds of walking sex.

Tate doesn't need my sympathy. He needs a kick in the ass, but he's going to have to get it from someone who isn't me. Other than the polite best wishes I sent him on opening day, I'm not speaking to the guy.

I wouldn't want him to get the wrong impression about my feelings.

I take one last look at the laptop screen and snap the lid shut.

No. Feelings.

He'll get the wrong impression that I *have* feelings. I'm a Brewster. We don't do that.

———

The next morning, I go for an early run, then shower and blow out my hair. I put on just the right amount of make-up—which isn't much, for this meeting—then slide my laptop and the contracts into my favourite Hermes bag.

I'm going for a drive in the country, but I still want to look every inch the part of a bad-ass silent investor.

The Ottawa Valley is full of small villages that are ripe for development, and I don't mean the overwhelming, soul-destroying construction that my father would put his money into.

I'm all about making the most of what's already there. Today I'm driving to the hamlet of Metcalfe. It's quaint and quiet, and Mabel's office won't change that.

I don't miss that the storefront beside it is empty, as well, and I make a mental note to see who holds that lease.

One of my other investments may need an out-of-town location, too, and it's always good to control who your neighbours are.

Mabel arrives shortly after me. She parks her car behind mine, and the difference is striking. For a two-time Juno winner, she drives a shit car. I want to change that for her, and that's what this meeting is all about.

Mabel Whitaker—Canadian singer and songwriter. It's a sad statement on the music industry that such a talented performer has turned to gaming and app development. Radio's loss is Metcalfe's gain, though. If she likes this building, with its turn-of-the-century charm and oodles of space at a bargain basement price, then she just might start Ottawa's next big tech company in the middle of nowhere.

And I want to be her silent partner.

I wave and give her an enthusiastic smile as she spots me.

"This isn't at all what I was expecting," she says as she joins me on the wraparound verandah. We're still waiting for the real estate agent, so I might as well start with my outside pitch.

I do a quick run down of the benefits, then I acknowledge the drawbacks—distance from the city being the main one—before finishing with the dealmaker fact. "The listed lease price is less than a quarter of any similar space in the city. And I bet we can negotiate that down even further."

"No way," she breathes.

"Yep." I wink at her. "Finding a good real estate deal is kind of my thing."

She laughs. "Isn't your thing supposed to be finishing a PhD?"

I wave my hand. "I do that on Mondays and Tuesdays."

I wouldn't say that to most people. But to the handful of women I partner with in business, it's a selling point. I'm juggling a lot of responsibility, and so can they.

"If you really want to look inside the city limits, I'm down for that, too. But I think you can do something special here. You won't need to limit yourself to one showroom at first. There are four rooms on the second floor just dying to be turned into tricksy puzzles. I know your focus isn't direct entertainment, but you could do something special for the locals and the media. And then it will be even more worth the drive out here for your corporate customers. Build it and they will come—and if you establish yourself as a reason worth looping through Metcalfe, the community will benefit, too, and then you'll have loyal, local customers, too. Loyalty is hard to come by in the city."

She nods. "Okay. I'm officially interested. But I don't want *me* to be the reason why people come here, just to be clear."

"Totally. I get that. When I said 'yourself', I didn't mean Mabel the singer, I meant Mabel the game designer. You'll make a name for Weirdaker Games on its own merits. But, my unsolicited advice is that you should leverage all the tools at your disposal."

She shifts uncomfortably. "The fame thing is a double-edged sword, you know?"

Oh, I know, although my own brush with the spotlight was at the infamous end of the celebrity spectrum years ago.

I think of Tate, more recently, shell-shocked at his trade news. Of how I'd invited him back to my apartment so he could process the news in private, and everything that had happened after that… "I know," I say softly. "And it's totally up to you how you use that or don't. There are a lot of different ways to run a marketing campaign, and I'm not going to meddle in that for you. It's up to you, completely, but I'm happy to be a trusted counsellor as needed. And a part of that is sharing the advice and then letting my opinion go." I wave my hand in the air. "Gone."

The conversation pauses there as the real estate agent arrives in a crunch of tires on gravel. Noisy—something to remember about the verandah. Maybe the parking lot could be paved.

I add that to my mental notes list, too.

The agent introduces himself to Mabel first, then me, then punches in the code to open the door.

My phone vibrates, and I check the screen as I step inside. A message from Tate.

Mabel looks at me. "Do you need a minute?"

I shove my phone back in my bag and shake my head. "No. I'm good. Let's see what we've got here."

4

---

TATE

*Vancouver*

My gut twists as the clock runs down the final seconds of the game.

It's been amateur hour out here tonight.

Even after weeks of pre-season training and play, there is zero fucking synergy between me and my linemates. Every shift is a clusterfuck of one sort or another. So many missed and intercepted passes.

The horn signals the end of the period and the end of the game.

Fucking hell.

It was bad enough losing to Calgary on Saturday in the season opener, but to lose tonight against my old fucking team on home ice is mortifying.

The silent disappointment echoes through the inside of The Pulpmill louder than any cheers ever could. I'm gutted, too, right along with the fans. I'd made a commitment to myself and them that if I didn't get to play with the Senators, I would crush them at every opportunity. And because that's what I'd decided, I had no doubt that's what would happen. I'm cocky like that.

Fucking hubris finally caught up to me. Really, that happened in August, when I was blindsided by the trade, and I'm still reeling from it. Instead of starting the season leading the team of my heart to another chance at the Stanley Cup, I'm stuck on the other side of the country on a team that hasn't made the play-offs in the eight years it's been around.

I can already hear the commentators, and they're not wrong. *Nilsson needs to do something soon to show he's worth that hefty contract he brought with him.*

If I force myself to think about it analytically, the trade was a good one for Ottawa. The Lumberjacks got me and a player to be named later in exchange for their number one overall draft pick. But it was still a slapshot to the balls for my ego. Especially given Ottawa had the chance to pick me in the draft. But in their infinite wisdom, they went with Sam Kettering, a hotshot forward who crashed and burned in his first season.

I push those memories away. They're toxic. I make my way to the dressing room and focus on getting home and away from people. I tell the Lumberjack press office guy I'll take questions as soon as I shower, and I make good on that promise. When I saunter back into the locker room, one towel slung low around my hips and another in my hands—to dry my hair, but also a prop to buy me a second once the vultures descend—I give him the nod and stand in front of my stall.

The first question is, of course, about how it felt to play against the Senators. I turn and stuff the towel in my hands into a nook, ensuring that the question itself doesn't make the video of this. I only want the news to run my answer. "I'm finding my footing here in Vancouver. We've got a lot of strength in our defence—some crazy big guys behind me, which I love. That's where my focus was tonight. We're only two games in. It's a long season. We're figuring out what works. The goal at the top of the second period is an example of that, and obviously, that's where our focus is. On the long season, on getting into the play-offs."

"You didn't answer the question."

I wink and adjust my towel. Buying another beat of time. "How about that, eh? Obviously, I know Ottawa is a well-oiled machine and full props to them for bringing their A game tonight. They clearly tried some new things in pre-season and that worked." Translation: They've moved on from me, and I see that. Not my team anymore.

From behind the flashing lights and shove of microphones, I hear another question, about deflecting what's really a personal problem of adjusting. I know how to play the game here. Acknowledge and reframe. I take a deep breath and aim my eyes just above the cameras. "At the end of the day, I can compete at a higher level, and I know that, but that's not the story you guys are making it out to be. Right now, I'm thinking, okay, that was game two. Eighty to go, and I'm excited. All right? Thanks, guys."

I turn around, and there are a few more pictures taken of my bare back as I reach up and grab the smaller towel I'd shoved in the nook above my head. By the time I'm done wiping off my face, they've moved on.

When I get home, I throw my bag down in the entryway and stalk through my apartment, closing the blinds, shutting out the twinkling lights of downtown. Twinkling is too happy for my mood tonight.

I grab a beer from the fridge on my way to the living room and loosen my tie as I flop onto the sofa. After jabbing at buttons on the remote, the TV comes on and tonight's game is queued up on the PVR.

What better way to rest after the work-day is over than to watch it all over again? I'll torture myself by watching every gaff and misstep in slow-motion instant-replay on sixty inches of in-my-face high-def.

Before I push play, I need to catch up on the rest of my life. I fish my phone from my pocket and take it off airplane mode.

Early on in my career I made it a policy to stay completely disconnected from the outside world until my work-day is over and I am safely out of the public eye.

I hate having to say "no comment" when blindsided by reporters looking for a quote about a trade, a bad hit, or even off-ice scandals. I refuse to lie, but that phrase always feels like one. It's better to be able to honestly say I know nothing and walk away.

A few swipes of my thumb later, the notifications start flooding in.

Most of them I can dismiss without checking because they are for my public social media accounts which my long-time friend and assistant, Rob, handles. I click on the voicemail.

"Tate, it's Max. Give me a call as soon as you get a chance."

Out of habit, I check the time and add three hours. The time difference bullshit got old real fast.

Midnight for me means it's three in the morning for Max, so I fire him a text.

**Tate: I'm around until noon my time. Call me when it's convenient - unlike you, don't have a tiny baby disrupting my sleep cycle.**

Moments later, my phone lights up, and I answer it. "Hey Max, what's up?"

"Me, with the baby." He doesn't sound like he minds, though. "How's my hometown treating you? Been to any clubs?"

"Not yet."

"Why not?"

Sasha. But I can't tell him that. "Still getting my bearings."

"Bearings? Jesus, Tate, it's not like you're some new high

school graduate leaving home for the first time. You've got connections in every hockey town in North America. In fact—"

I cut him off. "Connections—not friends." I don't really mean to admit that. "It's not just bearings. Things aren't going so smoothly with the new team, so I'm not really up for socializing."

"What you need is some playtime. I can hook you up with my buddy, Reid Porter. He's got a club in town that should be right up your alley."

"I'm fine, Max. Really. Now, I'm pretty sure you didn't call me in the middle of the night to make sure I'm getting my kink on. So, what's up?"

"Actually, that is why I called, in a manner of speaking. You know how Noah's arrival required all new basement furniture?"

I chuckle. Their basement went from fully-equipped BDSM dungeon to ultra-vanilla family room in a single weekend. "Yeah…"

"Let's just say the old furniture is no longer homeless."

"That's great news, because I have to tell you, I was so worried about its fate it was keeping me up nights. Thank you for not making me lose another night's sleep over it."

"I'm going to ignore that, smart-ass. Because we just took possession of a property today. All of that play furniture, and a hell of a lot more, is going to have a new home in that club I talked about opening back in the summer. Plans are quickly coming together for something spectacular. Porter—the guy from Vancouver I mentioned—made me an offer I couldn't refuse. His company will handle the day-to-day management of it, and we should be up and running soon. Like…next week, for founding members. You're in town next week, right? I wanted to see if you can squeeze a night of debauchery into your schedule before your game in Ottawa."

Well that's completely different. I might not want to go out and get laid here in Vancouver, but hanging out with my tribe back home? Fuck yeah. "Absolutely, I can. Just email me the details."

"Will do," Max says, then I hear Noah crying. "Gotta go. Parenthood calls."

---

Our third game is another bad loss at home, against Winnipeg, on Thursday night.

We spend Friday having our asses kicked by the coaching staff. It starts with a team meeting first thing, where the coach lambastes us over our shitty performance, singling out players to point out the fuck-ups and what they should have done differently, and then we're put through a bruising practice.

I spend Friday night watching game tape on my iPad, while I sit in a bathtub full of ice.

My poor fucking legs.

My poor fucking nuts.

Saturday's morning skate before our game against Edmonton is better. I even stick around for a bit after, drinking a protein shake with Andrushko before I head back to my apartment to chill.

*Bzzzz.* From my sprawled-out position on my couch, I glare at the intercom.

Something I wasn't prepared for with condo living was the incessant buzzing. My priorities for finding a place to live out here were proximity to the arena, a private parking space, and zero home maintenance.

All of that apparently comes at the expense of people pressing all of the buttons on the board in the lobby.

I may need to move.

For now, I ignore the latest round of noise because I know it's not for me. It's never for me.

It's always either the wrong condo or someone looking to get into the building who doesn't have a legitimate reason for access. Neither scenario requires me to get my ass off the couch, so I just wait it out until whoever it is gives up and moves on. I'm supposed to be napping, anyway.

I can't rest, though. I went to bed too early last night and got plenty of sleep.

My entire routine is so fucking different than it was back home.

*Bzzz.*

Different and irritating.

A minute or so later, my condo is blissfully quiet and I feel another hard stab of the loneliness that's plagued me since August.

The trade didn't just uproot me from my team, it yanked me away from my entire social life. My family.

Sasha.

I can't afford to let my thoughts head off in that direction. It's a game night and at oh-and-three, we're sitting in last place in the entire league—an unfamiliar and uncomfortable ranking for me. I need to keep my mental shit together if I have any hope of turning things around.

The silence is broken by a rhythmic knocking on wood, and it takes a moment for me to register that the sound is coming from my door.

Reluctantly, I get up from the couch and trudge through the condo. A huge grin stretches across my face when I look through the peephole and see Rob and Trevor, two of my closest friends who should be in Ottawa instead of on the other side of my door.

Up until I was traded to Vancouver, we saw each other at least a couple times a week whenever I wasn't on the road. Now, it's been nearly two months since we last hung out.

I swing the door wide. "What are you two doing here?"

Rob smiles back at me. "It's hockey night in Canada. Where else would we be?"

My stomach sinks a little, but I manage to keep the frown off my face. "You did not fly across the country just to take in a hockey game."

"Told you he wouldn't buy that," Trevor says.

"A little birdie told us you might appreciate a little company."

Fucking Max. "Since when have I ever been short of company?"

"Since you left Ottawa, apparently."

"I'm fine."

Rob shrugs. "In that case, I guess you'd rather travel to Ottawa with the team on Monday instead of coming back with us tonight."

"There aren't any flights to Ottawa tonight." I know this because I'm already travelling ahead of the team, and I booked the very first flight out after the game. It doesn't take off until mid-morning tomorrow and worse, won't arrive until mid-afternoon. Fucking time-zones.

"There are when you've got Jack Benton's private jet at your disposal," Trev says as he pushes past me into my condo.

Rob follows, making no secret of the fact he's checking out the place.

I close the door. "How the fuck did you get Jack's plane?" I've been on it twice before. It's kitted out to the nines, including a sweet master bedroom with a king-size bed.

"Who cares? He offered, we accepted, and now we're here. Are you coming back with us tonight, or not?"

A whole extra day to soak up the comforts of home, and track down Sasha? Hell yes. "Damn straight I am. And I get the bedroom."

By the time I arrive back at the arena, I'm flying high. An afternoon of shooting the shit with my buddies was just what the doctor ordered. I'm looser, more relaxed as I dress for the game.

Up until now, I've tended to just keep to myself and ignore

everything going on around me if it didn't pertain directly the performance of my job.

But tonight, I listen to my teammates as they yammer on about everything from advice to Leclerc, our starting goalie, on his impending fatherhood to the drama with Wade Gibson, who was traded to Edmonton in a deal that precipitated the Lumberjacks grabbing me from Ottawa.

This last bit grabs my attention.

It sure as fuck explains why Gibson, a rising star with twenty-two goals and thirty-seven assists in his rookie season with the Lumberjacks, got his ass booted.

Turns out there's more riding on this game than just the need for us to rack up our first win of the season. My pulse slows as I focus in on what they're saying. As the banter continues around me, I realize the best way for me to truly be a member of this team is to pull my head out of my ass and connect with them where they are at.

It's been eight years since I've been the new guy. But even then, I was still really young. And as part of a three-player trade, I didn't feel like an outsider because we were already like our own mini-team.

I'm not actually the only new guy starting this season with the Lumberjacks. But I may as well be considering the other guy is the head coach.

And speak of the devil.

Dan Cooke strides into the locker room and the chatter dies down.

Standing six-foot-six, he's big even for a hockey player, and with his arms folded over his chest, he's a formidable presence in a dressing room full of posturing alpha males. "I'm going to keep this short and sweet so it's easy for even the thickest skulls in the room to remember." He scans the room, stopping to catch the eye of a couple players. "I want good, clean hockey out there." Another pause. More scanning. More eye catching. "So, don't antagonize the other team over Gibson's appetite for other players' wives and girlfriends. Also, don't be asking Gibson whose wife or girlfriend he's fucking because he's probably just cocky enough to say something stupid."

This time when he stops, he's looking straight at me.

Holy shit. His eyes are twinkling and his tongue is so deeply planted in his cheek, there's no question this is his game plan. Tacit instructions to goad the other team into fights while he maintains an air of plausible deniability.

"Now go kick some Edmonton ass."

As soon as the coach is gone, Zack Moore comes over and sits next to me. "Just in case it wasn't obvious, Cooke wants us to—"

"Yeah, I get it." I grin. "Do everything he told us not to."

"FYI, Gibson gets no mercy over this—he's an asshole. Unattached puck-bunnies galore, but he went after a teammate's wife. Laski's marriage was on rocky ground, and Gibson took it beyond redemption."

As we line up during the national anthem, I'm optimistic about the outcome of tonight's game.

My first face-off of the night is against Gibson and it's obvious he hasn't learned a thing from the trade. He's more than cocky. It's like he thinks he's untouchable and can get away with whatever he wants. He hasn't absorbed that this trade was a step down for him. I know that he was put in Edmonton's first line in an attempt to psych me out. Fuck 'em. He's still a baby player— and I fully intend to make him feel it.

I win the face-off and haul ass to where the puck *will* be. For the first time since coming to Vancouver, I'm confident that it's will, not should.

I breathe easy when I get my stick on it. A couple of steps forward, then I flick it left to Simec. He taps it back to Landvic, who sends it up ice to where Moore is waiting. Moore takes the shot, but it's deflected wide. I push in for the rebound. The puck bounces off an Edmonton player, and the goalie smothers it.

"I hear Gibson's popular with the wives and girlfriends," I say to an Edmonton defenceman as I skate past him to the face-off circle. I don't stick around for his reaction. I have a face-off to win again.

I do just that, and race to the front of the net. Moore sends the puck my way, but I take a big hit and go down, the puck stolen by Gibson in the process.

By the time I'm on my feet, he's in the neutral zone. But not for long. Landvic slams him hard into the boards, drawing a five minute major for charging.

I can't blame him, but fuck, we're supposed to be drawing the penalties, not incurring them.

Simec, Moore, and I head back to the bench for a line change.

We manage to kill Landvic's penalty, and forty-three seconds before the end of the first period, Edmonton gets a minor penalty for hooking Moore.

Even though we start the second period on a power play, we don't score, and spend the rest of the period unable to gain any significant advantage.

At the end of the second, Coach stalks into the dressing room and room goes silent. "One goal," he says. "That's all we need to win this. More would be better, but one goal and solid defence gives us the win along with a shutout." He spins on his heel and leaves without another word.

Of course, we've been fighting for the last two periods to get one goal. But then, so has Edmonton. It's going to come down to who wants it more—and who will do whatever it takes to get there. That's us on both counts.

The opportunity comes well into the third period when Simec intercepts a pass deep in our own zone. He spins and snaps the puck to Moore and we take off up the ice. Moore dekes Gibson, then fires to the puck to me. I send it up to Simec and head for the front of the net.

Simec gets caught up in to the corner, but manages to flick the puck back at Moore who immediately sends it to me in front of the net.

It's a perfect pass. The puck hits the tape, and with one quick snap of my wrist, it flies over the Edmonton goalie's shoulder to the back of the net. Top shelf, baby.

My first goal of the regular season. Perfect.

When the horn marks the end of the game, we're still in last place in the league, but we're no longer sporting a big ol' zero in the win column.

One-and-three, and the season is young. Next up, I get a rematch with the Sens, and I've got fire in my blood to win that one, too.

5

---

SASHA

I SLEEP IN SUNDAY, after watching Tate finally—finally!—kick some ass against Edmonton the night before. The only thing on my agenda for the day is a girls' night at Ellie's place later in the evening, but before that I should do some shopping, and I've got some writing to do, too.

My dissertation is coming along nicely. Secretly, of course, because I'm in no hurry to graduate. But since my advisor approved the framework, I've been steadily writing away at it and it's probably more than half done now. I've got a goal of another five pages today, and unless something comes up, that's totally going to happen.

I can feel it. Today is going to be a rock awesome day.

But as I make my second coffee, there's a knock at the door, and as soon as I open it, I'm reminded that I do not, in fact, have the ability to predict if a day is going to be awesome or not—because something has most definitely come up.

Something—someone—who knows he shouldn't be here.

"Tate." I say his name just like that, a flat acknowledgement that he's standing on my doorstep.

He ducks his head and gives me a totally calculated, perfectly bashful grin. "Hey, Sasha."

"This is a surprise."

He nods. "We have a game here."

In two days time, but I'm not going to show my hand. He doesn't need to know I'm following the Lumberjacks' season. *Tate's season.*

"But not here in my apartment," I say dryly.

"No." His grin widens. "I'm *here* to see you."

Oh, crap. "You want a repeat." Another flat acknowledgement. He's made no secret of that fact.

He glances around the landing, and I reflexively step back, letting him into my apartment. This isn't a conversation for the hallway.

But it's not a conversation I want to have in private, either. I don't want to have it at all. "Tate..."

He closes the door behind him, and instead of moving into my living room, he just leans back against the heavy wood and holds up his hand. "Hear me out."

I cross my arms. "Okay."

"I know you're not up for..." He swivels his wrist in an encompassing motion. "Whatever. A relationship, public expo-sure, or regular text messages."

I nod. "Yep, and everything in between, too."

He gives me a baleful look. "Well, not everything. I think I can make a solid argument for an orgasm exception."

"Pardon?" I blink at him. "A what?"

"I don't want to push you, Sasha." He drops his voice, his words sliding into a lower, sexier pitch. "I just want to make you come. On your terms, whatever you want."

"I—" I gape at him. I'm speechless.

He waits for me to catch up, and I take my time. I look him over. Expensive jeans, perfectly cut to his narrow hips and powerful thighs. Even more expensive boots and belt. A casual

Henley stretched across his chest and arms—sculpted muscles I haven't forgotten since the last time he was here.

Haven't stopped thinking about, to be honest.

*I just want to make you come.*

Of course it's that simple for Tate. He's an unrepentant sexual being. He's so orgasm-centric that it's probably an offer he makes to everyone.

"No thanks," I finally spit out. I'm not interested in being a casual hook-up for an overgrown boy-child who gets everything he wants. What we did in August was a very hot exception to my no celebrity rule.

He nods mock-solemnly. "No hat trick for Sasha, then."

And then he smiles, and it lights up his eyes. They're hazel, but today there's a mossy green glint to them that is too fresh, too pure for someone as deviant as Tate.

I can't believe I'm falling for this. "What's a hat trick?"

"Three orgasms. One with my tongue, one with my fingers, and one with my cock."

"That doesn't sound so impressive."

He grins. "Of course it is. I'm the Gordie Howe of sex." He holds up three fingers and ticks them off, one by one. "The first one's in your clit. The second is in your pussy. And the third one, the one that makes you scream so loud your neighbours call the cops? That's where I'm buried deep in your ass."

"That is never happening."

"Never say never."

"You're a pig."

"Definitely. But your panties are soaked right now."

He's not wrong.

Why am I more turned on by his disgusting over-the-top ways than I ever have been with anyone else? This is the universe punishing me for setting aside my principles to sate my horny curiosity.

I need to change the subject. "Why…" God, my voice sounds

weak. I frown and try again. "Why does that perverted monstrosity of an answer make you the Gordie Howe of sex?"

He winks. "Because Howe's version of the hat trick was an assist, a goal, and getting in a fight."

Oral, vaginal, and… "Are you saying that anal with you is like getting in a fight?"

He frowns. "No."

I laugh, and he scowls at me.

"Anal with me is *excellent.*"

"I bet it is. You need to work on your advertising."

"I don't need to advertise my abilities."

"And yet you've got a little catch phrase for your sex trick anyway."

I point to the door. "Out you go."

Yes, I'm showing him out. No, I don't care that he flew across the country to see me. He didn't ask first, and if he had, I'd have told him to stay in Vancouver.

To try his hat trick pick-up line on someone who would fall for it.

"Sure thing. You've got studying to do, I bet."

I nod, because it's a good excuse.

He reaches for the handle, and pauses. His expression shifts, from playful to serious. "You must be getting close to the finish line on your dissertation, eh?"

I take a deep breath, and it catches in my chest. I don't want to think about that. "Yeah."

"You want any help?"

I try to laugh, but I can't. "Uh…"

He moves closer—something he hadn't done when he was offering me anal sex. Heat radiates off his big, broad body. "All joking aside, Sasha. I'm here for two more days. If you need a distraction, feel free to call."

I won't. I can't.

"Or you know…any time. If you just want to talk." I must have done a terrible job of hiding my surprise at that, because he reaches out and brushes his thumb against my hand—the slightest of touches before he retreats again. He's knocking me off-balance with this good guy routine, and I don't like it. "Hey, don't be so surprised. I like to talk."

"About sex."

"About anything. I'm a social guy." Something flickers in his eyes and I'm reminded again, for a second, that Tate might be lonely out in Vancouver. But then he winks, and I remember that if he were lonely, he could just pick up a puck bunny or three and fill that void with blow jobs and spanking, or whatever else he likes.

*Nails in his back, pleading for release...*

He's not done with his full-court press, either. "Let's have dinner tonight."

"I've got plans."

His jaw flexes. "Break them."

"I don't want to."

"Whatever they are, I'll do you one better. I'll take you to the nicest place in the city."

I bet that line works on a lot of women, but it's the exact wrong thing to say to me. I point to the door. "See you never, Tate. Don't let the door smack you in the ass on your way out."

He gives me a long, hard look, then nods. "All right. But I'll see you round, so…you know. Friends?"

I can't handle his relentless optimism. "Sure."

He gives me a long, curious look, like he's not sure if he believes me. That makes two of us. "You know what? You should come to Rapscallion tomorrow night."

That doesn't sound like something I would touch with a ten foot pole. "What is Rapscallion?"

He grins. "Max's new sex club."

6

———

TATE

SOMEHOW, my plan to show up and seduce Sasha for a fun Sunday morning fuckfest turned into her dressing me down and reminding me I was a once-and-done screw.

Fine.

But I don't think I imagine a hurt look flash across her face as I give her a cocky wave goodbye.

I'm still thinking about that look as I pull into the garage at my house.

My house, where I'll be lucky to spend a week in total over the next nine months.

Fuck.

I text Rob, and he says he'll be over soon.

I should grab a nap or squeeze in a workout. Instead, I flop on my couch, legs spread wide, and I close my eyes and think of the fire in Sasha's eyes.

My instinct is to send her flowers or send her an apologetic text—but since she didn't like the flirty ones, she won't want that, either.

I'm fucked.

This is the first time since I started playing pro that I've let myself get twisted up about a woman, well and truly, and she can't stand me.

And now I need to sit with the uncomfortable possibility that my distraction over Sasha has been a part of my rocky start with the Lumberjacks.

Fuck.

Last night's win in Edmonton was much needed. *That's* where my head should be. On my job.

I grab the PVR controller and turn on the television. Sure enough, the last few Sens games are recorded. *Good job, Rob.*

Somehow this is different than watching them on my laptop, on the road.

That should be *me* in that jersey. When Brandon skates onto the ice at the first line change, I can see myself right behind him. Now it's the fucking Russian with the fucking gap-toothed grin. The one whose smack talk got to me in Vancouver.

I'm not a big fighter, I let the goons handle enforcement, but that guy? I want to smash him in the face at the first opportunity.

I watch him closely, memorizing the sway of his body. He's fluid and fast for a big guy. I can't underestimate his speed again.

I hear the front door open, and I raise my hand. "Watching some game tape," I call out.

"Good deal," Rob says. "I brought you lunch."

"Thanks, man." And that's it. He leaves me to watch the game while he unpacks food, then quietly brings me a water before sinking into the recliner on the other side of the room with his phone.

At the next commercial break, I pause the game instead of fast-forwarding, and I glance over at Rob. "Hey, want to go out for dinner tonight? Somewhere nice?"

He grins. "Fuck yeah."

Sure, he might not have the sweetest pussy I've ever sunk into, but he doesn't give me grief. "It's a date."

He chuckles. "You that hard up?"
Apparently so.

41

## 7

## SASHA

I'm still reeling from Tate's unexpected visit when I arrive at Ellie's place Sunday night. Coming here for a girls' night means going through a quick RCMP security check, because my best friend is married to the prime minister of Canada—a fact I mostly find no big deal, but every so often it's kind of surreal.

"You're good to go, Ms. Brewster," the young constable says.

I pull my car ahead, and by the time I'm parked, I see our friend Violet Roberts driving in behind me. She gets out of the car and then opens the back door, where I see a baby bucket seat. She covers it with a blanket to protect wee Noah from the chilly October night.

I wait for them, then we walk up to the front door together. I'm dying to ask her about what Tate said, because Violet is Max's wife. Max, who now has a sex club called Rapscallion, apparently.

What a ridiculous, tantalizing name.

But I can't ask her right now because we're standing outside 24 Sussex, the official residence of the prime minister of Canada. This is not the place to talk about over-the-top kink club names and secret news I was not aware of.

Sure, the entrance is protected from the road by a stand of

trees, which makes this as normal as it can possibly be, but still. Not the time or place.

Ellie answers the door herself. "Come in, come in," she says, her hands making a grabby gesture at the portable baby bucket.

Violet hands Noah over with a laugh. "Your favourite person has arrived."

"I just can't handle how *cute* he is," Ellie says. We kick off our boots and coat while she gets the tiny bambino out of his buckles and blankets. "Yes you are. Yes you *are.*"

Oh the baby talk is going to drive me to drink. If she keeps this up, I'm going to need to be driven home by an RCMP constable—which might be a nice treat after the day I've had.

Violet laughs, and I look over at her. "Did I say that out loud?"

"Maybe."

Ellie sticks her tongue out at me. "Don't be a baby party pooper."

I stick my tongue right back in her direction. "Get me booze, stat."

She points toward the back of the house. "Beth is mixing martinis in the family room."

"God bless her." I leave the new mom and the barely-pregnant but mucho-excited mom-to-be in the foyer and go in search of booze. Of course Gavin knocked Ellie up, and of course she's glowing, and of course I'm happy for her. I just have a limit for baby talk, and apparently it's one minute.

In the family room, I find Beth Evans and Corinne Smith. Beth works in Gavin's office and Corinne is an RCMP officer who plays on his hockey team. I don't know Corinne that well, other than having seen her at Max and Violet's kinky Christmas party last year.

*Don't think of Tate.*

I'd done a decent job all afternoon of shoving our fight to the back of my mind. And all it took was seeing Corinne and, whoosh, he's right back in the fore again, and all I can think about is sitting next to Tate on the couch in Max's basement. I think by the time she was bent over the spanking bench, Tate's thigh was pressed up against mine.

That's all that happened between us that night. Sitting together, watching. A press of thighs and a few glancing touches of shoulders, arms, hands. A roiling churn of confusing heat that had kept me up all night after I left.

Want that had percolated for eight long months after that, until he wound up in my apartment and I propositioned him.

One afternoon.

How stupid had I been?

*And will there be couches at Rapscallion?*

"Hey Sasha," Beth waves a silver drink shaker in the air. "Lemontini?"

Hell to the yes. "Make mine a double."

"Corinne was just telling me about the progress Max has made with the new club." Beth's eyes light up as she pours my drink into a sugar-rimmed martini glass. "Have you heard about it?"

"Briefly," I manage to say. Ten hours earlier and I'm still reeling. As Ellie and Violet come in, I point a fondly scolding finger at my best friend. "Eleanor Montague, is there sex club news you may have forgotten to tell me?"

She frowns. "I don't think so. You know that Max bought an estate out of town."

"No I do not know this!"

Violet laughs and looks at Corinne. "You might know more than I do, actually. I haven't had a chance to read Reid's latest email, but we're having an inaugural party on Monday night, just for founding members."

"Reid?" I take a big swallow of my drink. "Who's Reid?"

Ellie makes a squeaking sound. "I may have forgotten to tell you about that, too. Reid Porter is a friend of…Max's? Gavin's? I think they both know him from Vancouver. He owns two clubs there, and in his day job, he runs a security firm."

My mouth drops open. "Reid Porter of Power Edge Security?"

Runs a security firm is an understatement. He's rich enough to run in my father's business circles, and when we expanded our manufacturing into Indonesia, Power Edge Security was a big part of making that transition safe and smooth and profitable.

Corinne leans in and takes a sip of her drink, her eyes wide. "You know him?"

"Not in a kinky way," I say. My eyes must be equally wide. "But he's…I mean, I can see it. He's super dominant. He's got that vibe."

Corinne gives us all the run down. Apparently, Max has bought a river-front estate, a big-ass house surrounded by enough grounds that it can be totally private, and Reid Porter's team is currently retrofitting it with high-tech security. Then his other team—from the club side—will convert it to a lavish dungeon, with multiple rooms set up for parties, as well as some private spaces.

The whole time she's talking, Ellie is rocking baby Noah back and forth in her arms.

This life is surreal on multiple levels.

But I'm excited for them, even though it's not really my world —outside of normal curiosity, of course.

After we're all caught up to date on the progress of Ottawa's newest and most exclusive BDSM club, the conversation turns to Ellie's pregnancy, which the PM's office will be announcing next week, once she's officially moved into her second trimester. That leads to her decision to take a full year of maternity leave before returning to her doctoral research, which in turn steers to the conversation to me, and my work.

"It's coming along," I say. "But I'm sure there will be a lot of re-working it as my advisor digs into what I've written so far."

"You must be close to being done," Violet says, and the echo of what Tate said hours earlier makes me shift uncomfortably.

I like the idea of moving through life as anonymously as possible. It's weird to have friends paying such close attention to what I'm doing—and I need to remind myself that's where their inquiries come from, a place of friendship, and not because they're spies for my father, or the press, or anyone else who has a vested interest in sabotaging my success.

"Some days it seems like that," I say lightly. "And then others bring that seriously into question. It's the way of academia."

Ellie laughs and nods. "So true."

Violet disappears into the kitchen to assemble a tray of munchies, and when she returns, the conversation drifts back to the club, and kink, and Corinne's eternal hunt for the right guy.

"It's so tricky, because I don't want a weekend warrior, but I don't want a 24/7 dynamic, either," she says. She lifts her martini glass into the air. "Universe, I beg of thee—please deliver me a big, strapping, alpha Dom who wants an alpha sub. Thanks."

"Are those a thing?" I ask, not caring that my voice is full of shocked awe.

She shrugs. "I keep hoping. I think they might be a bit of a unicorn in the kink community, but one day..." She clears her throat. "And what about you?"

"What about me?" *Claw me up all you want.* Was that kinky sex that we had? I don't think so. And I'm not having orgies with anyone, so whatever I have with Tate, he's not the right guy for me, not in a kinky, forever kind of way.

No, not the way Corinne means it. But...damn it. *Get out of my head, Tate.*

"Are you seeing anyone?" Beth asks, her eyes dancing as she watches me. She might think I'm freaking out, and I am, but not for that reason.

I drain my glass. "Nope."

Ellie gives me a curious look. "Nope?"

"What?"

"You always have someone."

That's true. Over the two years we were roommates, I always had a fuck buddy. I like sex, and I prefer serial monogamy without any strings. "Guess I'm going through a dry spell. Haven't got laid in months." Seven weeks and three days, to be exact.

And before that…

Nope, not thinking about how long Tate occupied my thoughts before I succumbed to my baser instincts.

"There's a guy in the PMO I should set you up with," Beth says.

Ellie gives her a curious look. "Who?"

"Craig, the new speechwriter."

"Ooh, interesting," my traitorous bestie says.

"No, not interesting," I say, waving my glass in the air. "Another Lemontini, please."

"Okay, no pressure on the guy front."

Ellie has her phone out, though. "Here, look at him." She holds it out, and there's his Facebook account.

I take the phone, because I'm not dead inside. And he is cute. I click on his profile picture to make it bigger.

"He's definitely your type," Ellie says, and Beth nods.

I give them a curious look. "What's my type?"

"Smart, quiet, not too flashy," Ellie says.

"Mmm." That does sound like most of the guys I've dated.

Beth adds, "Like he'd be really considerate in bed."

I groan. Yeah, that's familiar, too. Which is why Tate was so damn memorable because he was…well, not inconsiderate. But rough and demanding and…interesting. *Not boring sex.* He delivered in spades, the bastard.

And this morning, he was more than happy to deliver again, and I pushed him away.

I take another look at the image. Then I scroll right, and groan again. "No."

"What?"

I hold up the phone so they can all see. His last profile picture was him staring adoringly at Gavin. "We all deserve someone who looks at us like this guy gazes at your husband, Ellie. But anyone who puts a picture of themselves crushing on their boss as their profile picture is a hard nope for the Sasha Dating Game."

## 8

## TATE

A KEY FOB had been waiting for me at my house when I returned to Ottawa, along with a handwritten note with the address of the estate Max has purchased. The invitation is for me and my trusted guests, so Rob drives, and we pick up Trevor and Oliver on the way. All of my friends have played on Gavin's hockey team and attended get togethers at Max's place. Heading out for a night of partying like this is even better than them showing up to surprise me in Vancouver.

We're missing Brandon, but it's too weird to go out with him right now when we're going to go head-to-head tomorrow night. And I'm going to dominate out there.

It's a nice thirty-minute drive into the country, and when we pull up to the address, there's a heavy iron gate blocking the drive —and a high-tech sensor post that, when I hand over my keys and Rob sweeps the fob over it, opens the gate.

Fancy.

The circular drive already has a few cars in it, so Rob pulls around to the side and parks there.

At the front door, we're greeted by Max, holding Noah.

"Hey there, little man," I say, tugging on the toe of his cotton sleeper. He gives me a spit-bubble grin. "I thought this place was strictly eighteen and over."

Max chuckles. "An exception for tonight. Once Violet nurses him to sleep, we'll join everyone downstairs." He gestures at the sweeping double staircase behind him, and the hallway beyond. "All the space on this floor is public-friendly. We had caterers in earlier setting up the dinner buffet and they had no idea they were in a den of iniquity. Let's head on back, everyone else is already here."

A den of iniquity. Yeah, I've needed this. When Max asked me if I'd checked out any clubs in Vancouver, I wasn't ready. But after yesterday's blow up with Sasha, fuck it. I need to get back into the scene.

I know almost everyone mingling in the great room.

Lachlan Ross, an RCMP officer I've known in the kink world since he arrived in Ottawa, and the guy who introduced me to everyone else here via the prime minister's private hockey team, is leaning against a raised bar in front of the open kitchen. His arm is around his partner, Hugh Evans, who has his arms wrapped around their third, Beth.

I shake all of their hands, and Beth gives me a quick kiss on the cheek.

"You're all in on this, eh?" I ask.

"Of course," Beth says, her eyes twinkling. "Although Lachlan is doing double-duty tonight. He and Max also have to cast Gavin's vote by proxy."

In addition to cutting loose tonight, we're also going to vote on the club by-laws. The prime minister is a founding member in absentia until he retires from public life—so it makes sense he'd get a vote even though he's not here. I'm sure he and Ellie will find a way to visit on days when the club is officially closed, though.

Next I greet Corinne, another Mountie who plays hockey with us. She's an evil goalie, but take the pads off her and put her in a club, and she's a serene submissive. Max's invitation for dinner said semi-casual, so I'm wearing a blazer over jeans and a dress shirt, but the women all clearly got together and discussed little nods toward fetish in their outfits. Corinne's dress is fitted and covered in zig-zagging straps that reveal slices of skin. Beth is wearing leather cuffs on her wrists that match a wide leather belt around her waist, and Violet's black cocktail dress is blinged up in a big way by a diamond choker that I'm sure Max gave her as a public collar.

I wonder what Sasha would wear if she were to come to something like this.

If only she didn't despise me, we could have a lot of fun here.

Max claps his hand on my shoulder, dragging my attention back to the other guests. Jack Benton raises his glass in a somber acknowledgement of my arrival. In a bittersweet small-world twist, the billionaire lumber tycoon, and former owner of the Lumberjacks, now lives in my hometown and I'm all the way across the country playing for his old team.

"Jack," I say, holding out my hand.

"I didn't know they'd make a play for you." He takes my hand and gives it a firm shake. "But that was a hell of a game against Edmonton. Best of luck tomorrow."

I give him an easy grin. "The Sens will need it more than me."

He laughs. "That's the spirit." He gestures his glass toward the man approaching us—the only guest I haven't met before. "Do you know Reid Porter?"

I shift my attention to the other man, and extend my arm as I size him up. Big guy, older than most of us. Maybe in his early forties. "I'm Tate Nilsson. Haven't had the pleasure."

"The newest Lumberjack." Reid shakes my hand. "I definitely know of you. You're all over my morning news every day."

"You're from the west coast?"

"West Van, born and raised." He points at Max. "It's how I know the good doctor there, and Jack here."

"I like your plans for this place."

"You should come and check out my clubs at home."

*Home.* No, this is my home. But yeah, I should try to find a new tribe while I'm out west. Nine months of the year for the next however many years of my life is a long time to not have a space like this, where I can be exactly who I want to be without any need to self-censor. "I'll do that."

"The key fob for this estate will work at any of my properties. We have a great club in New York, another in Los Angeles. Denver, Miami, Toronto."

"Slick." That also means our members from those cities will get to come here. It was raised as a point of possible concern by Max, but I'm down with it. The more the better, as long as they're all properly vetted and checked out by Porter's team.

The conversation swirls through Porter's standard by-laws for all his clubs, and we add a few extra ones specific to Rapscallion to protect Gavin.

As we talk, I'm reminded how much I value this community. Only in the kink world have I ever felt truly comfortable in my own skin—well, unless I have skates on my feet.

After dinner, Noah wakes up, and Violet lifts him out of the swing. "I'll just take him over to the residence," she says to Max.

"I'll follow along in a minute after I show everyone downstairs." He points in the direction of the driveway as he turns back to the group. "We have a nanny waiting in the private apartment above the garage. Parenting logistics."

That right there sums up the value of this tight-knit group. Max invested in an entire property, a business, just to keep this alive for him and Violet now that they have a child.

Downstairs, we find a dungeon in the works. Most of the space is still open, waiting for custom furniture, but there are the familiar pieces from Max's basement. A St. Andrew's Cross, a spanking bench, and some furniture.

But there are new pieces, too—and some built-in cabinetry

that lends itself perfectly to storing fun hitty things, like crops and canes and whips and floggers.

I wonder if anyone here tonight would like some impact play. My hands are feeling restless.

*Not just your hands.* No, all of me is vibrating, anxious to work out some of the shit that's been clogging up my brain lately.

Hugh and Beth are the first to take the step from exploring to playing. They claim the spanking bench, making Lachlan groan as they roll it into the centre of the main room.

They're not in any rush, though. There's so much energy zinging between them as they tease each other and Lachlan about how they should choreograph a three-way pain-and-pleasure romp that everyone else slows down, too.

Lachlan's a big, tough guy. Watching him blush as Beth wiggles a cock ring at him is a lot of fun.

"You want it on him now?" she asks Hugh as he prowls around the dungeon, picking up and discarding various implements of torture.

He winks at her. "Up to you."

She closes the gap between her and Lachlan and whispers something to him I don't catch.

He shudders.

I saunter over to where Rob is leaning against the wall and join him. From this new vantage point, I can see Corinne quietly negotiating a scene with Reid.

Well, damn. I was going to ask if she wanted…

Doesn't matter now.

For the best.

I'm not in a good head space to dominate anyone tonight.

And really, when Hugh is on like he is tonight, watching is just as good.

He picks up an evil stick, a thin carbon-fibre wand that will pack a nice, biting snap against Lachlan's skin, and he twirls it in the air as he makes his way back to his lovers.

"Let's try this," he purrs at Beth.

She takes it from him, and he holds on, so she pulls him in against her and Lachlan.

The big guy pulls them both into his arms for a back and forth kiss so intimate it's hard to watch. Luckily we don't need to, because Max and Violet have returned.

And they aren't alone.

Everyone else in the room falls quiet when they see who is trailing behind our hosts.

I'm silent, too, but not because Ellie Montague just walked into a kink dungeon.

I couldn't care less if the prime minister's wife put on...angel wings, apparently, and a gauzy mini-dress that made her look just like a woodland fairy.

No, all of my attention is on her best friend.

Sasha doesn't even pretend she's not here to torment me. She shoots me a *don't even dare* look before beaming at Beth. "Don't let us interrupt."

Ellie winces as Lachlan scrubs his hand over his face, shifting right back into responsible Mountie.

"What are you doing here?" he demands to know.

I want to ask Sasha the same thing.

"Uh..." Ellie smiles. "Well, Gavin's out of town. And I was bored."

"Did you at least discuss this with him?"

Her smile gets even wider. "No."

Lachlan swears under his breath, then mutters something about pregnant women and deliberately bratty behavior.

Oh. Interesting.

Maybe the PM hasn't been kinky enough with his bride since he knocked her up. Well, her visit here tonight will almost certainly earn her some spankings I'm sure they'll both enjoy.

Her former roommate, on the other hand, isn't looking for a spanking.

Or biting.

Or any other hold-me-down, fuck-me-up good time.

But I'm not bitter.

It's a damn shame this dungeon is dry. A swallow or five of bourbon would make that fact she still hasn't looked at me again a fuck-tonne more bearable.

I'm not making any pretence of not looking at her, though.

I'm looking my *fill*.

Earlier, I'd wondered what she'd wear to a dressy kink event. Now I know. She's just as polished and classy tonight as she always is. But there's something about her dress that makes my blood turn right up to a lusty boil.

At first glance, it's a sun dress, sort of. It's made from over-sized silk handkerchiefs in jewel tones. Two triangles make a halter top, and the skirt is made up of many pointy swatches of silk.

But then she moves again, and each of the swatches moves independently of each other, and I realize I can see glimpses of her thighs. The whole stretch of thigh.

Her skirt has slits all the way up to her waist every few inches.

And I can't touch her.

Can't slide my hand between those silky wisps of fabric and stroke her to a clutching, satisfying orgasm.

She's cruel to deny us both that pleasure.

Apparently Lachlan is more generous than her, because he's decided not to make a federal offence of Ellie's sneak appearance, and now Hugh's getting them back on track.

"Where were we, beautiful?" he asks Beth.

She cups his cheek and gives him a soft kiss. "We were about to tie Lachlan up and mark up his ass."

Their lover groans, but he strips off his shirt and rolls his shoulders before placing his forearms together behind his back.

Eager, much? I chuckle under my breath.

I slide my attention surreptitiously towards Sasha. Her eyes are wide and her lips are parted, with the tip of her tongue peeking at the corner. Pink and curious.

Her head twitches in my direction, and her eyes flare even wider.

Shit.

She twists away and heads to the self-service bar as Beth drops to her knees in front of Hugh.

That'll hold everyone's attention.

I follow Sasha.

She snags a bottle of water and keeps going, but she doesn't hit the stairs to go back to the main floor.

Instead she stalks down a hallway I haven't explored yet. It leads to a quiet room that is currently empty, but from the book-shelves half-assembled along one wall, and a couch still wrapped in plastic, I'm guessing this is will be a library.

I have no doubt at some point in the near future I'll watch someone get railed against a wall of books, begging for release from their professor or naughty teacher.

I get hard just thinking about it.

---

## 9

# SASHA

COMING HERE WAS A MISTAKE. When Ellie called, I thought I could handle seeing Tate, but the truth is he brings up way too many feelings I can't control.

If only all of them were negative.

He leans against the door frame, taking up way too much space in this dark, intimate corner of the house. "What are you doing here, Sasha?"

"Ellie wanted to come and check this place out before strangers had access to it." It sounds weak to my own ears now. *I wanted to show you I don't need you.* And I don't.

"I didn't think this was your scene." The room is lit only by some dimmed pot lights in the corners, and his eyes glitter under the shadow of his pulled-tight brow.

"I don't know what my scene is."

His jaw flexes.

He could help me figure that out. He came by my place yesterday with pretty much that exact offer. No strings, just sex.

And I turned him down.

I'll do it again, too. Tate is not the man for me to explore my sexuality with. "Go back to your fun," I snap.

"I don't want to," he says silkily, and the rest of that pout is clear as a bell. *It's not fun now that you're here to be a burr in my side.* "You missed dinner."

"Yeah, we decided at the last minute to come out here. It's fine." Ellie ate before we left, because her pregnancy has her eating dinner at five like a senior citizen. She'll probably stop for a bedtime snack on the way home, too.

"Do you want to get out of here? We could go into the city."

I laugh. "I just got here. Why would I want to leave?"

His jaw tightens again, this time the hard cut below his cheekbone holding for a few beats before he relaxes. "I don't know. It was just an idea. I keep forgetting that you don't like me."

I turn my back on him. *Let it go*, I tell myself. He's not going to care or learn.

But then there's the part of me that always wants to be right. I hate that part. I take a deep breath, then look back at him.

Big, brawny. Stupid.

Stupidly hot, too.

I hate my ovaries for how they flutter in his presence.

"It's not you, okay? It's not that I don't like *you*. It's not personal."

He huffs a laugh and uncrosses his arms, swinging his jacket back as he stuffs his hands in his pockets. He makes jeans and a blazer look criminally good. "You've put your claw marks in my back, Sasha. I've been inside your body. It sure feels personal."

Heat slams into me. Yeah, he's been inside me. And it was the best and worst decision of my life, because I can never forget how good that day was.

"What do you want me to say? Nobody will ever compare to you? You rocked my world?"

He prowls closer. "We both know I did. And I'd do it again in a heartbeat, because I like your fire."

I can't breathe. I move backwards and bump into a piece of furniture covered in plastic. I look down. A couch. And when I look back up, Tate is right in front of me. Even bigger and brawnier than he looked across the room.

A visceral, hungry memory crawls up my insides. The way he felt on top of me. His weight. The aching press of his cock inside me as he pushed me into the bed.

It's just too damn bad that outside the bedroom, he ticks every single item on my no-go list.

Celebrity.

Wealthy.

Cocky.

"I'm not interested in your money. Don't ever try to impress me with a fancy dinner or anything like that."

He gives me a hard look, like he can see inside my head and he knows I'm thinking uncharitable thoughts about him right now. Too bad they war something fierce with filthy thoughts, too. "Fine."

"You shouldn't toss your money around for anyone else, either."

"That's none of your business."

I nod. "I know."

His jaw flexes again. "Maybe I'm just a generous guy."

"No. You're wasteful. You do stupid things like employ grown men who are otherwise unemployable because they have gigantic cases of loser-itis."

"Whoa, what are you talking about?"

"Your hangers-on." The same group of them are here tonight as were at the holiday play party at Max's house. It's ridiculous. And I've read about them since, in blogs, but that knowledge verges on inappropriate stalking, and I've probably said too much as it is.

Except Tate has never met a barb he can't top, and it's on. "They're called friends, and they're my most trusted support system. Novel concept for you?"

I snort. "Try another insult."

"You've had your nose stuck in a book too long, baby. You don't know a good thing when he's standing right in front of you."

"When a good thing is standing right in front of me," I purr, "I take full advantage of the rare opportunity and ride it for all it's worth. I'll let you know when that happens."

"I was just offering to take you out for dinner. How you turned that into back and forth sparring—"

"You were offering to buy me food before you asked me for a blow job," I snarl, stepping right into his personal space. "Totally transparent and uncool."

He smirks down at me. "Maybe I just want you fed before I crawl between your luscious thighs and make you come on my tongue. Gotta keep your energy up. But it's fine. You don't want my mouth on your pussy, that's your loss." His gaze drops to my dress. "Or my hand up your skirt as you watch people get spanked."

"Is that what you thought?" My words slam out of me in hot, offended whispers. "You thought I'd let you touch me here? In front of people?"

"Not in front of anyone. At the back of the room, when everyone's attention is elsewhere." He leans all the way in, until the heat radiating off his body is pulsing against my skin and his mouth is right beside my ear. "You'd come so hard on my hand, you'd have to bite me for a change. Just to keep your pretty little mouth quiet."

I squeak in outrage as his breath brushes against my cheek, and then he's gone, turning and stalking out of the room before I can get a retort in.

## TATE

I CAN FEEL her glare against my back as I storm away.

She makes me so crazy. I have a nearly irresistible urge to spin around, slam that door, and let her shove me against the wall until this tension between us finally evaporates.

Did she even know she was licking her lips as she dressed me down? The last time she did that, I had her on her knees. That's not happening tonight.

Fuck, her mouth. I smirk at myself, because that's exactly what I'd like to do. Fuck her mouth. Her cunt. Her ass, if she wanted…because I sure as hell do. Even mad as I am, that thought makes things twitch hard for me.

I want to shake Sasha loose from whatever hangups she has about me as a person—because fucking hell, that doesn't matter —and find a way to scratch our mutual itch again.

But wanting doesn't make things happen.

It's a waste of energy now.

So. Fine.

I lean against a pillar near the back of the main room and take stock of where everyone else is at.

Lachlan is bent over the spanking bench, and Beth is

torturing his ass. Hugh is on the other side, crouched in front of him, and he's laughing about something. I love how casual they all are about the dominance and submission in their relationship —since it's something they live every day, with Hugh being a bossy, demanding motherfucker and Lachlan naturally wanting to serve both of his partners, they have a lot more fun with it than people who are high-protocol.

They're my kind of people, for sure.

But I like watching people who are more rigid in their expectations, too. There's something beautiful about the formality in which someone like Corinne submits to a master.

Tonight, apparently, that's Reid.

Corinne has stripped down to a black sports bra and boy shorts, and she's standing at docile readiness in front of the St. Andrew's Cross.

Reid is taking his time preparing the scene. He keeps stopping in front of her and checking in, which is good communication from a first-time play partner, but it's more than that—

Out of the corner of my eye, I see Sasha return.

That damn skirt interrupts my thoughts about Reid and Corinne. The colourful silk pieces swing hypnotically, baring teasing slices of thigh. By the time I drag my attention up Sasha's body, she's noticed that I'm looking at her.

It's a free country.

I glare at her, daring her to pick another fight.

Maybe it's not just the skirt which has distracted me.

I make no apologies for how I live my life. I work hard and I play hard. But I try to be a decent person, and I'm generally drawn to other similarly decent people.

I know that Sasha is kind. She's a good friend, and crazy smart. I've seen that in glimpses here and there, even though she'd never toot her own horn.

But when it comes to me, it doesn't take much to fire her up.

We're like oil and water.

I want to know why.

I'm not chasing her again. But I hold her gaze and make it clear from my body language that she's welcome to join me.

She takes her time making that decision. She looks around the room before warily approaching and leaning against the opposite side of the pillar.

"I won't bite," I murmur, and her cheeks flush.

"I'd rather you bite than talk." She says it under her breath and I almost miss it.

We're not so different when it comes to sex. It's just all the other stuff we clash on.

"I don't know why it has to be one or the other."

The corner of her mouth flexes up in an almost smile and she turns her attention to where Reid is flogging Corinne. "It's kind of weird that everyone I know comes here and fucks in front of each other."

"Not everyone."

"Enough of them."

"You know, some people value that kind of friendship, that kind of openness."

"Some people?"

"Me, for one." I wait for her to give me a surprised look, and I smile gently. "I know you're still sorting out what you like and what you're into, but this...?" I gesture around the dungeon. "This is important to me. Judge with caution."

"Point made. I'm not judging." She holds my gaze, although it takes effort, I can tell. "Just figuring it all out."

"It's okay if none of this is for you. Everyone's kink is different."

"Do you think everyone is kinky?"

"No. But you are."

"How are you so sure?"

I'm not sure, exactly. "Just a solid hunch backed up by significant data."

That gets a laugh out of her. "Anecdotal data can't be trusted."

Oh, it's on again. I can't resist her, no matter how often I get burned. I push off the pillar and stick my hands in my pockets. It's the safest way to ensure I don't touch her as I prowl around to her side. "Then you might want to dial back the wide-eyed hungry look and the way you keep biting your lower lip," I whisper as I get almost close enough to touch her. Definitely close enough for her to feel my breath on her skin. "Your body is definitely sending mixed messages compared to the snark coming out of that pretty little mouth."

She stiffens, just for a second, then sighs. "Damn it."

I chuckle. "What do you hate more? That I noticed or that you're conflicted?"

"So hard to decide. Both are annoying."

"There's a couch over there we could go sit on. Watch from a better vantage point."

"I don't know." She flicks her hair over her shoulder. "And don't think I didn't notice you trying to trick me into sitting next to you again."

"It's not a trick." I sigh in exasperation. Never have I understood the appeal of spanking quite as much as when Sasha is pushing all my buttons. But she's not being a brat on purpose and I don't have any interest in actually disciplining her, so I'll have to deal with my hard-on on my own, later.

"Maybe I just don't know how to do this." She frowns, and I want to rub that little crease in her forehead away. She glances towards me, away from the display ahead of us. "What do you like?"

"That's a dangerous question."

"Because you might actually answer it?"

"Exactly." Right now I'm incredibly turned on by innocently bratty behaviour, but that's a temporary thing. That's a Sasha-specific thing, and when a woman has turned me down is not the time to tell her that *she* is my kink.

She glances over at the couch I'd pointed to. It's in the shadows, and I can tell she wants to go and sit there.

I lean in again. "I'm a hedonist, Sasha. I like dirty talk, dirty deeds, and dirty friends. And we don't need to fuck again if you don't want to, but you are one of those dirty friends. I'm going to sit over there and watch people be joyfully kinky. I suggest you join me."

I grab two bottles of water on my way to the sofa, and when she sits down next to me—again, not too close—I hand her one of them.

We don't talk. She watches Reid and Corinne, and I watch her. Not directly. My eyes are looking forward. But my gaze isn't focused on the obvious kink ahead of me. All my attention is keenly focused on the quiet, newbie kinkster next to me on the couch.

She's made her position totally clear. She doesn't like me, doesn't want me, and I can stop trying any time. She's made that point twice.

The problem is, I don't believe her.

I let that roll around in my head until Corinne's scene ends.

Max and Violet get up from where they were sitting with Ellie, and as Max goes to open his mouth, a pager goes off on his hip.

"Baby or hospital?" Violet asks.

He glances at the screen. "Baby."

"Of course," she says with a smile.

Max waves at the wall of whips behind them. "Have at it. We'll be right back."

As Trevor and Jack move into the sunken part of the basement—where the ceilings are taller, and perfect for a skills competition with a bull whip—Sasha watches Max lead Violet back upstairs.

"He's so attentive," she murmurs.

"He's pretty happy to be a dad."

"I think most guys would just let Violet go and feed the baby on her own. Stay here and keep partying."

"Yeah, some might."

She gives me a challenging look. "You don't agree?"

"I just said that some might. Some would, is that better?"

She rolls her shoulders in a vague kind of shrug. "Whatever, I don't want to get into it with you."

"You've got a big ol' chip on your shoulder, don't you?"

Something dark flashes in her eyes. *Definitely* not a comfortable topic. "Maybe I do. Maybe I have good reasons for being wary of men. And I'm one year away from being Dr. Brewster. So when you're done being a media darling, I'll have my own business empire. Got it?"

"Media darling? That's just the job, princess."

"Not one I would pick."

"Noted." I rock my jaw back and forth as I look at her. I refuse to be goaded into fighting with her again. "There's a story there, isn't there?"

She sips at her water and searches my face before answering. "It's not a big deal."

Liar, liar, pants on fire.

"Tell me some of those reasons," I say, my voice low and only for her. "Tell me about the jerks and the assholes."

Her eyes tighten up and she glances down. I follow her gaze and watch as she flicks one of the silk slices of her skirt into just the right spot. Always careful. Always controlled.

"It's not really about other people," she says, surprising me. "There was a period of time a few years ago where I was a bit reckless and splashy with my social media."

I can't keep the surprise off my face. "You?"

She gives me a rueful smile. "Yeah. Youthful indiscretions were fun right up until they weren't. I got a ridiculous reputation. The good thing about the internet, though, is it has the memory of a goldfish. Nobody remembers that I was once billed as Canada's answer to Paris Hilton."

I definitely don't remember that. "You've done a good job of rebranding yourself."

Her eyes tighten again. "It wasn't all me."

Ah.

She waves her hand, affecting a coolness that feels fake. I don't like it one bit. "Whatever. It wasn't like I filmed a sex tape. But it was distracting, and at the end of the day, it interfered with my MBA. I ended up switching schools and starting again. So before I decided to pursue my PhD, we—I scrubbed myself from the internet as much as I could. Now it's my goal to be as boring as humanly possible."

"You aren't boring."

She pauses as a whip cracks in the background, then gives me a half-smile. But before she can respond, Max and Violet return. She strips down to her underwear, just like Corinne did, all the energy in the dungeon shifts in their direction.

For the best. I've probably pushed my luck enough.

And tomorrow is a game day—maybe the most important game I'll play this fall.

I should worry less about why Sasha doesn't like me and more about how I'm going to dominate on the ice tomorrow night.

## SASHA

I CAN'T SLEEP when I get home. I finally drift off in the early hours of the morning, and when my alarm goes off, I feel like death warmed over.

I'm sorely tempted to go back to sleep, but I'm a teaching assistant for a first year course, Social Context of Business, and I need to be on campus in two hours anyway.

I'll nap this afternoon.

I put on gym clothes and pack everything I need for the day into a backpack, then run to campus as a warm up. The gym is busy, but the flat-screen mounted above the free weights is on a sports channel and they're talking about Tate's return to Canadian Tire Place tonight, so I elbow my way in there.

I've got earbuds in to discourage people from trying to talk to me, but I'm not listening to music. All my attention is focused on the muted television.

Expectations are low for the Lumberjacks tonight. Everyone thinks their offensive lines are a mess—which is code for Tate has messed up their already-fragile dynamic—and now they're talking about what kind of non-wins would be wins-enough.

That makes me laugh.

Only a win will do for Tate, I'm sure of it.

———

Eleven hours later, I'm proven right.

I had no doubt.

Watching hockey has never been better than porn—at least, not until tonight. And I might be the only person in Ottawa who thinks so. We're at the start of the third period for the Senators' home game against the Lumberjacks, and Tate and his gang of oversized thugs from the west coast are dominating his former team.

I'm more than a little turned on. He's fast and aggressive tonight, totally in their faces, and I'm standing up in front of the couch because I was getting dangerously close to jumping on it when I was trying to sit.

There's no sitting when Tate Nilsson is wearing a Lumberjacks jersey and owning the Senators' end of the rink.

Right now he's circling, waiting for the ref to set up a face-off, and he's watching them. He's oblivious to the fans booing him, the cameras, anything else. He's laser-focused on his former teammates.

They're so going down.

Be still my traitorous ovaries, who want to go down, too.

*Not happening.* Tomorrow, he'll get on a jet plane and head to Buffalo. Pretty soon he'll be back on the other side of the country, safely out of temptation.

The face-off is going to be against a young kid they brought up to replace him, and Tate's not having any of his attempts to own the space. It might be his house now, but it was Tate's for eight years.

The kid skates in front of him, then stops, bumping against Tate's chest.

Tate shoves him back, hard.

The camera zooms in as the ref slides in between them, and his mic catches the last bit of their exchange. Tate's voice is vibrating and savage. "Seriously, you gonna keep that shit up? Andrushko's gonna pound you into the fucking ground, you clown. Get the hell out of my way."

It's not the classiest thing that's ever been caught on a hot mic, but where the announcer is blathering on about it not being a good use of Tate's energy, I see something else.

He's pissed, on behalf of his team—his new team, his *now* team—and he doesn't care that the guy across from him is wearing his old jersey.

This moment might not be elegant, but it's important. Right now, tonight, is maybe when Tate becomes a Lumberjack for real. He had an awesome game against Edmonton, sure, but this was a real test, and he's passed with flying colours. Ottawa might be frosty at the end of the game tonight, but I bet everyone in Vancouver is cheering pretty damn loud right now.

I know I'm grinning as the refs push them apart.

Definitely better than porn.

As soon as the game ends, I reach for my phone.

**Sasha: You were amazing tonight. Good job.**

He doesn't respond right away, and I ignore the pang of disappointment I feel over the silence. It's silence of my own making, after all.

But when my phone lights up an hour later—long after I'd accepted he wasn't going to reply, and that was fine, because it's for the best if he doesn't—there is no ignoring the anticipation that soars inside me.

**Tate: Thanks.**

What?

That's it. No lewd suggestion, no leading comment.

My pulse pounds as I start a new message back. He might be done with me. He'd have every right to be.

**Sasha: Are you celebrating?**
**Tate: The guys are going out.**

Who is this monster, and what has he done with gregarious Tate?

**Sasha: Are you going with them?**
**Tate: Are you asking me something here? Because…**

A text message bubble appears, then disappears, as he writes the rest of that thought. I cut him off at the pass.

**Sasha: I know I shut you down before. I won't tonight. If you're interested, come over.**

And then to make it even worse—or better, really, because we both know what I want, I add—

**Sasha: Any time. Late is fine. Go out first with your teammates.**
**Tate: I'll be there in twenty minutes.**

## TATE

Hᴏᴛ. Fucking. Damn. I just got home, but I turn around and head right back out to my garage, arming the security system on my way out.

Sasha wants another night? I'm in.

We're going to do a better job of talking about some boundaries this time, though.

I park on the street across from her building. She buzzes me up, and I take the stairs two at a time.

When she opens the door, all my plans to talk first and fuck later get wobbly, because she's wearing not much of anything—black volleyball shorts that are painted on, and a loose, swinging tank top through which I can see the outline of her nipples—and my brain short circuits.

"Nice suit," she manages to say before I pick her up and turn us, pressing her against the door a beat after it clicks shut.

Her mouth is hot and sweet and wet. As we kiss, I fist one hand in her hair and palm her ass with the other. Her leg is warm and smooth to the touch, and I can touch a hell of a lot of it because her shorts barely cover her ass.

So much skin. I love those shorts. I love her ass.

"We need to talk," I growl as I move my mouth down her neck.

She cries out when I bite her gently, then not so gently.

I press my entire body into hers as I suck on her flesh and try to get a fucking handle on myself. Breathing hard, I finally bring my mouth to her ear. "First. We need to talk, *first*. Before we fuck."

"Don't be crazy," she whispers. "We've tried that a few times and it doesn't go well. Let's stick to our strengths."

"You want me to fuck you so hard your eyes cross?"

"You know I do."

But I know there's a solid chance she'll have second thoughts after. "No regrets tomorrow."

She stills in my arms. Then she nods. "No regrets."

I nip at her skin again, because I can't get enough of the taste of her, and I love the way she squirms in my arm. "You sure?"

She waits long enough that the silence is agonizing, then she says a single, quiet word. "No."

I tighten my grip on her and lift her away from the door.

She buries her face in my neck as I carry her to her bedroom.

I dump her on the bed and cross my arms. "Why did you invite me over?"

She flops out on her back and waves for me to undress. "Because you had a good game. Strip off that fancy suit, Mr. Victorious."

I'll show her victory. The adrenaline rush from winning a big game can keep me going all night—and tonight was a big game, no matter how much I may have downplayed it to the press.

I tug my tie loose, then toss it at her. "Hang on to that. We might use it."

She bites her lip and tugs her tank top up, until I can see the bottom curve of her breasts. She trails my tie over the creamy pale skin of her belly, and I grit my teeth to keep in the dirty, filthy, fucking perfect things I want to say to her.

*Show me your tits.*

*Show me your cunt.*

*Touch yourself.*

*Lick those fingers and tell me how you taste.*

No, my brain doesn't want to talk right now, but that's what we need to do. I shrug out of my jacket and hang it on the back of a chair she has in front of a dressing table. "I'll make you a deal," I say, my voice full of gravel as I unbutton my shirt. "We can talk about two things. All the dirty things you want me to do to you, and how long I want to be able to do them."

She slowly wraps my tie around her hand. "The answer to the second point is not just tonight, is it?"

I shake my head. "Not by a long shot."

Her lips part and her eyes darken as she searches my face. "I'm not an easy girl to date."

"I'm an easy guy to please. You let me worry about whether or not I'm happy."

"I have rules."

"I bet your rules have rules. That doesn't faze me."

"I want you to go down on me. Like, all the time. I could just date your tongue and be perfectly happy."

"Lies. You like my dick inside you too much for that. But I love the way you taste, tiger. You can ride my face as soon as we agree that we're dating."

"We're not dating." But she smiles. She smiles, and the room lights up. I drop my shirt on the floor and crawl onto the bed, onto her. "You're the devil," she whispers before I kiss her. She says it again as I tug her shorts over her hips and down her legs.

Then I roll us over, so I'm on my back and she's sitting astride my chest, her legs spread and her pussy so close I can already taste her.

"I want to do this again," I growl. "I want to know that when I'm in town for Christmas, you're going to be in my bed. When I'm on the east coast, I want you to consider meeting me." I pinch her hip before she can protest. "On your own dime, because you're building a business empire and I don't want to impress you. I just want to fuck you."

"Oh." Her eyes flare wide and her lips part in surprise.

I squeeze her ass and nudge her pussy closer to my mouth. "Come on, Sasha. Let's do something crazy and start seeing each other like normal people do."

"Normal people do not bribe each other with oral sex."

"Pretty sure this is how marriages are held together, babe." I turn my head and kiss the inside of her thigh. "But really, zero expectations. We can keep this quiet. I just want you to answer your damn phone once in a while."

"You haven't actually called me," she says, another smile threatening to curl at the corners of her mouth. "Just texted. A lot."

Well I missed her. A lot. But I'm not going to admit that. "And I'll keep texting."

"Next time try calling, and I'll answer."

"God fucking damn it, you are a stubborn woman."

"Mmm." She rolls her hips, and now she's within an inch of my mouth. "I'm definitely considering letting you do this again."

I breathe in the scent of her and lust jams all my brain circuitry. Negotiations can resume later. The celebration needs to begin now. I lift my head and squeeze her ass in my hands, serving her pussy to myself like the delicious treat it is.

Above me, her hand connects with the wall, and she leans in, shifting her weight as she spreads her thighs on either side of my head.

Heaven.

She's wet, her entrance slick and swollen, and I lap my tongue against her in selfish, wolfish licks before remembering myself. Then I slow down, settling in to giving her the best head she's ever had. So good she'll need to have me back, even if there's a long list of reasons why us being together shouldn't work.

None of that matters.

This matters. Her cunt rubbing against my face, her clit getting hard for me. Her pussy soaking my chin as I slide my tongue along the frilly ridges of her inner lips. And she fucking likes that. She gasps and shivers under *my* touch, *my* tongue.

*Mine* is a dangerous thought when it comes to a woman who barely tolerates me most of the time.

I shove it away and think about how good her pussy is going to feel gripping my cock. Fucking. This is what we have together, and it's hard enough to negotiate. Nothing else is on the table.

That's okay. We're going to make fucking so damn special it's going to be enough.

I work her over until she's grinding against me and then I give her my fingers. She's got such a greedy cunt, she takes two right away, even though that's effing tight. She squirms and whimpers as she fucks my hand, as I suck her clit, and when she comes in a gasping, clutching mess, I lick it all up.

All of it.

Every fucking drop, because she's delicious.

When she slumps, I catch her, and roll her onto her side. She reaches for me immediately, her hands greedily going to my belt. I haven't even taken off my shoes yet. I catch her hands. "Hang on."

I swing up off the bed and quickly strip, palming a condom before I drop my suit pants on the floor.

She's up on her knees by the time I turn around again, and we meet in the middle of the bed. She's still wearing that nearly see through tank top, but I like it. I like the way it shows me side-boob through the arm holes, and hints at turned-on nipples, and casts delicious shadows on her hips and over her sweet, swollen, well-kissed pussy.

I really like that tank top.

But it has to go.

I haul her against me, kissing her mouth hard as I give in to my urge to squeeze her tight. To hold and maul and contain her, just for a second, in the hard confines of my arms.

Then I fist the shirt with my hands. "Is this like the bra? Any rules about ripping it?"

She hesitates for a second, but she's caught up in this moment, too. I've driven her just crazy enough to give me this. She shakes her head. "It's old."

The fabric gives a small protest, but then gives way. I tear it right down the front, baring her soft, perfect breasts I've been thinking about for months. How good they feel and taste in my mouth as I drive my cock deep into her belly.

The way she'll claw up my back if I suck on them long enough.

I give her the condom as I tumble us to the bed. I fall on her, getting a heady charge out of how she feels beneath me. Lithe and soft against my big, hard body. She makes me feel like a conqueror, something primal that pushes my buttons in a new and interesting way.

Sex is a chemical reaction. Two or more people coming together and making magic together, and the magic I make with Sasha is something else. I buck into her hand as she rolls the slick condom down my length, her fingers nimble and light.

I need to be inside her. I roll onto my back and she follows, our bodies tangled together. Limbs entwined, hands grabbing at slick flesh. I grip her hips and drag her against my cock. The rub of sex against sex is deliriously good, and it gets even better when she rolls her hips and catches the tip of my dick right at her entrance.

Her breath catches as I thrust into her, that little gasp telling me I'm almost too big for her, almost too much, but then her body makes room. She welcomes me inside, her body going pliant as I move in and out, each intrusion deeper than the last. There's that little voice again. *Mine.* For tonight, anyway. For the holidays too. I've got so many plans. So much pleasure to give her.

I squeeze her wrists in my hands, holding her arms like reins as she rides me. I could watch her on top of me for hours. Bouncing flesh, swollen lips, bright eyes. All that perfect hair mussed up and tangled because of my hands, because of how we tangled and rolled and rubbed against each other.

She looks wanton, undone and sexy. Polished, perfect Sasha is a sex doll right now, and I'm going to pretend that's all my doing. That she's never like this for anyone else.

I trace my fingers over the shadowy curve of the inside of her thighs, the dip where her legs meet her torso, then over her smooth mound and up the tight curve of her belly. Her skin tenses and contracts beneath my touch, and I keep going, up to her soft breasts and those puffy, pink nipples I want in my mouth.

Tugging her down, I change my grip on my her body. I slide one hand into her hair, winding the golden brown strands around my fist, and with the other, I curve around her hip and squeeze her bottom.

Fuck, I want her there, too. *Nothing says possession like claiming her ass.* Want roars inside me, fierce and loud, and my fingers drift over the crease between her cheeks, finding her softest, most sensitive skin.

She gasps, but she doesn't pull away.

"Is this okay? Do you like that?" I ask as I nip at her breasts. I glance up at her and give her a charming grin.

Horny uncertainty is written all over her face. She drags the tip of her tongue over her bottom lip and nods shakily. "Yeah."

"Feels good, doesn't it?"

Another nod, and her eyelids flutter shut as I circle her tight rear hole, slowly, in time with the dragging thrusts of my cock in her pussy.

She sways above me as I fuck her, as I explore her ass with my fingers and suck on her tits, and my dirty, perverted brain is so happy I can hardly handle it. Deep down, Sasha is as hedonistic as I am, I'm sure of it.

"Come on my cock," I growl as I slam up and into her. "I want to feel your pussy squeeze me so tight it hurts."

She rolls her hips, pressing against my fingers before grinding down. Clit, ass, pussy. I want her to feel this orgasm in all of them. In every cell of her body.

I want her to feel pleasure like she's never felt before, so she'll need me to come back and do this again.

I want to be her fuck toy, her dirty secret, her perfect escape.

"God, yes, Tate…right there," she gasps, slamming her hand into the headboard just behind me as she tries to fuck down on my cock, but she's shaking now, her thighs trembling hard.

"I've got you." I roll her over, pressing her into the bed. I hitch one of her thighs up, squeezing the back of her leg as I hold her open and drill into her, hard and fast as she convulses beneath me.

Yeah, that's the fucking good stuff right there. Sasha coming on my dick as I'm buried deep inside her, my balls churning fast to join her. My own climax rips up my cock, a powerful spasm that turns the edges of my vision black as I fall on top of her.

Heavy breathing and sweat-slicked skin might just be my idea of heaven. I kiss her neck, tasting the salty proof of how hard she worked for both of those orgasms. I want to lick every inch of her until she's ready to do that again.

"Fine," she says, her voice sex-slurred and happy. I roll to the side so I can look at her, and the expression on her face is worth it. She's so adorably disoriented right now, not quite sure of what to make of this, of us. "We can…see each other. Naked, anyway."

"I was hoping you'd say that." I kiss her hard on the mouth. "I'm calling you as soon as I get to Boston tomorrow."

"That sounds like a threat."

I grin. "Take it however you want." I weave my fingers through hers and squeeze her hand. "And I want to take you to the Rapscallion play party."

Her eyes widen, and I'm not sure if that's alarm or surprise or something else in her expression. "That's...public-ish. Definitely not secret."

"It's just our friends. And what happens at Rapscallion—" I stop myself before I push her too far. "If you don't want to, I'll understand, no questions asked."

She searches my face, her eyelashes sweeping low against her cheeks every few seconds in lazy blinks. Finally she shrugs. "Okay. Let's go as friends. And you're not flogging me."

I grin. "Okay."

"Is that something you do?"

"Nah. I mean, I have." I've done everything, pretty much. "But I don't seek that out. I'm pretty flexible when it comes to kink. I'm a top, but beyond that, I just really like dirty sex, and the kink community is the safest place to explore that."

She gives me a long look. I know curiosity when I see it, but I know nerves, too—and there are some things that people need some time to work up the courage to say. Finally she breaths in quickly, then lets it out with determination. "I have a question that might sound selfish."

I give her my most disarming smile. "Hit me with it."

"I don't want to have sex in front of others. At all. Ever."

"Okay. That's a statement, not a question."

She shoves at my shoulder. "I know. That's the establishing statement. The thing is, is it weird to want to go and just watch, without ever...participating?"

Oh, sweet Sasha, who thinks she's selfish as she worries about other people's feelings. "No, that's not weird. But..." I draw her close, so she can feel my cock hardening against her belly. "Watching is participating."

"Not really."

"Yes, really." I try to think about how to explain it, and then decide it's better if she just experiences it herself. "Kink is a lot more than a four letter acronym. It's everything outside of the vanilla paradigm. It's people experiencing sex in a whole new way, and yes, freaky is celebrated. But lots of kink is subtle, and lots of kink is private. And what you'll find is that everything has a counter. So you like to watch. In order for that to happen, someone else needs to like to be watched. You are satisfying that kink for them just by being there."

"That turns you on," she murmurs.

I glance down between our bodies. Fuck yeah, it does. My cock is hard and wet at the tip, pre-come leaking all over her belly.

That's crazy hot. I reach between us and fist my dick, rolling my thumb across the slick head.

Her breathing changes, her chest rising and falling faster as she watches me jack off for her.

"I like the idea of you watching me," I tell her.

She jerks her gaze back to my face. "I don't want to watch you with anyone—"

"Settle down," I say with a chuckle. "I meant like this. No, when we go to Rapscallion—"

"As friends."

"As friends," I repeat. I don't care what she tells herself or others, I'm fucking her sideways when we leave there. Maybe I'll hire a limo for the night so I can rail her on the drive back into the city. "I won't touch anyone else. I'll sit right beside you on a couch, touching you when nobody is looking, and watching you get so turned on you'll slide right onto my dick once we're alone."

"You've got such a romantic way with words," she smirks.

Whatever. She's turned on and not even pretending she's not.

She leans in toward me, her eyes hooded and her lips parting. The invitation to kiss her is crystal clear. I sink into her, closing my mouth over hers as she winds her legs around my body.

"Get another condom," she whispers after she kisses me stupid. "I'm not done with you yet."

## 13

## SASHA

As PROMISED—OR threatened, depending on how one were to reflect upon last night's sex-bribe-a-thon—Tate calls as soon as he arrives at the hotel in Boston. I'm walking across campus on my way to a meeting with my advisor, but I've got enough time to talk for a bit.

"I'm at the university," I tell him as soon as I answer it.

"Is that meant to be some kind of warning?" His voice is low and dirty and entirely dangerous to my self-control.

"I'm just saying, I'm in public."

"So I shouldn't tell you that I can still taste your pussy on my lips?"

My cheeks burst into flames. "I walked right into that, didn't I?"

"Of course you did. Actually, I was calling to ask how late I can call you, because some of the guys want to go to an oyster bar that doesn't take reservations, so we're going to need to put our name on a list and wait. We'll be out for a while." He drops his voice even lower. "But I've got a bedtime story to tell you, and I wouldn't want to miss the opportunity."

I know how important team bonding is for him. If he's got an invite to hit the town with his new teammates, he should take it. "I'll be up late. Call whenever."

I'm still blushing as I end the call. I put my phone away and detour to the next building, where I can get a coffee and buy myself a few minutes to compose myself.

Except in line at the coffee stand is none other than Ellie, and she's looking straight at me.

"What's up?" I ask totally nonchalantly.

"Who were you talking to on the phone?" Her eyes are sparkling. Dancing, really. Her body parts are having a disco bash at my expense.

"Nobody."

"I'm starting to doubt your assertion that you aren't seeing anyone." She turns around and orders a decaf pumpkin spice latte from the barista. I do my best not to make a gagging sound, and then add my own order to hers—a latte with an extra espresso shot, because I'm staying up late tonight.

*Don't ask her why she thinks that...* But I don't need to, because Ellie's proud of her detective work, and tells me anyway.

"You did this girlish head bob as you hung up the phone. And you smiled at the air around you. If you'd have kicked up your heels, I wouldn't have been surprised."

"It's cold outside. I was probably just moving to keep warm."

"Mmm." She doesn't believe me. That's fine. I'm not going to crack under interrogation, but it's a good warning that I shouldn't take Tate's calls in public.

*Or just tell your best friend you're banging a hot hockey player.*

No, that wouldn't do. There would be questions I don't have the answers to. I change the subject. "I'm heading over to Joan's office. Are you walking that way?"

"I am."

We grab our coffees from the other side of the coffee stand, and head out the south doors. Two very casual RCMP officers, Ellie's security detail, follow at a close distance.

On the walk over, we talk about conference season. I'm presenting at two—Seattle and San Diego, which means I need a new wardrobe. "We should do a girls' weekend in New York."

Ellie gives me an amused look. "When have I ever taken you up on that?"

"Never. You just like to borrow the clothes I bring back. But you're the prime minister's wife, now. Your wardrobe could use some upgrading."

"I do just fine raiding your closet." And the Ottawa and Montreal designers that are knocking down her door, too. I've raided *her* closet a couple of times now. "But I wouldn't object to something in a Christmas red."

I clap my hands. I love shopping like other people love pumpkin spice or taking naps. And if the shopping needs to solve a puzzle, like the best way to dress a growing pregnant belly over the holidays, I'm all over that. "Deal."

We stop inside the lobby of the Faculty of Social Sciences. "I've got a meeting with an undergrad," Ellie says. "Are you going to the seminar on women and migration this afternoon?"

"Yep, I'll see you there." Waving goodbye, I head for the stairs. My advisor's office is on the tenth floor, but I'd rather take the stairs than wait for the elevators. Between non-stop texting with Mabel about her launch plans and watching hockey, my gym routine has been seriously disrupted. I'm going to need to break down and get the NHL app so I can watch Tate play and stay healthy at the same time.

As I climb the stairs, I rehearse what I'm going to say. This is a trick I learned years ago from my father, not that he'd appreciate it. No matter who calls a meeting, no matter how powerful they might be, you go in with your own agenda.

I find myself doing this even when I know the meeting is going to be positive and supportive, like today. I really like my advisor, Joan Turnbull, but I'm just naturally on edge.

And every so often, my caution is warranted.

When I knock on her door, she waves me in. "And you can close that," she says. Uh oh. A closed-door meeting isn't usually a good thing.

*Set your own agenda.* I don't want to be rushed towards defending my thesis. I can afford to take my time and get it right. I need more publications under my belt.

"I have a colleague at the University of Washington who's quietly planning an early retirement, and the subject of continuing her research came up on a conference call this morning. The India paper is what we're working on together."

My brain shifts gears, my catalogue of Joan's current projects whirring to life.

"I want you to meet with her when you go to Seattle. Have dinner with her. She'll invite some of her colleagues along." She smiles at me. "It would be good to bone up on their undergraduate offerings."

A job. That's what Joan is talking about. I'm speechless. I don't have enough research done yet to graduate, let alone interview for a tenure-track position on the sly. "They'll need to have a proper search..." I finally say.

"Yes, of course. But if you've already met with them, that would give you some advantage in that process. Just think about it." She leans in. "I know you've always been on the fence about going into academia full time, but you have a real affinity for research and rigorous academic debate. I think it would be a good opportunity to at least consider."

"Of course." I nod and give her a sincere smile. "I'm shocked, to be honest. But grateful. And I will do my research as you suggest."

"It will mean accelerating your plans to publish and defend your dissertation."

My chest tightens. "Yes."

"How do you feel about that?"

We've never talked about my father or his plans for me. It

doesn't matter, really. His plans are not my plans, and I'm a grown up.

Mostly.

I'm a grown up in that I'm *not* going to do whatever he wants if it isn't also what I want.

I'm a total chicken in that I haven't exactly told him that.

"It's complicated," I say.

"It often is. Fear of the next step is normal, but you're ready. You've excelled here, but it's time to leave the nest, so to speak."

In more ways than one, but she doesn't need to know that. And I've already been working on a plan in a completely different direction. My stomach twists at the thought of leaving behind my investments here. "There is something I should tell you, though." I take a deep breath. "Over the last two years, I've invested in a few local business start-ups. This is completely separate to my research, and for the most part, I'm a completely silent partner."

She chuckles. "For the most part and completely don't go together."

"Fair point. I—" I glance down at my lap, where my fingers are twisted together so tightly my knuckles are white. "I like to be helpful to my partners, to be a sounding board as needed. Moving across the continent would make that more difficult."

"Ah."

"I'm not ruling anything out. This is why they invented airplanes. But I've put down roots here in Ottawa, and it would take a lot to make me leave."

"Nobody will expect you to commit to anything based on one dinner."

I let out a sigh of relief. "Then I'm really looking forward to meeting her."

---

When I get home after the grad seminar, I'm antsy and distracted, and I still have hours to go until Tate calls. I go to the gym and do a punishing boot camp class, then fall into an extra-hot bath when I return.

By the time he calls, I've come up with a plan. I'm going to bite the bullet and go to Toronto to have a real conversation with my father. Then I'm going to read everything I have yet to read by this prof out on the west coast.

And each time I take another step toward real independence, I'll reward myself with phone sex with Tate. Maybe even in-person sex, too. Frequent flier miles couldn't be put to a better use.

He calls at eleven, and my heart leaps when I hear my phone ring. That won't do at all, so I take my time answering. "Hey," I say after the third ring. "How was dinner?"

"Amazing. We packed away an alarming amount of seafood."

"Good protein."

He chuckles. "For sure."

"Who did you go with?"

"Simec and Moore, and one of the defencemen, Andrushko. It was a bigger group that headed out at the start of the night, but we lost a couple of guys at the pub we went to first. They made friends with the locals."

"That's fun."

"Calling you is better," he says, low and smooth.

"I'm glad you did."

"Do you have your computer handy? I want to send you an email."

"I do." I grab my laptop off my bedside table and open it up.

"What's your email address?"

I tell him, and ten seconds later, a new message pops up from Tate, with the subject line, **Open in private (and then maybe delete this message).**

"What did you send me?" I ask suspiciously as I hover the cursor over the message. I don't click on it.

"Just a link." He is enjoying this way too much already.

"Is it filthy?"

"Of course."

I click into the email, then shake my head. "I'm not watching porn that you sent me."

"It's a visual aid."

"It's degrading to women."

"Just watch it. She's having a pretty good time."

She. Jesus. He hasn't even sent me video of a guy jerking off, which I would totally watch. But I'm curious about what he thinks I'd like, so I turn off the speakers on my laptop and hit play on the video. He doesn't need to know I'm watching it.

"It's pretty hot, eh?"

"I'm not watching it."

"Liar."

"Shut up." On the screen, a woman is making out with a guy, and it's…gorgeous, actually. They're taking their time, and the video quality is top-notch. "Okay, what's next in this ridiculous plan?"

"I'm going to talk in your ear as you watch the video."

"Are you watching it, too?"

"No. I'm imagining you. I bet your cheeks are red."

"Because I'm embarrassed."

"I know. That's what makes it hot, right? You feel filthy."

I do. An achy, annoying heat slides from my belly, up to my chest. It swirls into my breasts, leaving them heavy and tight.

"I missed you today," he murmurs, and that feels filthy, too. Sweetly filthy, like I don't have any right to that longing, but I like it.

"I didn't miss you at all."

He chuckles. "How was work?"

I can't answer a question like that right now, but I like that he asks. "Uh…"

He smoothly slides the conversation back to the porn playing on my laptop. He makes my head spin. "Is she naked yet, or are they still teasing her?"

They? There's only—oh, nope, there's another guy now, knocking on the door. Of course there is. "The second guy just arrived."

"Who do you think he is?"

"Someone who needs to get tested for infection on a weekly basis?"

"No judging. I bet he's the best friend."

I chew on the corner of my lip as I consider the dynamic on the screen. "Her best friend or his?"

"Ah. Hmm, interesting. Yeah, let's say he's her best friend. I like that. Maybe her roommate, too. I bet they knew he'd come home and interrupt them."

I watch him join them on the couch, as they shift towards him in invitation. "Maybe he's watched them before…"

Tate groans. "Yeah. Fuck, see? Now you've got me hard as I think about that."

I like that. I swallow around the lump in my throat. This is hot, but also nerve-wracking. What if I say the wrong thing? "Tell me how hard you are," I finally whisper.

"Painfully so," he says, his voice catching. "And I haven't even unzipped my fly yet."

"You should do that. You should touch yourself."

"Soon. You should, too."

I smile. "I'm already naked."

"Fuck. Next time lead with that." He laughs, and I roll onto my side, settling in to watch the video.

Now I know why he picked this particular one. The first guy is a biter. He's kissing her neck—although kissing hardly feels like the right word for what he's doing. Sucking, nibbling, devouring…but it's hot. It's hot because it's winding her up, and when he stops, she pushes into him.

Practically begging for him to mark her.

"What's happening now?"

"He's biting her."

"Yes. That's so fucking hot. Do you ever wear turtlenecks?" Tate asks in my ear. "I'd love to leave a line of marks from the back of your neck all the way down to your ass."

I have a number of tops that would cover that kind of delicious abuse. "Never," I whisper.

"I'll buy you some."

"Do you ever take no for an answer?"

"Almost always." He clears his throat. "If this too much—"

"No." I say hastily. "No, this is good. Hot. This is very, very hot."

"Good."

"I may have some shirts that climb my neck," I admit. "I was just being difficult."

"I like difficult. You're an amazing puzzle, Sasha."

The truth is, I'm not nearly as complicated as I pretend to be. "I don't mean to be."

"That wasn't a complaint." His words promise something dangerous—that he's already on his way towards figuring me out.

What am I going to do with him then?

I need to get us back on the right track. Dirty, simple fun.

"So I mentioned that I'm naked," I murmur. "But I may have forgotten to tell you how wet I am, too."

He bites off a curse. "Yes. Tell me all about that."

I slide my hand between my legs and squirm as my fingers glance against my swollen clit. I watch the three actors on the screen get naked, and I tell Tate all about how watching them is turning me on.

In my ear, his voice gets coarser and his breath grows heavy. Before the end of the movie, I'm coming against the hard press of my fingers, and in a hotel room in Boston, Tate climaxes with a shout.

"Fuck, I just shot come into the air like a fucking fountain," he says with a laugh. "Good job."

"That was fun," I whisper as I close my laptop and roll onto my stomach, trapping my hand between my body and the bed. *I wish you were here so we could do it all over again. I wish it was your fingers I'd just ridden. I wish I could kiss you goodnight.*

"Sleep tight, Sasha."

"Mmm."

"I'll text you tomorrow."

Tomorrow is a game day. "Good luck. I'll be watching."

## 14

## TATE

THE ROAD TRIP at the end of October comes to an end with a loss in Minnesota, and when we return to Vancouver, I call Sasha.

I expect her to say something about the game.

She doesn't. She asks about the flight, and the weather. Safe, easy conversation where I can just close my eyes and absorb the sweet sound of her voice.

When she pauses, I ask her if she's in bed.

"Yep. Just finished composing an email to my advisor where I had to admit that I may have been inappropriately snarky with a student today."

"There's gotta be a good story there."

She laughs. "Maybe. It depends how amusing you find a robust defence of logic."

From her? I think I'll find it highly amusing. "Test me."

She tells me about how this kid, a second year university student, kept refusing to see the point of a lesson, because it didn't jive with his life experience. "We were getting to the end of the tutorial hour, and frankly, he was being deliberately obtuse. So I said, 'Next thing you're going to tell me is that you need a parachute to go skydiving.' And you can guess how that went."

I frown. "Well, yeah. Of course you do."

She giggles. "No. You only need a parachute to go skydiving *twice*."

Fuck. I walked right into that one. And so did the cocky undergraduate student, too, I bet. I bark a laugh of my own. "So you're sending a cover-your-ass email about that?"

"Here's hoping my advisor finds it as funny as I do."

"I'm sure they will."

"Mmm." She's still laughing, and that does funny things to my insides. Then she sighs, and there's nothing funny about what that does. That's a straight-up lightning-bolt-to-my-dick sound.

"You should put your computer away," I say, dropping my voice to a husky, make-no-mistake-I-want-to-voice-fuck-you level.

"Okay," she breathes.

And then I do. Slow, and sweet, until her sighs are filthy and well-satisfied.

There's something about phone sex to make my bed feel like home, and after, I sleep like a baby.

I wake up at seven the next morning totally jazzed for the day ahead. Practice is scheduled for ten, so I have plenty of time for a leisurely breakfast of eggs and bacon and still get to the arena an hour early to give me some bonding time with the boys. Even though we racked up more losses than wins on this trip, it afforded us as a team an opportunity to connect.

There are a bunch of guys in the player lounge when I arrive. I greet each one as I make my way through the room towards the coffee machine. After making myself a cappuccino, I snag an apple and drop onto the sofa next to Moore.

I go with the safest small-talk I can think of, because that thing with Gibson fucking Laski's wife is still really raw with the team. "I bet your family was happy to see you last night."

"Yeah. Liam, the little brat, woke up when I got in and he

insisted on sleeping in our bed." He says it with a rueful grin. "All night."

"Oh," I say as I clue in to what he's not telling me. Kids complicate your sex life.

"Yeah. I don't mind, though. He's the best part of me, and kids grow up way too fast."

"Did he like his special edition Percy?" I went shopping with Moore to get a present for his son when we were in Boston. I zeroed in on the Thomas the Train display and found a brand-new issue train that lit up and talked. After helping Max with the world's largest teddy bear, I may be developing a knack for this kind of thing.

Moore chuckles. "It was perfect. Thomas makes me super-dad every time, but this one was an extra hit."

"Super-dad? I need to learn this soon," Leclerc says as he parks his ass on the sofa opposite, coffee in hand.

"You're going to be just fine," Moore tells him.

I have nothing useful to contribute to this conversation, so I drink the last of my coffee and excuse myself to get ready to head out onto the ice.

Practice goes really well. While Simec, Moore, and I have a long way to go before we're as slick as my line on the Sens, we're getting there. By the time practice is over, I'm feeling pretty good.

"We're done for the day," Coach says, then turns to me. "Tate, my office once you're finished in the locker room."

My gut twists. True, I hadn't been playing to my abilities, but between that last home game against Edmonton and today's practice, I thought I was getting back in the groove.

I shower and dress quickly, because *when you're finished in the locker room* really means *get your ass moving.*

The door to coach's office is ajar and he looks up when I knock. He motions me in. "Close the door and sit down, Tate."

I nudge the door until the latch clicks, then take the seat across the desk from the man who holds my future in his hands.

"You've been here the better part of two months. The schedule doesn't really have room for a leisurely adjustment period."

Fuck. Just when I feel like things are shifting. "Yeah, it's been more of a struggle than I expected."

"Look, I get it," he says. "After eight years, you got comfortable, and thought you were going to live out the rest of your career as a Senator. So, the trade was a bigger blow to you than some of these guys who get passed around more than a doobie at a Grateful Dead concert. But trades are a fact of life. Take Mike Sillinger. He played on twelve different teams over his NHL career. Even Gretzky got traded. You're not the only new guy here. Between my years as a player and a coach, this is my eighth new team. It's time for you to suck it up, settle in, and make Vancouver home. Understand?"

I nod my head. "Yeah, I get it." He's right, and there's no point in me telling him I'd already figured this shit out for myself. Sometimes you just have to let the coach be the coach.

"You know the Senators weren't looking to trade you."

Maybe not. But at the end of the day they did. This is a business, and I'm just a commodity.

I don't say any of that out loud, of course. But Coach can read it on my face. "In fact, they really didn't want to let you go. But the Lumberjacks want a serious a run at the Cup. This is a multi-year plan we're working, and you're a big part of that plan—no matter the cost. You, of all people, should understand just how much it means to give up first pick overall in the draft."

I do know. But at the time, I didn't give a fuck what they'd given up to take on my contract, so I didn't connect it to my own value, both with the Senators and the Lumberjacks. Coach saying all this out loud actually helps cement my resolve to fully commit to life in Vancouver and with the Lumberjacks. If I didn't understand that this trade wasn't a rejection before, I do now.

"There's more to being a Lumberjack than wearing the jersey,"

I say, holding out my hand. "And I'm ready to commit, heart and soul."

"Glad to hear it. I'll see you in the morning."

I leave his office feeling a little lighter, more grounded, and determined to really connect with my team and my new city.

I head to my car, but home will have to wait. My work-day isn't over yet. I have an appearance on the CBC's *Home Ice Advantage*. I'm looking at it as a warm-up for the busy weekend of public appearances I have ahead of me.

I head downtown to the studio, and I'm glad I scheduled the extra travel time. Traffic across the bridge is a nightmare, because unlike Ottawa, Vancouver's construction season never ends, even in the early afternoon, before rush hour, it's brutal. But I'm quickly learning, and by the time I'm parked and escorted to the studio, I've still got a few minutes to get my head in the game.

Roger motions for me to come in.

"Glad you could make it." He stands and we shake hands, then both take our seats as a staffer puts a bottle of water on the table in front of me. "We're up after the news. Any questions before we get started?"

"No, I think I'm good." After ten years in the NHL, I've done enough of these shows to know the way this goes. I'm going to get asked about the trade, there's no way in any universe that doesn't happen and I'm as prepared as I can be to handle those questions.

I put on my headphones as Roger does the intro.

"Welcome to *Home Ice Advantage*. I'm your host Roger Brown, and we're here with the Lumberjacks' new centre, Tate Nilsson. Tate, great to have you on the show."

"Thanks for having me."

"Let's get right down to the burning question. How did you react when you got the news of your trade? I mean, was it something you were seeking, or was it a surprise?"

Seriously? How could anyone think I had been looking to get traded away from the Sens? I'm careful not to let my irritation show, and I take a moment to formulate an answer that won't get me saddled with an image consultant. "I was shocked, but hockey is a job. If you look at the NHL in terms of the corporate world, it's a bit like being transferred to a different division where they need my skillset."

"Do you look on it as a demotion?"

"No, not at all. I'd say it's more of a lateral-motion."

"But you no longer wear the C on your sweater."

Wow, this guy is really going for the throat. And it's at this point I'm grateful for coach pulling me aside after practice for that pep-talk. It also occurs to me that his little chat coming directly before this interview might not be coincidence. Tricky fucker. "No. But I have a lot on my plate settling into a new situation, so I think it helps some by not having the additional responsibility."

"You've been here for two months, the Lumberjacks are in the basement, and you've only scored two goals. Considering you were one of the top scorers last season, fans have to wonder if your heart is still in Ottawa."

"I'll be honest, there's always going to be a piece of my heart in Ottawa. I have friends, family, and my roots are there. But Vancouver is my new home, and as with every major life change, it takes time to adapt and find a new groove. We've just come off a very successful road trip—"

"Successful? How can you say that when you lost more games than you won on this trip?"

"One of those losses was by a goal late in the third period, one was in overtime, and another went to a shootout. We've really tightened up as a team and we played every bit as well as the teams we faced."

"I know it's still early in the season, but how do you see the Lumberjacks' chances making a run at the cup this year?"

I give him an even look and ignore the smirk I get back. "Our chances are just as good as any other team in the league. We've got plenty of talent and drive, and we've got nowhere to go but up."

"And that's all we have time for today. Tate Nilsson, thank you for being with us today. And good luck against Washington tomorrow night."

"Thanks. We'll give it our best shot."

"And that's it for this edition of *Home Ice Advantage*. Join me, Roger Brown next week when Lumberjack enforcer, Boi Landvic will join us in the studio. Stay with us for *On Location*, coming up after the local news, here on CBC Radio."

I gather my jacket and rise before offering my hand. "Thanks for having me," I say with more alacrity than I feel.

He grins. "Hey, I know I was rough on you there, but you did great."

I'm still irritated, but he was just doing his job. And it's going to be a long season of more of the same. I need the Vancouver market on my side, so I resist the urge to squeeze his fingers until his knuckles pop. "No problem. Comes with the territory."

---

The next night, we chalk up a win against Washington and I want to go straight home and celebrate with phone sex with Sasha, but that will have wait. A bunch of the boys are heading out for beer and wings, and I feel obligated to join them—for a little while, anyway. We had a great game, and it's important we continue that connection off-ice as well.

Landvic, Leclerc, and Onetti are already sitting at a large table when I arrive. "Grab a seat, wings are ordered."

Nodding, I take a seat next to Leclerc. "Great game tonight. You made some righteous saves." And I'm not bullshitting. He more than held his own in those few plays where our defence failed him. I'm tempted to poke at him a little about keeping his mojo for the next game, but we've got three days off and I don't want to risk putting him off. Players can be superstitious fuckers, and Leclerc already has a few…quirks that we accommodate.

After a basket of wings, a beer, and a bunch of good-natured ribbing, I say goodnight to the boys, and head home.

Friday morning, the sun is shining and I decide to take advantage of the nice day before it's time to go to an afternoon appearance at the team store. I pull out my rollerblades and head over to the seawall.

I'm not the only person to have the same idea, but I'm sure it would be even more crowded if it were a Saturday or Sunday.

The temperature is perfect for a leisurely skate.

The views of the North Shore mountains are particularly amazing and I can't resist a selfie. I pull out my phone and fire up Instagram. I double-check the photo of me grinning wide and caption it. Loving #Vancity. I look happy. I am happy.

Saturday night, I do a last check in the mirror before the limo comes to get me for the gala, and I can only think of Sasha. She'd be all over this. Dressed to the nines and one of the first to make a big, fat donation. I have selfish reasons too. Having her here would make this less far less tedious.

Don't get me wrong, I like dressing up, especially for worthy causes, and the glitzy gala scene opens a lot of wallets, but I'm unsure of how to conduct myself.

Back in Ottawa, I had a reputation—attending these shindigs stag often meant pussy at the end of the night, and I'd spend the evening scoping out my opportunities.

Here, I can make a new start. A new reputation.

My alarm goes off at seven on Sunday morning and I struggle to shake the grogginess. It wasn't a particularly late night, and I'd been judicious with the alcohol, but it's been a full weekend of public appearances, and they take a lot out of me mentally.

Sometimes, I think they are more exhausting than playing hockey.

I'd really like to bail on the breakfast I'm scheduled for, but it's to raise money for the Lumberjacks' charity that funds equipment and participation fees to remove economic barriers for kids to play sports, and that's something I can totally give up some free time to support.

I have the world's fastest shower, then head out again to conquer Vancouver traffic, Vancity hockey fans, and my own mental head game.

I'm going to figure this out.

And I promise myself that by the next road trip, we're going to return with more wins than losses, so Roger Fucking Brown has to eat his fucking words.

## 15

## SASHA

NOVEMBER ROLLS in with a wintery blast. For me, at least.

I stare out the window at the swirling whiteness as Tate tells me about the balmy sunshine he's just landed in for the Lumberjacks' southwestern road trip. He sounds tired already.

"Tell me that the traffic is horrid, at least," I say.

"Brutal."

"That's some small comfort. I'm wearing sweatpants over long johns right now."

He chuckles in my ear. "And I'm sure they're sexy."

I glance down at the grey cotton pants and imagine Tate peeling them off me. "I need to move to an apartment with a fireplace."

"I have two fireplaces at my house in Ottawa. One of them is in my bedroom."

He's made the invitation before. We've talked almost every day since his game here, and more than once, me staying at his place the next time he's in town has come up.

I don't know how I feel about that.

When it comes to Tate, I have ugly, vicious waves of jealousy. How many people have been fucked in front of that fireplace in his room? How many at one time? How many on back-to-back days?

Of course, there have been other men in my room, too, but they all pale in comparison to Tate in every way.

"Or…" He rolls right over the silence that I give him instead of an answer. "You could come and stay with me in New York, and we could get a suite with a fireplace."

"When are you in New York?" It's such a farce that I ask him. I know he's there for a week after American Thanksgiving, playing games against the Rangers, the Islanders, and the New Jersey Devils.

"End of the month."

"Mmm." I already have my flight booked, of course. Shopping trip with a side of dirty banging—there was no way I wasn't going to make that happen. "That could work."

"Email me your flight details and I'll have a car pick you up at the airport."

I smile. "Email me your hotel room details and I'll show up wearing nothing but lingerie under my winter coat."

"Okay, have it your way. Will you stay with me the whole time?"

I don't hesitate on this point. I'll put up a lot of walls between us, but I'm not going to lie about how much I want him. "Yes. I can arrive late on Friday and stay until Monday morning."

"Do you want tickets for the Friday night game?"

Any tickets he could get me would be too good. Probably sitting next to wives and girlfriends and visiting parents, and exactly where the cameras would focus over and over again for reaction shots. "I probably won't be able to make the game, but I'll find you afterwards."

"For sure. I can't wait." And that's why I can't lie to him about how much I want him—because he's an open book about being into me, too. For all his frat boy tendencies, Tate is way more emotionally available than anyone else I've ever dated.

He'll need to learn to harden up if we're going to be hooking up on the regular. Because we're going to burn out. We have to. We're too different.

I tug a blanket around me and hunker down against the cushions of my couch. "Tell me more about L.A. Are you going out tonight?"

"We'll definitely go out for dinner. Nothing crazy, though. We didn't get much sleep last night, or the night before." He tells me about the back to back games at home in Vancouver—a win against Detroit—and then a hard-fought loss in Calgary last night, followed by a second late night flight to L.A. He groans as he admits he was up reading until almost five this morning. "And then we had a team meeting."

"That's exhausting."

"Yeah. But we're finally gelling. Even last night, we held our own hard against the best team in the division. They want to keep us focused on what's working, but also keep adjusting the game play so the other teams can't read us."

"That's something I didn't realize before," I say as I burrow deeper into my blanket nest. "How dynamic and fluid the plan is. What lines start, that kind of thing."

He makes an impressed sound. "Someone has been paying attention."

Ooops. "Maybe."

"I like it." He clears his throat. "Are you maybe going to take a nap, too?"

I wriggle my hand under my many layers of clothing. "Is that code for touching myself to the sound of your voice?"

"It is now." He pauses, and when he starts talking again, he's shifted position, because his voice sounds different. "You don't have anything else to do right now, do you?"

I have like six other things I could be doing. None of them trump Tate's dirty talk in my ear as a blizzard rages outside. "Nope. I'm yours until you need to sleep."

## 16

## TATE

"Yo, Nilsson, hurry the fuck up!" The guys hammer at my hotel room door again, and I shake my head.

I'm grinning, though. Good-natured harassment is a form of love in the NHL, and getting to this point was a real challenge. I'll take whatever they want to dole out.

I swing the door open and gesture for Simec and Andrushko to come into my room. "I need two more minutes."

"Pretty boy has to be pretty," Andrushko rumbles.

I flip him the bird.

Simec whistles as he lifts one of the four bottles of hand-crafted reserve bourbon I'm taking with me to Moore's house for Thanksgiving dinner. "What is *this* good shit?"

It's five-hundred-dollars a bottle of gratitude and appreciation. After a rocky fucking start to the season, the Lumberjacks made me an alternate captain yesterday before our game against the Flyers.

"A little something for after dinner." I put my tie on and pocket my phone and my wallet, making sure I've got my hotel key before we grab the bourbon and head downstairs.

Zack Moore grew up in South Jersey, just across the river

from Philadelphia, and he has a sprawling house in the same neighbourhood.

The entire team will spill into his home for Thanksgiving, because we're on an east-coast swing and he happens to be the only guy from this corner of the world.

I'm definitely aware that Moore—the team captain, and the Lumberjack who has been with the team the longest—pulled this dinner together in part because of me. We had a rocky adjustment when I joined the team in August. That was all on me. My head was elsewhere. Back in Ottawa, for reasons.

Now my head is right where it needs to be—in the game, eyes on the prize at the end of the season.

Our hired car pulls up behind another identical one, and there's one behind us, too.

Inside, we find Moore in the kitchen, pulling the biggest turkey I've ever seen out of the oven. "We got some help with the rest of the food," he admits as he sets the pan holding the roasted bird on the stove. "But it wouldn't be Thanksgiving if I didn't do this myself."

His wife drifts by, a kid on her back, and he grabs her and gives them both a kiss.

"All right," he says, clapping his hands. "Let's go check out a bit of the game while that rests, and then we'll eat. Sound good?"

"Sounds great." I hold up one of the bottles of bourbon I brought. "And I have a little something for after dinner."

His eyes light up as he takes the bottle. "Damn good stuff, this."

"Thought it might be worth a little indulging."

Andrushko plunks the two bottles he was carrying on the counter, too. "Hardly a replacement for a warm body, but since this is only action I'll see tonight…come to Papa, bourbon baby."

"It's come to Daddy, you Russian freak," Simec says. "And we'll be back at the hotel with plenty of time to head out, if you want to find a warm body." He shoots me a look. "You could come out with us, Nilsson. I've got some numbers from the last time we were here…"

"Nah, I'm good, man."

"Doesn't need to be anything raunchy."

I almost choke on my tongue. Actually, it would, but I'm not available.

Simec keeps going. He's got his phone out now. "Yeah, this girl." He flashes me a picture of a blonde. "She's in the PR department for the 76ers, I think. She's really sweet. And gorgeous."

"Yeah, still not interested, but thanks." I shake my head. "Much appreciated. Seriously. But I've got a friend back in Ottawa. It's all good."

That turns three heads towards me in a hurry.

Andrushko frowns. "You got a girl? Did we know this?"

Shit, no. And I've said too much. I roll my lower lip between my teeth to keep from telling them all about Sasha.

How she's a Valkyrie with fire in her eyes. How she takes zero shit from anyone. How she's suspicious of men and money, and men with money most of all.

But also how she's sweet when she thinks nobody's looking, when it really counts. How she's nice when someone's world has been rocked. How she's smart all of the time, but never wants anyone to notice.

And she's gorgeous, too.

Instead of telling him any of that, I wave off Andrushko's frown and Simec's curious look. I point them toward Moore's oversized family room, where the rest of the team is watching a football game. And I change the subject to the new cross-training regimen our physical therapists are on about. Work. That's where my focus is.

Not in Ottawa, and the secret friendship I have with Sasha.

Not on how my head is here now, but my heart might be somewhere else.

She doesn't want my heart.

My cock, yes. And that's hers whenever and wherever she asks for it—with the caveat that I've got sixty NHL games to play in the next four months, and we live on opposite sides of the country.

Details.

## 17

## SASHA

I FLY into New York on the day after American Thanksgiving.
Tate has an evening game against the Islanders, so instead of
interrupting his pre-game routine, I catch a cab to the mid-town
building where my father owns two condos. The concierge
recognizes me immediately.

"Ms. Brewster, we weren't expecting you, but this is a pleasant
surprise."

I grin and wave my hand at my suitcase. "Don't panic, I'm not
staying here. I just need to ditch my bag for the evening." I scrawl
the hotel name and room number that Tate had texted me on a
piece of note paper. "And I can swing by later or tomorrow to
pick it up, unless…?"

He gives me a patient smile that I will definitely reward him
for handsomely with a Christmas gift when I leave the city. "We
will see it delivered there at your convenience."

"You are the *best*. I'm heading out for the afternoon. I'll have
some purchases delivered here over the weekend, too. They can
be forwarded to Ottawa as usual."

With a grateful wave goodbye, I return to the steady flow of
foot traffic on Fifth Avenue. All the shops are decorated for the

holidays, and I glide in and out of familiar department stores. By the end of the afternoon, I have three holiday dresses for Ellie, a couple new work outfits for myself, and a tie for Tate. Of all my purchases, it's the only one I keep on me. The others are sent back to my father's building.

The tie is green and purple, just like the Lumberjack jerseys, and I might give it to him this weekend, because it's not really the right Christmas present for him.

Besides I'm not sure if we're going to exchange presents.

I mean, of course I'm getting him something, but the trick with gift giving when you're not sure if it will be reciprocated is to keep it light and thoughtful. A token of sorts. Not a tie. Something that shows that you've been paying attention in a non-creepy, casual observation kind of way.

Something that says, *I notice you. I see that you're—*

I come to a dead stop in the middle of the sidewalk, and people swerve around me. At least two of them curse, because hello, New York, but I don't care.

I know exactly what to get Tate for Christmas.

Now I just need to find it—and I don't have time today, because I need to get out to Brooklyn.

I slot that shopping task into my calendar for Sunday. It might be something best ordered online, but if I can find something one-of-a-kind here, that would be even better.

Feeling quite proud of myself, I hail a cab.

At the arena, I dodge and weave around the Islanders fans thronging toward the entrances. I know there are a lot of tickets still available for tonight's game, so I ask the young man working at the box office window to give me three of the cheapest seats and hand over cash.

Inside, I make my way up the top level and find my seats, right in the middle of the row. I sit in the middle of the three, thus ensuring I don't have to share an armrest with anyone.

One can afford to be a diva when one sits in the nosebleed section.

I pull out my phone and catch up on some emails while I'm waiting, but as soon as the teams are lined up and ready to come onto the ice, I tuck it away.

Tate is announced right in front of Andrushko, a defenceman. My favourite centre charges onto the ice, and when Andrushko follows, he pats Tate on the ass with his hockey stick, and Tate gives him—and the crowd—a flirty smile in response.

I'm going to tease him about that later.

———

The Lumberjacks win, and so easily it's hard to remember that they're still trailing the bulk of their division. My cheeks hurt from grinning. As the final buzzer sounds, I pull out my phone again. I'm not fighting my way through the drunken crowd.

**Sasha: I've arrived in the city. Will meet you at your hotel at eleven. Saw the game, too. Good job.**

Let him think I've just landed and I watched the game on the airplane. It's for the best he doesn't expect me to show up in person.

Once the din has died down, I make my way back to street level and catch one of the waiting cabs. I give him the name of Tate's hotel, then sit back and think about how I want this to go.

Naked, really. That's my agenda.

When I arrive at the hotel, I find the ladies room and strip out of my clothes, carefully folding them into my bag before I button my coat back up.

As promised, I'm only wearing a bra and skimpy panties underneath it.

As I press the button for the elevator, Tate replies.

**Tate: At the hotel and freshly showered. Where is your gorgeous ass?**

I don't reply, but I'm grinning when I knock on his door a minute later. "It's right here," I say, peeling my coat open and cocking my hip to one side.

He takes a step back, and I look my fill of him as I move inside and hand him my jacket. He's bare-chested and his sweatpants are hanging low on his hips.

That's even better than lingerie.

"You had a good game," I said, ignoring the way my heart is trying to hammer its way up my throat. What is this weird feeling battling at my insides?

Oh, sweet merciful crap, I really missed Tate.

And now he's here, and we're both half naked, and I'm trying to make stupid small talk.

"You watched, then?" He hangs my coat up, then sits wide-legged on the bed and pats his thigh.

My heart does that thumping thing again. I stop in front of him and put my hands on my hips. "I did. My favourite part was right before the start. I liked the way Andrushko hit you with his stick."

"You know, listening to our conversations, some people might get the mistaken impression that you don't like me."

"How about that?" I climb into his lap and kiss him, because I can't pretend I don't need his mouth right-the-fuck-now. "Mmm."

We kiss long enough for us both to be breathless, and for his heavy erection to grow to distracting thickness between my legs. But I'm not going to get it just yet, apparently. He tugs at my ponytail. "Are you hungry?" The corner of his mouth twitches. "Do you like me enough to buy me dinner?"

"Yes."

"I want steak." He gives me a slow, filthy appraisal that tells me we're ordering room service instead of going out. "And maybe lobster."

"Whatever fuels you best, alternate captain."

"You noticed the A, too?" He grins. "Excellent."

"Don't read too much into my interest. It's all purely physical. I can't help it if your body is a gift from God that demands my attention."

"Of course not." He tumbles me sideways. "Strip out of that very sexy lace while I order us in some dinner."

I peel my bra off first, as he picks up the phone. Then I stretch out on the bed and wait until he's on the phone with the kitchen before I begin tugging my panties down my hips.

His gaze turns hot, but he doesn't skip a beat in ordering. "And we'll have some ice cream," he says, looking at my breasts, then my belly, and finally at the pink skin between my legs. "What do you have in a berry flavour? Perfect. Thank you very much."

After he hangs up the phone, he leaps on top of me and lightly slaps my hip.

"What?"

"Bad girl. Distracting me when I'm ordering steak you're going to have to pay for."

"And ice cream, too."

"Raspberry," he whispers as he presses his mouth to the sensitive spot behind my ear. "Just like your nipples."

Okay. I'm here for this. I stretch beneath him as he kisses my neck, then my breasts, licking and sucking at my nipples until I'm panting for more. I get it. I get his fingers and his mouth between my legs, and an orgasm so good it makes my thighs shake and little bright spots dance in front of my eyes.

But it's what he says after I catch my breath that really makes my head spin. He looks up at me, his cheek pressed against the inside of my thigh, and he gives me a funny half smile. "You were a little testy when you arrived."

"Was I?"

"Mmm. Nothing an orgasm won't fix."

I grin at him. "Definitely not testy now."

He doesn't ask me what my barbed sharpness was about. I'm glad. I don't really have a good answer, other than he shakes me to my core and I miss him. I don't want to tell him *that*.

But he's not done with the hard questions. "What are we doing?"

I hold his gaze and give him the truth. "I don't know."

"Do you like it?"

"Yes." I wrinkle my nose, because we both know how reluctant I am to admit even that much, and he laughs. Then he crawls up my body and my breath catches in my throat. My eyes burn as he too-gently finds my gaze and holds it. I more than like it, and we both know it.

I like Tate so much it hurts. And I don't know how to handle these feelings.

He rubs his thumb at the corner of my mouth as he looks at me with what can only be described as tender awareness. Damn him. "Are we having an old-fashioned, secret affair?"

That's too heavy. "This is a fling," I whisper.

"Friends with benefits?"

Are we friends? I'd be more comfortable calling us frenemies, to promise myself there's no way I can get close because this is just sex.

A frenemy fling. Four years ago, I would have hashtagged that bitch on Instagram. Now I don't have any social media accounts and the label feels a bit...cliche. Somehow, I don't think Tate would like me calling it that, so I tug him closer and let him kiss me instead.

We both like that. And when we're kissing, the labels for whatever this is don't matter at all. When his tongue quests deeper into my mouth and that hungry yes-yes-yes feeling roars back to life inside me...nothing else matters.

# TATE

I WAKE UP TO A WARM, soft body pressed against my side, and cool, nimble fingers exploring my muscles.

"What time is it?" I mumble as I grope Sasha right back, because I'm not dead and she feels amazing.

"Almost seven." She whispers it, but I can tell she's wide awake.

"You're a morning person."

"I'm also a morning sex person, if that helps. And a nap person, too."

I roll her onto her back and kiss my way down her body. "Excellent," I mumble, but it comes out sounding something like *sesellent*.

"What do you have to do today?" She gasps as I lick her instead of answering. "Tate!"

I lift my head and blink blearily at her. "Yeah?"

"That's it? You ask me what time it is, accuse me of being a morning person, and then go down on me?"

It wasn't an accusation so much as an observation, but that sounds about right. "Yeah. Shhh. Busy."

"Okay." She sighs and drops her head back, and I return to kissing her pussy, because doing Sasha is my entire agenda today.

Coach gave us the day off since we won last night.

And now I'm winning again. Go me.

I do have an idea for tonight, but it'll go over better after an orgasm and some breakfast.

---

She makes a cryptic phone call before we hop in the shower, and when we get out, there's a somber looking gentleman in a black suit waiting outside my suite. She just opens the door and he's there. She gives him a beaming smile and he rolls a large suitcase into the room before departing.

"Who was that?" I ask as she shrugs out of the fluffy white robe she'd put on to answer the door.

"The concierge at my father's building."

"Here in New York?"

"Yes." She says it simply, without her usual bite, but I know better than to ask any more questions.

I grab the suitcase and lift it onto the sofa for her. My shoulder screams from the hit against the board it took last night, and while she gets dressed, I dig out the horse liniment I carry for just this reason.

"What's that?" Sasha shoots me a quick glance. I tell her and she laughs as she holds out her hand. "Can I rub you down?"

"Be my guest."

She climbs onto the bed behind me and smooths just the right amount of the herb-infused salve over my muscles. "Like this?"

"A little harder." Her thumbs dig in and I groan. "Yeah. Right there."

"I like that sound," she whispers in my ear.

I twist my head around and catch her mouth for a quick kiss. She sighs as I pull away, her eyes a little hazy. "I like that sound," I murmur as I touch her lips. "Hey, I have an idea. I was going to suggest it later, but the sounds have me turned on again."

I love the way her face lights up. "What's your idea?"

"You know about the plans for Rapscallion, right? How it's part of a chain of private clubs?"

She pauses, then slides around to sit on the bed next to me. She gives me a guarded, cautious look. "Yes."

"Reid has a club here in New York." I search her face for any clue as to how she's feeling about this, but I get nothing. "We could go tonight."

Sasha should play poker, the way she can hold an absolutely nothing expression for way too long. "Maybe," she finally says. "Let's discuss over breakfast."

She climbs off the bed and finishes getting dressed. Out of her suitcase comes a pair of tall black leather boots, which she pulls over her skin-tight jeans, and then she puts a big, touchable sweater over her long-sleeved t-shirt.

By the time I'm dressed in jeans and a dress shirt, she's got a touch of make up on and her hair is perfectly twisted up into a big bun on the top of her head.

"We might run into guys from the team as we head downstairs," I tell her.

She shrugs. "Then introduce me as a friend who knows her way around New York."

"Oh yeah?" I tug her close and give her a searing kiss. Friends. We need to work that out between us, because nobody's going to believe we're just friends—not the way I look at her. "Tell me what you know about New York."

"I know the best breakfast places are in Tribeca," she murmurs with a smile. "And if you're going to take me to a kink club tonight, I'm going to need a new outfit, too."

Oh, fuck yeah. Fine, we can be so-called friends. Whatever she wants, however she wants it, if she gives me that kind of a kick-in-the-gut filthy feel with a simple promise of a new outfit.

Instead of grabbing a cab at the hotel, she slides her fingers through mine and tugs me towards the subway. Only in New York City would Sasha feel anonymous enough to hold my hand.

We should come here again.

I'm grinning by the time we're on the train. It's crowded, so we stand next to a pole.

She catches my stupidly happy expression and sways into me. "What's that grin about?"

"You. This." I kiss the top of her head. "I wasn't sure you'd come down to spend the weekend with me."

She doesn't say anything to that, but when we get to our stop, she takes my hand again and doesn't let go until we reach our destination.

We're seated at a small corner table, adjacent to each other, which makes it easy to talk quietly once we order.

"So you want to go shopping after this?" I brush an errant lock of hair off her cheek as I lean in.

"Depends. What do you think the dress code is for a club like..."

"It's apparently called Miscreant."

Her eyes go wide. "That's fun."

"Mmm."

"So is it gothic? Like *Eyes Wide Shut*?"

"Probably. The clubs I've been to in Toronto and Los Angeles have been pretty theatrical. The Ottawa scene is way more laid back."

"I didn't even know there was a BDSM community in Ottawa."

Kink is everywhere.

"What will you wear?" She runs her hand over my arm. "I like you like this. Buttons to undo..."

"I can wear a suit."

She makes an appreciative sound low in her throat. "Okay. I'll match that."

Our food arrives, and we dive in. Sasha tells me about her favourite things to do in New York at Christmas, and I tell her about the last time I was in the city, with the Senators. We went skating at Rockefeller Center and acted like kids. It was fantastic.

"I bet that was something," she says with a laugh. "How many of you went?"

"Most of the team. People caught on to the fact that we knew a thing or two about skating, and we ended up taking pictures for a while after."

"Do you like that side of it? Meeting fans?"

"Yeah. Although I wouldn't be recognized here if I was out by myself, or with just you, and I like that, too. The celebrity is confined to being situationally specific." She hasn't fully confided in me, but I know this is a big deal. I hold her gaze. "I like my freedom. I don't need to be public all the time."

She nods, but there's something in her eyes, an edge of concern.

"I know you keep your life private." I get that. My life doesn't need to be hers just because we're fucking. "I won't do anything to risk that."

One side of her mouth hitches up in an almost-smile. "As much as you can."

"Sure. I'm not going to promise something I can't deliver."

"I know." She leans in and kisses me lightly. "I'm a pro at being invisible. It's fine."

"So going to a kink club is…"

"Not something I'd do with anyone else," she says quietly.

I take her hand. "Reid's club is members only. And it's not just money that gets someone in. There's a vetting process for membership, and you need to be nominated by two existing members, no exceptions. It's private. And there are ways to be even more anonymous, although I don't think you need a mask. Nobody will be looking at us. There will be plenty of spectacle put on by those that want to be seen."

As I'd hoped, she has a gorgeous reaction to that. Her lips part and darken, her pupils dilate. Sasha can't wait to watch other people be kinky, and I can't wait to watch her.

But first, we've got an entire day in New York City together. "I bet if we went to Rockefeller Center today, nobody would know who I am," I tell her. "I'd just need to make a stop first."

## SASHA

TATE SENDS some quick texts as I pay for breakfast—something he only questioned for a second, and only silently, with a glance.

"Okay, the assistant equipment manager can meet me at noon to get me my skates." He tucks his phone away and slings his arm around my shoulder. "So we've got until then to do some shopping."

I guess an NHL player doesn't wear rentals, even for a recreational skate.

We hit up a couple of my favourite boutiques in SoHo. At the first place, Tate prowls through the store and picks me out a few things to try on. He's got good taste. But at the second store, I know exactly what I'm looking for. This is the New York location of a chain of stores, and I bought the dress I wore to Rapscallion at the Ottawa location.

If we're going to Miscreant tonight, I want something just like it.

I want another chance to try Tate's brand of kink, at a club and all dressed up.

"There's a chair back by the dressing room," I tell him. "Go have a seat."

He raises one eyebrow in amusement, but does as I request. I describe the dress I bought in Ottawa to the sales girl, and she nods. "We've got a couple of other dresses from that line, they're over here."

I know the one I want as soon as I see it.

The silk handkerchief skirt is variable lengths on this one, showing more leg on the right than the left, and the entire thing is overdyed in a rich dark red.

I shield it from Tate's eyes as I sweep into the change room and shrug out of my winter clothes, but I need someone's help with the zipper—because the bodice is that snug, there's no way I'm doing it up myself—and I might as well use this opportunity to tease him.

Holding the dress against my body, I open the change room door.

He's sprawled like a king in the arm chair, big thighs spread wide, but as soon as the hinge creaks, he snaps to attention and gives me a heated once over. "Now that's a dress with kinky potential."

I wink as I turn around. "Zip me up?"

He stands and stalks towards me. I watch in the mirror as he stops close enough to radiate heat against me, and I wiggle my hips, enjoying how the panels of my skirt swirl around my bare thighs.

He catches his lower lip between his teeth and slowly zips up the dress as he, too, watches our reflection. "The boots give it an extra something, too. Wear those tonight."

I vamp in front of the mirror. Yes, I think I will.

"That's two kinky dresses you own," he murmurs as he sets his hands on my waist. The heavy weight of them makes my chest tight and hot. Makes me hungry for more of his touch, his gaze, his sex.

"That you know of," I whisper back.

His jaw flexes and he gives me a hooded look. "We'll make a deviant out of you in no time flat."

I'm well on my way. "But first a wholesome holiday skate, right?"

His eyes flare bright, and I think for a second he might cancel the whole thing and just drag me back to the hotel for filthy afternoon activities. "Right," he says slowly. "Wholesome is my middle name, after all."

I laugh at him as unzips, his fingers teasing a decidedly *not* wholesome trail all the way down to my ass—and then a little lower, following the fabric of my thong until I'm gasping for him to get out.

He does, retreating to his chair to resume his ridiculous sprawl. Nobody should make sitting look that good, I think as I close the change room door and try to catch my shuddering breath.

---

After meeting someone from the team at Madison Square Gardens and retrieving Tate's skates, we head to Rockefeller Center, where we're ushered into a VIP igloo next to the rink. Tate poses for a quick picture with the couple who had apparently booked this time slot—and who didn't mind sharing it with an NHL player who could get them tickets for Sunday night's game, too.

Once they head onto the ice and the concierge has returned with a pair of rental skates for me, Tate turns all his attention my way. "You want me to teach you how to do some fancy skating?"

I laugh out loud and bat my eyelashes at him. "Oh, Mr. Hat Trick, won't you please show me all your moves?"

He chuckles and pulls me close, his hand finding the bare skin at my waist beneath my shirt. He rubs his thumb back and forth, back and forth, stirring all sorts of dirty feelings in me.

But we're here to skate. I plant my hand in his chest. "Later, big boy. Put your skates on."

"Do you need help getting your laces tight?"

"Is that a euphemism for something?"

"Give me a minute and I'll make it one." He grins. Unrepentant and perfectly filthy.

"I think I can figure it out," I say innocently.

The rentals aren't great, but unlike him, I don't travel with skates.

Back home, I have two pairs, perfectly broken in.

He doesn't need to know that yet, though. I'm happy for him to "teach me" how to skate if it means his hands on my waist, his body curved behind mine.

We make our way to the ice, and he steps on first.

I've been around rinks my entire life, but there's still something impressive about the way he pivots backwards, holding his hands out for me. Pure confidence on blades of steel.

I'm going to enjoy this.

I take a deep breath and push off, gliding right into his arms. He turns me around and pushes off, his legs moving quickly on either side of me. I gasp, because he's really skating both of us, I don't need to do anything.

Damn it, he wasn't supposed to actually impress me, and now he's done it twice in as many seconds.

The rink is actually pretty busy, but Tate deftly weaves around the other skaters. When he slows around a family, I glide ahead, and he catches up again, coming beside me this time.

I reach for his hand and we circle the rink again, fingers linked.

"You can skate," he says when I do a quick step sequence around a stopped couple.

"I can."

"You didn't say."

"You didn't ask," I whisper as he twists me around, holding me in his arms so I'm skating backwards.

He drops a quick kiss on my mouth. "I'm learning that's key with you."

"How about that, eh?"

He laughs and spins me around again. This time I take off. There's no way I can out skate him, but it's fun to get up to speed and feel the cold air rushing against my cheeks.

It's more fun when he catches up again, and this time, he takes my hand.

<hr>

After a stop for coffee, we stroll back to the hotel, doing a last bit of Christmas shopping on the way. Tate buys a few presents for his parents, and I find a pair of cufflinks my father will appreciate.

"What are you doing for the holidays?" he asks in a totally obvious way as we step into the elevator in his hotel, and I laugh. I'm eager to plan our next opportunity to be together, too.

"I'll be in Toronto for Christmas Eve. How about you?"

"I'm flying back to Ottawa. My mom is bringing the Christmas dinner to my house on the twenty-fifth, and then there's the Rapscallion party on Boxing Day. I was thinking…"

I grin at him as he trails off. "I've already agreed to go with you."

"Not that. Although I'm looking forward to that, for sure. No, I was wondering if you wanted to come out to Vancouver. I don't know how much time you have off, but I've got a light week over New Year's, two home games and that's it."

We arrive on his floor, and that ends that conversation, because ahead of us are some of his teammates, strolling towards the elevator.

"Hey, there's pretty boy. Tate, we were just looking for you," a big guy says in accented, easy English. Andrushko, my brain supplies a moment later. He looks different out of uniform. "And..." he swivels his attention to me. They all do. "I am Vladimir. Nice to meet you."

I take his hand. "I'm Sasha. A friend of Tate's from Ottawa."

"Oh," Vladimir murmurs, and I swear he's thinking about lifting my hand to kiss my knuckles.

I pull back, because no thank you.

He winks at me. "We've heard a lot about Tate's friend from Ottawa. We weren't sure you were real, but you are, in fact, real and very beautiful."

My mouth drops open, and I snap it shut as I give Tate a sideways, confused glance. What the hell?

2 0

TATE

DAMN IT. I try to signal to Sasha with my eyes that it's not a big deal, and Andrushko doesn't mean it like that, except he does, and God fucking damn it, why did I say anything to them?

Also, Andrushko needs to get his pervy fucking eyes off Sasha, right fucking now. Obviously they don't know that this is a bad time to be social, but I have damage control to do.

Simec goes in for a handshake, too, but I cut him off at the pass. "We gotta go, guys. Sasha's just grabbing something from my room, and then she's got a busy afternoon. I'll see you later."

I don't wait for them to respond. Planting a hand in the small of her back, I guide her around them and down the hall.

Her back is extra straight, her shoulders stiff and squared off, and the normally soft plump of her lower lip is flexed and tight.

I got a bit sloppy. I promised her we'd keep things on the down-low, and I can see from her perspective how it may seem like that didn't happen.

But this isn't a big deal. I just need to explain to her that the language happened to match up. Friend. Ottawa. And she is beautiful, that's unavoidable.

Except when I let us into my room, she doesn't move very far inside.

Damn it. I take one look at her twisting her arms in front of her and shake my head. "Okay, first of all. I'm sorry. No excuses, I shouldn't have said anything at all to the guys. But I swear, they don't know anything about you."

"They know you have a *friend in Ottawa*. What else have you told them?"

"Nothing."

She chews on her bottom lip. "I thought we'd agreed to keep this quiet."

"We did. We are."

"Who else knows about me?"

"Nobody. They don't know anything, either."

She frowns, her forehead pulling tight, and she squeezes her arms tighter across her chest.

This won't do. I shrug out of my jacket, then wave for her to do the same. "Take your clothes off."

She gives me a disbelieving look. "What?"

"I can see your brain spinning hard, Sash. And fair enough— you set some parameters, and those got busted today. My fault. I'll own that. But we're in private again. And before you storm out of here pissed at me, I want a chance to remind you what's good between us."

"Sex can't save us from this being too complicated." But her voice hitches as she says it.

Oh yes, I think sex can do exactly that. It's not the worst hypothesis to test. "Are you sure? Because I'm pretty sure an orgasm or three would do wonders for clearing your mind."

She looks past me, towards the window. Her expression doesn't crack, doesn't give any clue. The seconds tick by as silence stretches to the point of what-the-actual-fuck, and then she looks down at the plush carpet. "We need to reconsider what we're doing here. I'm not going to storm out, and I'm not pissed, exactly."

"You don't look happy."

She looks up at me. "The last thing I want is to be the centre of a rumour storm."

"I'll shut it down."

"Please do. Our friendship is nobody's business but ours."

Friends.

I'd asked her last night if that's what we were, and she didn't answer me.

Now I know where we stand, and I'm not sure I like it.

But isn't that how I explained our relationship to the guys at Moore's house? *I have a friend back in Ottawa.*

It didn't feel wrong.

It didn't feel complete, either, but we are friends.

And I want to keep fucking.

The rest maybe needs to be off the table—for now.

Except she's not the only one who gets to name terms. If we're re-negotiating this thing between us—and apparently we are, because Sasha's all business now, cool and in control—then I've got some demands of my own.

"I need to know why." The words come out harder than I mean them to, but maybe that's *my* secret. Maybe I'm getting close to my limit of not knowing what the hell is going on in her head.

"I have a history of being in the public eye. I don't like it."

"That's bullshit. You're photographed with Ellie."

"That's different."

"How?" I peel off my shirt and prowl toward her. I'm not above using my naked body to get what I want.

"Tate, put your shirt back on."

"Sasha, take your coat off."

She rolls her eyes. "No, really, put your shirt back on. We need to take a selfie together."

"I thought you wanted to be private."

"Sometimes maintaining privacy means publicly establishing a plausible cover story."

"Fine." I turn around and grab my shirt from the bed. When I turn again, her coat is off. She doesn't hang it up though. So I guess she's still really planning on leaving. Damn it. I sigh and hold out my phone.

She takes it and moves us to in front of the window. "Try and hold it up like this—" She demonstrates what she wants. "So we've got the city in the background."

I take two pictures, then twist quickly and kiss her on the cheek as I take a third. "That one is just for me," I murmur as I pull her into my arms, dumping the phone on the side table.

We may not get to fuck right now, but kissing definitely makes me feel better.

"Tell me what I'm doing with the selfie," I rumble as I haul us backwards and fall onto the bed, pulling her with me.

"Posting it to your Instagram with a caption like, *Ran into a friend in New York. Got some Christmas shopping done.*"

I kiss her instead of telling her that I want to post the last selfie instead. *My girlfriend met me in New York. Having a stolen weekend in the Big Apple.*

"It's for the best," she whispers when I finally stop, and I tug her into the crook of my arm as I stare up at the ceiling.

"You think we're doomed."

She waits a beat before responding. "I think there's a natural end point to being—"

"Don't say fuck buddies."

"Intimate, then." She says it softly. "I can only do this if it's private. That's just who I am. I'm finishing up my schooling, and then who knows where I'll end up? We're in different places. Literally, figuratively. Geographically."

Emotionally, too. She doesn't need to spell that out. I've wanted more from the very beginning.

How the hell did I get to a place where *I'm* the sap. What the hell?

She takes a deep breath and sits up, turning to look at me. "Anyway, I don't like the word *doomed*. That suggests we have goals beyond the here and now, and I've been very careful—"

"Ever so careful." I sound snarky, and we both know it.

She raises one eyebrow. "Have I not been clear?"

Yeah, she has. I sit up, too. And I take her hand. "Crystal."

"So don't say we're doomed. We're not. We are exactly what we are able to be, and nothing more. And when we come to a mutually agreed upon end to our fling, we'll still be friends."

Mutually agreed upon nothing. My chest tightens. "Is that so?"

"Of course."

"Are you going to be able to see me bring someone else to Rapscallion? Fuck someone else, if she's into public stuff? Are you going bring someone around? Because I won't handle that well."

She frowns. "That's not fair. I mean, of course we'd both eventually have other relationships, but I wouldn't rub your face in it."

"You wouldn't need to. The second you start dating someone else, I'll *know*, Sasha."

"I don't want to think about that. I only want you. I don't want..." She gestures at the window. The outside world. "All of that. But I *do* want you. I'm here, aren't I? You knew I was upset, and yet I'm right here. I stayed. You said stay. You said come to New York, and I was here, no questions asked. I already had my plane ticket booked. There's a secret for you. I was coming here already, before you even asked. I was going to be here just in case you wanted me as much as I want you."

"I do."

"Then stop worrying about what we aren't. What we are is this, and it's everything to me. So stop pushing me to give you something else."

Something she never offered.

I tamp down my objection, because she's right. And what we are is something special. I can focus on that. "I still want to take you to Miscreant tonight."

She leans in, and this time it's her that topples me over. She stretches out on top of me and kisses me softly. "Of course. I'll meet you there, though. I need to go make sure I'm seen elsewhere."

That's something I'd never have considered, and it makes me curious all over again for what Sasha hasn't told me. "Where can I send a car to pick you up?"

She wants to protest, but the address is private and for members only. She kisses me one last time, then gives me the address of her father's building.

I'm about to protest again when she stops, her coat in hand, and gives me a coy, sideways glance. "I'll still come back here tonight, though, if we can manage that in secret. I just won't leave tomorrow, if you don't mind me holing up for a few days."

Relief blooms in my chest. "I won't mind at all."

"Then I'll see you tonight."

21

SASHA

Even though they weren't expecting me, the concierge team at my father's building is accommodating. I head back to the condo to do some work for the afternoon.

Tate texts me a picture of him, sweat-slicked and ripped post-workout, two hours after I leave his hotel room.

**Tate: How I'm spending my afternoon.**

I text back a picture of my laptop and research papers.

**Tate: You should study naked.**
**Sasha: You should go find some teammates to have dinner with.**
**Tate: I'd rather bring you dinner. I can feed you while you study naked.**
**Sasha: I'm wearing six layers of flannel. I'll see you tonight. What time is the car coming?**
**Tate: Nine.**
**Sasha: Can't wait.**
**Tate: Get naked.**

**Sasha: Leave me alone.**

---

At half-past-nine that evening, the towncar Tate sent for me stops outside a row of brownstones on a quiet street in Brooklyn. I hurry up the stairs and ring the bell. The ornate wooden door is opened by a tall, muscular man wearing a tux, who steps aside immediately and lets me in, but bars me from moving beyond the private foyer.

"Can I help you?" he asks.

"Yes, I'm a guest of Tate Nilsson. Sasha Brewster."

He pulls a phone from his pocket and swipes at it with his finger a few times before looking. He nods, then steps aside, motioning me through the interior door he swings open. "Welcome to Miscreant, Ms. Brewster."

I give him a quick smile at him as I enter a larger hallway dimly lit by crystal chandeliers.

"Sasha." I turn at the sound of my name. I should have known Tate would be here, waiting for me.

He helps me out of my coat and hangs it in a large open closet next to the door.

"Ready?" he asks.

I take a deep breath and nod.

He leads me around a sweeping staircase into a larger room, with matching chandeliers, lit a bit brighter here. The walls are covered in a creamy floral print damask, and there are groups of vintage style leather sofas and arm chairs arranged throughout.

Elegant. Classy.

And crowded. I'm surprised at how many people there are. My limited experience has been in the context of an intimate gathering of friends. This is both a bit scary and freeing. Scary, because it's unfamiliar, and freeing because it feels anonymous.

"Would you like something to drink?" Tate asks.

I nod my head. "Sure, a glass of red wine would be great."

With this hand at my lower back, Tate guides me to an empty sofa with an excellent view of the room. "I'll be right back," he says before heading to the bar.

I watch him walk away. He's wearing a black suit. The cut of the jacket accentuates his physique. My gaze quickly settles on his ass. Because it really is a very fine ass, and the fit of trousers show it off perfectly.

Out of the corner of my eye, I catch a flash of red, and I turn my head slightly. There's a woman wearing a deep red corset with a black leather pencil skirt and red spike heel pumps leading a man on a leash. He's trussed up in some kind of leather harness. Straps connected to metal rings cross his shoulders and circle his torso and connecting at his waist to a leather thong with a padlock. I'd been kind of fascinated by Beth's dynamic with Lachlan at Rapscallion, but this is a whole different level.

Tate returns with our drinks and hands me my wine before sitting next to me. "Not my kink," he says as he follows my gaze.

"Not mine either, but there's something about it…" I trail off as the leashed man glances up at me, then immediately back to the floor. His…mistress?…says something under her breath, then gives me a cool look. Not negative, just dominant. Whoa. I raise my glass at her in respect and she smiles.

"Do you know anyone here?" I murmur, turning my head slightly towards Tate.

"Nope. But I know people just like everyone here. See anything else you find interesting?"

I look around again. Standing just to the side of us, is an auburn-haired woman in a gorgeous school girl uniform. A blue and green tartan skirt, white socks, black patent leather Mary Janes. Her white shirt is undone enough to show some cleavage, and her navy tie, complete with a crest, is knotted loosely below her first fastened button.

There's the low hum of many voices resonating through the

room, but I do catch snippets of the conversation she's having with a guy wearing leather pants and a tight black t-shirt. Things like *role play, no single tail,* and *liver.*

I must look a little confused because Tate leans in close. "They're negotiating. Discussing what they will and won't do with each other. Safewords. Sounds like hers is liver."

I laugh. "That's a good one." Not a word I'd ever utter by accident during sex, that's for sure.

He grins at me. "Notice, she's not wearing a collar? Not everyone who comes to a club like this brings a date. She's free to play with whomever she likes, and from the looks of things, she likes," he says as the couple wander off towards the stairs.

I nod and take a sip of my wine. It's good—but then why wouldn't it be? Everything about Reid Porter is pure money, in an understated, knows-where-to-spend-it kind of way.

And he attracts an interesting crowd. One of the things that really grabs me is how elaborate some of the outfits are. Not in a fashion-conscious upstage-each-other-and-gossip-later kind of way. I know what that feels like, and this is different. I'm captivated by the un-self-conscious way people present themselves.

When we're finished our drinks, Tate takes my glass and sets it, along with his own, on the small table next to him. "Let's go explore."

"Absolutely." Between the glass of wine and the people watching, I've shifted from uncertain to eager.

Holding my hand, he leads me up the twisting staircase. There's a set of heavy doors on the first landing, and as soon as we walk through, the ambient noise morphs from the low hum of conversation to slap of flesh punctuated by moans, groans, and squeals.

On the next landing, there's a long hallway to the right, and the other side opens into a room nearly as large as the one we'd just left. The scene is not unlike the one at Rapscallion, or Max's holiday party. Only here, there is more equipment and people using it.

"Ah, the dungeon," Tate says with enthusiasm. "I think we should start here. Let me know when you're ready to move on to the next scene."

There is a clear route through the various stations, almost like a kinky IKEA, and each has a small area for spectators. We stroll along the pathway past two couples still setting up their scenes. The next is a female Dom and a male submissive, similar to the couple I'd been fascinated by downstairs, and Tate stops to watch.

I lean into his side, my pulse racing as I watch people I don't know do something incredibly private—in a pretty public way.

That's so hard for me to wrap my head around.

"Enjoying yourself?" Tate murmurs in my ear.

I am. But I'm more interested in the woman's leather corset than how she's torturing her sub, so I nod my head toward the next scene. "We can move on."

"Whatever you want," he says, his voice low and for my ears only. A dark, heady thrill runs through me. I believe he means that literally.

I don't know what I want, exactly, but the next scene is getting closer. It's like what I've seen at Rapscallion, only amped up a thousand percent.

A dark-haired woman is strapped naked and face down to a spanking bench, where she's being fucked by two men, and a blonde woman is helping them.

My breath catches in my throat as I try to take it all in. Straining muscles, guttural groans, and desperate, turned-on whimpers.

None of the casual restraints I've seen Max and Hugh use, either. This woman can't move at all. Her leather-cuffed wrists and ankles are attached by clips, and thick leather straps span her upper and lower back. In her hand is a rubber ducky, which is totally incongruous to the scene.

I tap Tate on the shoulder and rise to my toes as he leans down. "Any idea why she's holding that?" I ask him, quietly.

"It's hard to say your safeword when you've got a cock driving in and out of your throat," he says, completely straight-faced.

Good point.

Wide-eyed, I return my attention to the foursome. One of the men has a tight grip on the braid at the back of her head while he thrusts his hips forward. I'm kind of in awe of this woman, taking his entire length down her throat.

Behind her, the other man directs the blonde woman, who steps in and presses a vibrator against the bound woman's clit. The bound woman moans and as she tries to buck her hips, the man behind makes a cut motion with his hand. The blonde immediately pulls the vibrator away and moaning quickly changes to a growl, which elicits a huge grin from the man in charge. "Aw, you sound frustrated, pet. But it's only polite to wait for Master Geoff to come before you get your turn."

Geoff must be the guy with his dick down her throat.

How surreal to know their names.

Not-Geoff nods at the blonde and she goes back in with the vibrator until she's silently ordered to retreat again.

"Mmmm, I think I could go like this for hours," Master Geoff says, and now two of them have voices. There's something about that added touch of reality that makes me all tight and hot and wound-up inside. "What do you think, angel?" He's looking at the blonde as he says that. "Should I torture pet and keep going, or take mercy on her and come right now?"

The blonde gives him her full attention, and the puzzle pieces start to click together. She's submissive, too, but maybe not as much as the one they call pet. In my head, neither angel or pet is capitalized, and I make a mental note to ask Tate about that later. Too complicated for a whispered conversation right now, and I don't want to give up any of my attention. Not when…angel…has a decision to make.

Geoff grins. "But there is a catch. If you say she gets mercy, then you don't get to come until Master Colin gives you permission." Whoa. "Now, that could be sometime tonight, or it could be the next time we play together, or even longer."

My eyes feel like they're as big as saucers. And they get even bigger when the blonde says, sweet as can be, "Give her mercy, please, Sir."

"Fuck, angel, sweet and selfless as always." Master Geoff speeds up his thrusts and it's not long before he lets out a long moan, his hips held tight against pet's face. He withdraws and nods at Master Colin, who motions for angel to move in with the vibrator again. Without letting go of pet's hair, Master Geoff leans down and kisses her. He's so gentle, it's hard to reconcile it against the way he'd been fucking her face just moments earlier.

Tate takes the moment of quiet to ask me if I want to move on. I nod silently, eyes still glued on the foursome as they shift towards giving pet her well-deserved release. Tate doesn't shift a muscle until she gets it, and I squeeze his hand.

We stroll past two more scenes, but I'm on sensory overload, and he clearly gets that, because he leads me out of the maze of sex. We spill out at the far end of the hallway we saw before, and here there's a small nook that's well shadowed.

Tate tugs me into the darkness and presses me against the wall, shielding me from anyone who might pass by.

Without saying a word, I reach for him. Reach. Ha. I grab him, my fingers twisting into the thick waves at the back of his head as I crush his mouth onto mine. His hands go unerringly to where I need them. A palm, hard and hot against my breast. Fingers sliding under the ribbons of my skirt to find me wet and hot, swollen and desperate for release.

But he doesn't stroke me to a quick, furtive orgasm. He covers the whole of my sex with his hand and squeezes. "I know," he whispers against my mouth as I gasp. "I know you want to come. I know you're turned on. But I want you to wait until you don't have to muffle your cries. Until I can see your pleasure and drag it out."

"Those sadists have given you terrible ideas," I say, my voice hitching as I nip at his lower lip.

"Yep."

I laugh weakly and squeeze his hand between my legs. He rewards me with a slow rock of the heel of his hand against my clit, and I thump my head back against the wall.

"Tell me what you're feeling," he says as he kisses my exposed neck.

"I want you to fuck me."

"Mmm. Me too."

That's not what he meant and we both know it. "I'm kind of overwhelmed. And turned on."

"Good." He licks at the base of my neck, where my erratic pulse is hammering out of control.

I sigh, long and ragged, and try to pull my scrambled thoughts back together. "It's a little strange to take so much pleasure in watching others when I hate having my own privacy invaded. Don't you think?"

"Are you invading their privacy?"

"You know what I mean."

"We talked about this before."

"They need an audience…" I trail off. They need us to watch. "They didn't seem aware of us, though."

"They were kind of busy. And not everyone is interactive with an audience. But I bet we can find that for you, if you want."

"I don't know what I want."

He rolls his thumb over my clit and I leap like he's triggered a live wire. "Are you sure?"

"Shut up."

"Such talk from a pretty mouth."

I grin. "If you were a sadist, you'd push me to my knees and put my mouth to better use."

"Is that what you want?"

I want to watch someone else do that. I want Tate to leisurely finger me as I get wetter and wetter… "I want to go see more things."

He steals a kiss, hard and fast. "Then we'll do that. Maybe something more interactive? Or do you want a secret look inside other people's filthy lives? The majordomo told me there's a room upstairs where you can watch from behind glass."

"I don't know about that."

"Next time, maybe."

I nod.

"How about a good, old-fashioned orgy?"

Heat washes over me. "Yes. Please."

He straightens my dress, then we head to the other side of the townhouse. Tate points out some of the architectural modifications Porter has done. "He bought the adjoining townhouses to give some buffer space on either side of the club. Apparently he uses one side as office space and the other is his personal apartment when he's in New York."

Colour me impressed.

We enter a rectangular room with a floor to ceiling window that runs the entire length. Most of the room is empty, like a stage, with a single oversized leather couch on a raised dais in front of the windows. Smaller loveseats line the opposite wall, for spectating or maybe more active participation. I get the impression that anything goes at Porter's clubs.

There is one couple already there, sitting on the sofa on the far side of the room, and they're off in their own little world. Tate leads me to the loveseat closest the door. "If we sit here, we can move on without disturbing anyone else."

I look around the nearly empty room, about to say something snarky when a door at the far end is shoved open, loudly smacking against the wood panelling. In stumbles a nearly naked woman, a glorious smile lighting up her face even as she twists and tries to evade a man chasing her down.

Behind them follows a staff person in a suit. His ear piece gives him away. "Dungeon monitor?" I ask quietly.

Tate kisses my temple. "You catch on quick."

"Does that mean this might get—" Rough, I was about to say, but then it does, and the word dies on my tongue.

The guy catches the woman and hauls her back against him, his hands grabbing as much of her flesh as they can. His fingers leave white imprints on the fleshy curve of her hip and the top of her chest. "Caught you," he growls loud enough for all of us to hear. "And it seems we aren't alone, little one. Is that what you wanted? You wanted others to see you be pinned down and fucked like the good set of holes you are?"

I must gasp, because Tate covers my mouth with his hand. And he has to tug me back into his side, so maybe I was about to jump to the woman's rescue, too.

I shoot him a look, and he grins.

"Warn a girl next time," I murmur as I settle back against him.

"I didn't know that's what was going to happen." He winks and points back to them, where the woman is twisting helplessly and apparently blissfully happy for that fact.

The guy drags his very willing prey to the dais, where he folds her over the arm of the couch and presses down hard between her shoulder blades.

Then he looks right at me and smirks as he slides his fingers between her legs.

I stop breathing, and after what feels like a million seconds, but is probably only one, he shifts his attention to the couple on the other loveseat.

I follow his gaze, the tightness in my chest easing as I realize he's not going to return his gaze to me.

I'm the watcher, buddy. Freak other people out.

Or not. The loveseat guy says something to the couch guy. I miss it, because my head is still buzzing from the uncomfortable jolt of being caught in my voyeurism.

"You okay?" Tate asks quietly.

"Yeah." I sound breathless and horny, which is bang on.

"Do you want to—"

"Stay. I want to watch."

He drags his fingers up my neck and into my hair, stroking my skin gently. "Then we'll watch."

There aren't any straps or cuffs in this scene, but it's even more dominant than the first one we watched. Basic and primal in his aggression, the couch guy manhandles his partner, using his language and his body to push her buttons.

And then as if previously choreographed, and maybe it was, the other couple moves to join them. The second guy drags his partner along, ripping her clothes off her as they go.

Then there are two mating couples in front of us, grappling and fucking like their lives depend on it.

I can't look away. I can't stop squirming.

"You like it when more people get involved," Tate whispers in my ear. His warm breath grazes my skin, sending a flash of heat to my sex.

"Mmm."

"I'm putting that on my Sasha List of Approved Kinks. Group action is a thing for you."

"I...I wouldn't say a thing." *Liar.*

"It turns you on. The more people the better. I'd definitely call that a thing."

"Watching it turns me on," I confess.

"I hear you loud and clear, tiger. No touching. That's strictly for you and me."

Yes. I lick my lips and nod, but I can't look at him. My gaze is glued on the writhing foursome in front of us.

"But if we got closer..."

There goes my breath again. Gone. Vaporized.

He sinks his teeth into my earlobe and tugs. "Not tonight. But if you ever want to. We could ask people to fuck right beside us if you wanted."

I don't know what I want. On the couch, someone groans that they're about to come, then a female voice echoes the same thing.

It's a surreal tableau. As the last cries of ecstasy fade, Tate stands up, pulling me with him. He leans in. "We're done here," He says as he slides a hotel keycard into my hand. "The same car that brought you here is waiting outside. It will take you straight back to the hotel and in through the underground garage. Meet me in my room."

## 22

## TATE

NEED POUNDS through my veins as the elevator carries me up to my floor. I'm only a few minutes behind Sasha. How will I find her waiting for me?

Naked, maybe.

She likes to be naked.

Lingerie…she likes that, too. That skimpy little thong she was wearing under that dress might have a matching barely-there bra, and I'd happily sink my teeth into her through those scraps of fabric.

Or maybe she's still dressed, waiting for me to—

The elevator dings and the doors slide open.

I was wrong on all three counts.

Well, maybe not the last one. She's still dressed.

But she's waiting right in front of me, the empty hall stretching behind her.

"Sash?" I frown, wondering if something is wrong, but she doesn't say anything. She just stands there, a tentative smile curling her perfect mouth.

Her eyes sparkle, and it takes me an extra beat to catch on because all I can think about is being inside her.

But it's going to take a bit more work tonight.

She takes a step back, then another.

She wants a chase.

The already growly need inside me roars to life. I roll my lower lip between my teeth as I pace forwards. She turns and sprints down the hall. That's fine. She's gotta get the door open, and now nerves are probably making her hands shake.

I'm steady as a beast on the prowl.

She skids to a stop in front of my door, then fumbles with the key card. I grin when the light flashes red for her.

The ragged, desperate breath she takes sends a jolt of awareness straight to my balls. I've never played with primal kink, but for Sasha? I'll pin her down and make her fight me. I'll earn her scratches, her hisses, her cries of submission as I find her wet and ready.

She tries again, but I'm closer now. Close enough that when the lock clicks and whirs, it's my hand that closes over the handle and opens the door—only to push her through it, urging her to run again.

She can't run far, though.

"We're all alone now." My voice is rough and low, and my words send a visible shudder through her body.

Click. The door shuts behind me.

She whirls around, her hands balled into fists—and she's smiling even as her eyes go wide and her lips tremble. "I wasn't sure if you'd like that."

I unbutton my jacket and crudely cup my erection through my suit pants. Yeah, I liked it.

Pink dots bloom on her cheeks. Her next words slide out on a breathy whisper. "I don't know what to do next."

I've never wanted to be a teacher more than in this moment. "I've got a few ideas." I take my jacket off, then reach for her, one hand wrapping around the side of her neck as the other clamps down on her hip. My fingers slide through the ribbons of her skirt, and that's even better. I shift my grip until I'm squeezing a handful of ass, my fingers teasing the edge of her soaked panties. "You're wet. Is that for me?"

"Y-yes." She sways, and I tighten my grip, stilling her. Her eyes go wide and her gaze finds mine.

"Unzip your dress."

She reaches back and after a quick tug, the gorgeous red silk tumbles down her body.

No bra. I cup her breast, squeezing the flesh just hard enough to make her gasp, before I trail my fingers up her pebbling flesh and around her neck again.

She's so gorgeous. Sun-kissed skin, polished to perfection at the best spas, I'm sure.

"We've never discussed safewords," I murmur as I rub my thumb over the pulse point at the base of her neck. "But you need one tonight."

She swallows, a delicate working of the muscles in her throat. "Red works for me."

"Good. Yellow for caution, as well." I kiss her hard, then whisper against her mouth, "You may need that in a minute."

She gasps as I spin us both around. I sit on the bed, then pull her over my lap.

"Tate!"

I squeeze her ass as I push down between her shoulder blades, adjusting her position until she's nicely off-balance. "Yes?" God, she feels good. I push her legs apart, grabbing a good fistful of her thigh as she flails a bit, looking to get comfortable.

Oh, no, tiger. There's no comfortable tonight.

I slap the inside of her legs, and she gasps. "Did you have something to say?"

She shakes her head and presses her hips into the air.

I grin and spank the fleshiest part of her bottom.

I'm no sadist. I don't want to hurt her, or punish her. But the pink bloom that spreads across her skin? That's the hottest thing

I can imagine right now. Beneath her, my erection thickens again, heavy and hard. I'm going to fuck her into the mattress when I'm done.

I slap her ass again, reddening it. Marring that perfect skin.

This is gorgeous, too. Breaking down her polished veneer and mussing her up. I like Sasha wearing my mark. Three more spanks on either side have her squirming, and my dick is throbbing for attention.

Grabbing a fistful of her hair, I guide her to her knees while I use my other hand to free my aching cock. Her eyes go wide as she realizes what I'm doing now.

"I caught you," I murmur. "So I get to use you however I want."

Not really. She gave herself to me willingly. Maybe one day we'll have enough space to actually play pursuit for real. I'll chase her until she's breathless, and then fuck her in the wild.

But for now, we need to pretend that's happened. It's an easy fantasy to slip into. There are a dozen ways I want to lay my claim on Sasha.

Her eyelids flutter as she licks her lips.

Fucking hell, that's hot. I rub my swollen head against the corner of her mouth as I give her a fair warning. "Right now, I'm going to use your throat." I stroke myself, showing her just how much cock I'm going to make her swallow. She might gag, and the thought of that makes me even harder. "Slap my leg if it gets too much, understand?"

She nods and licks her top lip.

Fuck. Me.

"Good enough." I press gently against her lower lip, forcing her mouth open. She sucks at my thumb and whimpers when I pull it away, but I've got something better to stuff into her mouth.

Cupping her head, I push her down until the tip of my cock brushes against the back of her throat. It feels so good I want to fuck her face already, but patience will be rewarded, even when I'm acting like a primal motherfucking asshole.

I pull her up a touch, then push her down a bit farther.

She lurches slightly, and my cock twitches as her throat constricts, then relaxes a bit. Jesus, that sends shivers up my spine.

"One day I'm going to watch my entire length slide deep into your throat," I say. "Until then, I'm perfectly happy to make you slobber and gag as you learn to take me."

I push down a little more to make her gag again before I ease her back. "Suck," I tell her as I pump her head up and down my shaft a few times.

Her mouth feels like heaven, and I've been riding the edge all night. I'm not going to last very long.

She hums around my dick and the vibrations make my balls tighten. I push her head back down and make her gag one last time, then I settle her mouth into a steady rhythm up and down my cock. Fuck. I need to pull out, or I'm going to spill my seed down her throat, and that won't fucking do. Another time.

Tonight, I want to come in her pussy.

Using my hold on her hair, I pull Sasha's head backwards. She gasps and looks up at me. My gaze feels molten as I lean in and lay a hard kiss on her mouth. "So much more of you still to ravage."

I drag her up by her hair, and I don't miss that she's shaking. But every time she shoots me a quick look, it's accompanied by a secret smile, too.

We're both enjoying this.

"Hands and knees," I tell her with a growl as she tries to flop out on the bed.

She gives me a hard, pouty glare as she rolls onto all fours, then starts crawling away from me.

Grabbing her ankle, I lean forward and wrap my other hand

around her waist, then yank her back. I bite the fleshy part of her still pink ass.

She sucks in a sharp breath, and that sound sends blood straight to my already sensitive, on-the-edge-of-exploding cock.

I trace the mark with my tongue, then nip my way up her back until I reach her shoulder, giving it a slightly harder bite. "Behave," I warn her, not meaning it at all. We'll both enjoy it if she doesn't.

Releasing my hold around her belly, I move to grab Sasha's wrists. She twists and scratches at me, shoving her way free.

She doesn't get far. We wrestle until I've got her back where I want her, then I bring her arms roughly behind her back, trapping them easily in one hand while I use the other to free my belt.

She tests the strength of my hold, but sags when she realizes I'm not letting go.

"What are your safewords?" I ask as I secure her wrists with the leather.

She twists her head to look at me. "Red and yellow."

"And do you wish to use one right now?"

I get a smirk for that. "Hell no."

Good. Pushing her down, I kneel between her legs, and use my knees to spread her wide, then trap her ankles under my own.

"You're awfully wet," I trail my finger through her sopping pussy and slide it up and slowly circle her tiny puckered hole. "Maybe I should stake my claim here tonight." I circle again, and press my fingertip gently against the centre and she tightens up. It's tempting. But I'm not in the mood for gentle, and that's the only way I'm taking her there.

At least the first time.

Grabbing a handful of her hip, I squeeze. I want my marks all over her. I grab a condom from my pocket and quickly cover up, then I position myself at her entrance.

She bucks hard.

Game on.

I reach down for the belt secured around her wrists and use it for leverage as I slam home.

She's tight and hot, and the sounds she makes as I bottom out are better than any drug I can imagine.

I roll my hips and my balls slap against her even as they draw tight.

I'm not going to last long. Not a problem as long as I get her there first. Flexing my thighs, I pulse my hips, driving into her again. My cock feels big and rude inside her, an intrusion. Invasion.

Speaking of which…I rub my thumb over the clenching knot of her asshole, and she bucks beneath me.

"Nowhere to go, Sasha…"

She cries out as I press against the sensitive flesh, alternating with the driving thrusts of my cock inside her pussy.

"How do you want to come?" I ask her, my voice guttural and desperate. I want to spill myself inside her. Mark her from the inside out. "With my cock in your pussy? Or back here?"

"Ah…"

Fu-uuuck. As an out-of-control tremble takes over her entire body, I push in, fucking her ass with my thumb. Her pussy clenches down on my cock, and my control vanishes.

I tumble forward, shoving her into the mattress as I pound my hips against her, charging after my own release as she comes apart.

White spots light up the corners of my darkened vision, and I brace myself up on one arm. Jesus, my thighs are cramping up. Fucking worth it.

I deal with the condom, then release her arms, rubbing them all the way up to her shoulders. She rolls onto her back as I stretch out beside her.

"That was…" She laughs weakly and throws her arms above her head as she gives me a pleasure-filled smile. "What the hell was that?"

"A lot of fun."

"Yeah."

"You want to do it again?"

"Yes." She laughs under her breath, and I haul her close. She kisses me, then runs her fingertips over my collarbone. "We're both probably covered in scratches and bruises. You might get some looks in the shower tomorrow."

"I'll find a private stall."

She gives me a thoughtful look. "I may have overreacted about people knowing about us."

I don't care about that. I do care about the wall I can't seem to get over, that guards all her secrets. But that's a battle for another time. I haven't earned her secrets yet.

We'll get there, though. I push against her, pressing her into the mattress again, and she makes a happy little sound. We'll get there. We have to.

She's too perfect for me. I'll do whatever it takes to hold on tight.

## 23

## SASHA

Sunday is a game day, so Tate heads to Madison Square Gardens early for their morning skate. He comes back to the hotel for lunch and a nap before leaving again at three. The last time I dated an athlete, we lived in the same city and he didn't want me in his space on game days.

There are a lot of things that are different about Tate. The way his face lights up when he sees me after being away for a few hours.

I consider going to watch the game in person, because I know he'd like that, but there are some—a lot—of things I need to sort out before I can take that step. So I stay in his room, instead, and get work done right up until the moment the game begins.

Once it does, I'm glad I decided to stay behind instead of going to Madison Square Gardens. It's an epic disaster almost from the beginning and I have a hard enough time watching—cringing—in private, I can't imagine what it would have been like if I were there.

Over and over, I'm tempted to turn it off because it tears me up inside to see things going badly for Tate and his team. And every time I reach for the remote, I stop myself because it would be like turning my back on him when things are rough. And that's not me. What is me, is that little glimmer of optimism. That there's still time for them to pull it together.

Until there isn't.

When the final horn blows, the Lumberjacks head off the ice, heads bowed. The final score is five to one. A loss is a loss, but at least they weren't shut out. I don't know why that matters to me, but it does, even though Tate wasn't involved in that single goal.

I turn off the television. I don't want to see them interview Tate. It's going to be ugly. Everyone has high expectations of him, and I know he's already beating himself up. I don't need to watch the pile on.

More than that, I don't want to watch it. I know for Tate, it's part of the job to be accountable to the press and the public. But there's a level of discomfort for me that goes beyond that of witnessing the equivalent of him screwing up at the office. Between interviews and getting showered and dressed, it's going to be well over an hour before Tate gets back, so I haul out my laptop to do some work.

Nearly two hours after the game ends, I hear male voices in the hall. Tate's back. I close my laptop and put it away. Then I feel awkward. I'm not sure what to do with myself. If they'd won, I would have been naked, posing provocatively on the bed. That's exactly the wrong thing in this instance, and I hate that I don't know what to do.

The electronic lock clicks and Tate walks in. He looks miserable and my heart aches.

He shoots me a wan smile. "You're still here."

"I said I would be."

"We lost. Badly," he says as he shrugs out of his coat and lays it over a chair. His suit jacket follows.

I get up and go to him. "I know, and I'm sorry." Grabbing his hand, I lead him back to the bed and he sits on the edge. "Do you want something to drink? A beer?"

He shakes his head as he toes off his shoes. "No. Thanks."

I lie on the bed, and moments later, he joins me, pulling me into his side. I rest my head on his chest and let us both just be.

"It was a total shit-show out there tonight. And I was the star of the disaster," he says. There's a sadness in his voice. Disappointment. And anger.

From my perspective, he's overreacting, but that's not what he wants to hear. At least I can remind him the rest of the team bears some responsibility, too. "You've all played better, there's no denying that."

"You watched. I was kind of hoping you hadn't."

"Of course I watched." I stroke his arm as his heart thumps hard and fast against my ear. "I won't lie. It was hard, and it's possible I may have shouted at the TV a time or six and been tempted to turn it off. But I want to support you, and one of the ways I can do that is by watching you play—even when you're not at your best."

"I thought we were pulling it together. Even with our losses, I felt like we were gelling as a team. Tonight...I have no fucking idea what the fuck that was, but it wasn't professional hockey. At least not from my point of view. I let everyone down. My team, my fans...myself. You."

"I don't know about the others, but you can cross me off that list." He didn't let me down, and I won't be an excuse for him to get a few more hits in while he beats himself up.

"This team is counting on me for a run at the Cup."

"You'll need their help to get there." If I can nudge him towards talking about the team not gelling, that's probably more productive. I think. I'm no sports psychologist.

"I'm in a position of leadership."

"Is this loss harder because they put an A on your jersey?"

"Maybe. Yeah, I think it is. Fuck." His arms tighten around me. "Fucking hell, Sasha. I thought we were clicking. You know? And it turns out, maybe I don't fucking know anything at all. Because that was a mess."

"What can you do?"

He scrubs his hand over his face. "We'll have a team meeting in the morning. Coach won't pull any punches."

"Good."

"We'll probably have a long practice, too. I'm sorry, that's going to eat into our time."

"I've got boat loads of work to do. That's fine." I play with the buttons on his shirt. "Do you want to watch a movie?"

"No."

I swallow hard. "Do you want—"

"I want you." Three little words, rough and real.

Straddling him, I unbutton his shirt and he sits up so I can tug it off. He reaches for the hem of my t-shirt and pulls it over my head, then buries his face in my cleavage. I kiss the top of his head and hold him close as he tastes my skin.

His hands are hard and insistent, his touch almost selfish. He gropes me, squeezing my breasts together so he can mouth them at the same time.

I slide my fingers through his hair and give myself to him. He sucks on my flesh, pulling my nipples deep into his mouth, and deep inside, a new and strange fire begins to burn.

We tumble, shoving clothes up and off and away. He's still damp from his shower, his muscles bulging as he moves against me, and I give myself over to him fully. Pliant and ready to be whatever he needs.

Take it, I say with my body. Take me, however you want me.

It isn't like anything we've done before. This is raw and sweet and kind of scary. But I can't say no to him.

And as we move together, I realize, I don't want to. Not tonight. Not ever.

# 24

## TATE

The atmosphere in the Devils' visitors' dressing room at practice the next day is almost funereal.

There's none of the usual good-natured banter, only the occasional quiet exchange. Some players are sitting in the stalls, while others are on their feet taping their sticks.

My guts are roiling. It was hard to force down my breakfast. Last night, Sasha did an amazing job of reducing my stress, but this morning it has rolled back in on me, and now it's time to face reality.

When Coach walks in, he immediately gets down to business, starting with a film review.

"We need to be first on the puck, and the only way that happens is keeping up the hustle. They're going to do whatever they can to slow you down." The red dot of his laser pointer dances across the screen. "Nilsson, that means your line needs to dig deeper and find that extra boost of power." His gaze fixes on me for a moment and I give a slight nod. "We're under a lot of pressure, here, boys. Transform that energy to your advantage, and use it to push back."

When the film is done and the lights are back up full, Coach straightens to his full height and silently surveys the room, catching the eye of every player.

"This isn't about a single game. This is about a season. This is about climbing the ranks until we claw our way into the play-offs. It's going to be hard, and it's going to be long. Don't let one shitty performance knock you off your game. Now I want to see a hard practice out there. I want you to push each other. I want you to watch each other. Study your teammates better than you study your opponents. It's time to get inside each others' heads. Tomorrow night's game isn't against New Jersey. It's with your team mates. That's the goal. Know what your partner is going to do before he does. Got it? Good. Get out there and show me what you can do."

Practice is long and gruelling as we play through what feels like every possible scenario from every hockey game ever played. But it goes really well. Simec, Moore and I are tight and totally connected. Our defensive lines are rock solid, and Leclerc is on fire. Nothing is getting past him.

And when we get back to the dressing room, the atmosphere is closer to normal.

"Yo, Nilsson. We're going out for pizza. You coming?"

"Are you crazy, Simec? Why would he come with us for pizza when beautiful friend from Ottawa is here?"

Fucking Andrushko.

Moore swivels to to face me. "Wait, what?"

"Nothing, just another fine example of Andrushko and his language barrier," I say as I pull out my phone and fire off a quick text.

**Tate: Just finished practice. Going out for pizza with a bunch of the guys, unless...**
**Sasha: GO! Have fun. I'll see you when you get back and we can have a late dinner.**

Slipping my phone back in my pocket, I look up to four pairs of eyes staring at me.

"What?" I ask. Like I don't know.

"Well, are you coming with us, or going to hang out with your language barrier?"

I flip Moore the bird instead of answering him.

After we're all dressed, five of us hit a pizza joint one street over from Prudential Center. Being close to the arena and known for good food, it's been a regular stop for players for years.

We order a couple pitchers of beer and three large pizzas to get us started.

Moore makes a big deal about checking out my Instagram feed as we wait for the food to arrive. "Okay, pretty boy, fess up. What's the deal?" he asks.

"It's exactly like I posted—a friend of mine from Ottawa is in town, and we've been hanging out. Simple as. Meanwhile...I'm awfully curious to know why Andrushko and Simec are here. Given the vast quantity of fuck-worthy women stored in Simec's phone, I would think they'd be off getting some action."

"Don't worry about us," Simec says. "We've got plenty of action planned for later. We just need to fuel up first."

Andrushko's face lights up as he grins. "We're having split-roasted bunny with double stuffing tonight."

"Double-stuffed and spit-roasted, you walking language barrier," Simec says as he smacks the back of Andrushko's head. "And you don't say shit like that in a restaurant."

He's not wrong, but there isn't anyone around us. And if I have kinky teammates, that's good information to have. I lean in, careful to appear more interested in privacy than the group sex. "Threeway?"

Simec nods. "I've got a kinky hook-up here who likes to do hockey players in pairs. She's a wild one."

Landvic, apparently a horny little bastard, asks the next question, saving me from being nosy. "How so?"

Simec winks. "She likes to be watched while getting fucked. If it's a stranger, all the better. If you wanted to walk in on us, she'd fucking love that."

---

It's nearly five when I get back to my hotel room. Sasha's leaning back against the headboard, working on her laptop, which she sets aside as I shed my coat and jacket. "How was the pizza?"

I join her on the bed. "Tasty, as always." I lean in to kiss her. "But nowhere near as tasty as you."

"Flatterer. How did practice go?"

I grin. "Really well. I came out of it feeling pretty good. Like maybe we have a chance after all."

"Of course you have a chance, You're only a little more than a quarter the way through the season."

I love that she's developed an interest in hockey, but I don't bother to tease her about it. I've got something else on my mind.

"So," I say, drawling it out. "A kinky birdy told me there's going to be a threesome going on just down the hall tonight."

Sasha shifts in my arms and looks up at me, her eyes twinkling. "What? Who?"

"Simec and Andrushko."

"And you're telling me this, why?"

I grin. "Small talk?"

She doesn't buy that for a second. Nor should she. "You think I want to go watch." A statement, not a question. She's not wrong.

"I'm making the option available."

Sasha's body goes rigid against mine. "What did you tell them?"

"Absolutely nothing. Andrushko brought it up when we were eating, and Landvic was remarkably curious. I just listened."

"But you think you can just invite yourself along to watch?"

"Apparently, the woman they're hooking up with is an exhibitionist. Landvic is going to bust in on them at nine. They have a whole scenario planned out. I'm quite certain they wouldn't care if we happened to be in the hallway at the time. Or if we followed him into their room."

Her mouth falls open. She doesn't say anything, but her eyes sparkle as she searches my face.

She knows me too well. "That is a very intriguing fantasy, but I think I'd like a quiet evening in with Mr. Hat Trick instead."

Thank fuck. I hated the way my Andrushko and Simec looked at Sasha the other day, and truly, the last thing I want to do is take her to see them in all their naked and fucking glory.

But if she wanted to, I would have done exactly that.

Staying in and getting dirty in a very private way sounds heaps better.

Cupping her breast, I brush my lips against hers, then nip and kiss my way down her body.

Later, long after we've showered and eaten supper, I lie awake, Sasha asleep in my arms. I know this is a stolen luxury, but it feels right.

I want more of this, no matter what it takes to get it.

# 25

## SASHA

Ellie is waiting for me in my office when I return to the university on Tuesday. I'm surprised she wasn't waiting at the airport.

I give her a cool look that won't fool her for a second. "How long have you been here?"

"Forty minutes. I assumed you'd be an hour early for your office hours."

Instead I'm only twenty minutes early, which by my books is cutting it pretty close. But that's not why Ellie is looking at me like she doesn't really know me.

"What is it?" I know exactly what it is, of course.

She crosses her arms. "You know I love you."

"Yes."

"And obviously, your life is your own to worry about, and I'm not one to pry."

"Mmm."

"But you went away this weekend."

"I did. I do that a lot."

"You went to New York."

"I bought you pretty clothes."

"Don't distract me." Her eyes light up. "Tate was in New York, too. For three games."

I give her an innocent look. "You don't say."

"And you ran into him. You let him put a picture of you on Instagram."

"Yes."

"Sasha!"

"Yes?"

"Are you and Tate dating?"

"I wouldn't say that." We're fucked up. And fucked. And still fucking, even though that's a really bad idea. Except I'm sore in all the right places, and I can't wait to do it again. Sigh. "It's complicated."

She laughs. "I know something about complicated." Then she claps her hands. "Tell me everything."

"We've hooked up a few times."

"You flew to New York for a booty call?"

I'd fly to the moon to spend time with Tate. "And shopping. It's secret, so...zip it. The picture was a bit of damage control, because his teammates saw us together."

"Zipped." But she's grinning at me.

"Don't have happy-ever-after dreams for us. That's not what this is."

She frowns. "Why not?"

"For all the normal complicated reasons that most relationships don't work out in the long run. Don't worry about it. We're having fun, and that's all that matters. I'm going with him to the Rapscallion Christmas party."

She pouts. "Gavin says we can't go."

"What do you say?"

That gets a sigh. "He's right. It was fine when it was just our friends, but Rapscallion is now included in Porter's network of clubs. There will be people there that don't need to know that

Gavin is a member. Mutually-assured destruction only works to a certain extent. We'll get our public kink when we're old and retired."

I think about the sea of unfamiliar faces at Miscreant and nod. "Probably for the best."

She narrows her gaze and searches my face. "What aren't you telling me? What is that blushing about?"

I roll my eyes. "We went to the New York club. It's called Miscreant."

"Oh my God. Oh my *God*. Was it good? Tell me everything."

"It was…amazing. Very *Eyes Wide Shut*. Very classy. The costumes were out of this world, but personal, too, you know? Like the performative nature of the clothes was an intrinsic part of each person's kink. I can't stop thinking about it."

A dreamy smile softens her face. "That sounds like so much fun."

"I know it means you can't go, but I'm really looking forward to a bigger crowd on Boxing Day. It'll be interesting to see how the estate setting changes the vibe. The New York club is in a Brooklyn brownstone, and it was very…New York. Hard to explain."

"One day…"

I grin. "One day. Maybe you could go in a mask or something. There were some people disguised."

She bites her lip. "Oh, don't give me ideas."

I point to the door. "Go and tell your husband about that. I've got office hours in five minutes."

"I'm going." She stands up, and her belly is, I swear, bigger than when she sat down.

"When are you due again?"

"Late spring." My expression must give away my shock, because she laughs. "I'm not that big. It's mostly this outfit."

"If you say so. It's adorable, of course."

"Of course." She's still laughing as she heads down the hall, an RCMP officer following closely.

I take a deep breath and open my computer. Okay, back to work.

# TATE

Over the next three weeks, the Lumberjacks get our shit together. Coach told us to worry more about each other than the teams we go up against, and he was right. It makes all the difference.

The eleven games we play in December bring us up two spots in our division. Seven wins and four losses mean I'm flying home to Ottawa with a smile on my face on Christmas Eve.

My dad picks me up at the airport, and gives me a big Nilsson squeeze at the arrivals gate. When we get to my house, we're greeted by not only my mother, my brother and my sister-in-law, but also Trevor, Oliver, and Rob. My mom has put on a massive spread, and there are so many presents under the tree, the living room floor space has been cut in half.

It's loud and happy, and when a knock sounds at the door at quarter to ten that night, my pulse picks up. I'm not expecting her until tomorrow at lunch, after my family takes off. But if Sasha were here too, it would be fucking perfect—even if she did rip into my friends for being bros.

Hell, I think I'd like that.

But when I swing the front door open, it's not Sasha standing in a swirl of wintery whiteness.

It's Brandon Vance, my former Senators linemate.

"Hey," I say, holding out my hand as I step back to welcome him inside.

He takes it and gives me a firm handshake. "Merry Christmas."

"Same to you. You didn't fly home?"

"Nah, I sent my folks to Hawaii instead. I'll see them over the All Star Break. I just went out for dinner with a couple of the guys who are similarly on their own this week, and I was thinking of you."

"For sure. Come on in, man. Have a drink." I feel like a heel for not reaching out myself. "We've got a lot of catching up to do."

Rob shoots me a quick *are you okay* look when I introduce Brandon to the room, and yeah, I am. I'd avoided all my previous teammates on my last visit, because we were playing them, and it was too raw.

But we're all professionals. Trades are a part of the business. And when we're two broken old veterans of the game, I'll want to count Brandon as a friend. Hard to do that if I've shut him out.

He shakes hands with my father and gives my mom a big hug. "Mrs. Nilsson, nice to see you again."

"You're having a good season," she says before pointing at the fridge. "Tate, I put all the leftovers away. Your father and I are headed to bed. See you in the morning."

My brother and his wife also excuse themselves as we settle down with drinks, and suddenly it's like old times—me and my crew, shooting the shit. I tell my friends about Miscreant— leaving out that I wasn't alone when I went there—and then the conversation turns to the Rapscallion holiday party in two days time.

Which just leaves Brandon, suddenly silent.

Shit. I don't own the kink landscape in Ottawa, especially since I spend most of my time on the other side of the fucking country.

"You want to come, man?"

He shrugs. "I don't want it to be awkward."

"It won't be. We're good. I just needed to adjust to being on a new team. I'm sorry if that came across like I was shutting you out of everything, that wasn't my intention."

He nods, and I hold out my beer. He clinks our bottles together.

"Speaking of the party…" I take a deep breath. "You fuckers are going to have to carpool on your own. I'm bringing a friend with me."

I wake up early on Christmas morning, and the first thing I do is call Sasha.

"Hello," she says sleepily, after answering on the third ring.

"Merry Christmas."

"Tate." That's a gift right there, how she says my name like my voice is the best thing she's heard in ages.

But fuck, if it is, that's shitty. "How's your visit going?"

"Nearly over."

Uh-oh. "That good, eh?"

She sighs. "My father and I got into it last night. He gave me shares in the company as a present. That's not a *present*. That's an obligation. So we had words. I'll be glad to get out of here after breakfast. And I won't feel even a little bit guilty about taking his plane to get home, either."

"Are you personally going to steal it?"

"Ha. No. And don't feel badly for the plane crew, either. It's a relatively short trip, and I'll make it worth their while."

"I have no doubt." I stretch my arm across my bed, where I'm going to have her, over and over again, in just a few hours. "I can't wait to see you."

"Same."

"I hear my family waking up."

"I'll let you go and be social."

"I'd rather be social with you."

"Soon enough."

The warmth of her laughter zings through me, as I shove myself out of bed and get dressed for Christmas morning breakfast and presents with my family, I find myself aching to have her here, *now*. It wouldn't be soon enough. Could never be soon enough. In a few short months, Sasha had become the best and most fragile part of my day. A slice of a conversation, a teasing text.

It isn't enough. Not by a long shot. When it comes to Sasha, I'm getting greedier with each passing day.

## SASHA

Christmas morning at the Brewster house is picture-perfect. My mother's decorator outdid herself this year, although I think that every year.

This year's theme is silver and white, so I put on a dark blue silk blouse and white wool pants.

Picture-perfect. Actually perfect would be pyjamas until noon and unlimited buttery toast.

One does not eat buttery toast in dark blue silk. Or anywhere in the Brewster house, for that matter.

We do have unlimited mimosas, though. That's something.

I find my mother in the enormous eat-in kitchen, glass in hand. Excellent idea. I pour myself a drink from the fruit juice bar, top it up with champagne, and take a seat at the table. "Merry Christmas," I say, holding up my glass.

She gives me a warning look, like she knows I'm just waiting for my father to come downstairs so I can launch back into my argument with him. I'm not sure how she can anticipate that— I've never been fired up to fight with him in the past.

But she is my mother. Maybe she can sense that everything in my life is shifting.

New opportunities.

New friendship.

New passion.

*This isn't about Tate.* He invades where he doesn't belong, like my churning thoughts about what to do when I graduate.

I take a big swig of champagne and orange juice, wishing it were buttery toast instead.

"Your brothers will be here soon," she says, steering the conversation where she wants it go.

"What are we having for breakfast?" Besides booze.

"Your father requested crepes."

"Carbs? It's a Christmas miracle."

She laughs, and it's a genuine, warm sound. "And worth it to see that look on your face, my darling."

I wink at her, and that's when my father walks in. He kisses my mother, then goes to the mimosa bar. "What did you make, sweetheart?"

Oh, so we're pet-naming me this morning. "The classic. OJ and champagne in equal parts." Maybe not equal. I swallow another sip to be sure. Definitely more bubbly. Oops. "Mom says you want pancakes for breakfast."

She tuts at me. "I said crepes."

"I know, but I'm betting a shiny loonie that Dad asked for pancakes and crepes was your compromise."

He laughs, and I think for a second that we've done it, we've successfully navigated the start to a lighthearted morning. Except then he crosses his arms and pins me with a glare. "Sasha, I've been thinking."

I groan. "No. No thinking. It's Christmas morning. We're doing pancakes—"

"Crepes," my mother interjects.

"And presents, and then I'm flying back to Ottawa."

His mouth tightens. "To be with the hockey player?"

You could hear a pin drop in my parents' kitchen right now.

I'm staring at my father, my mother is staring at me, and the skin around his mouth has turned white.

What the ever-loving hell? "Excuse me?"

I rise from the table, glass in hand, because I might need more booze for this conversation, but before my dad can answer, the house is filled with the noisy arrival of my brothers, who probably stayed out late partying with their friends, but manage to look pulled together enough that my mother will take a formal family picture of us in front of the fireplace and post it on—

Instagram.

My mother loves Instagram.

Fucking hell.

I give her a wide-eyed, jaw-clenched glare, and she waves her hand. "Oh, Sasha."

"Don't Oh, Sasha me, Mom! What did you tell him?" I turn back to my father, ignoring the greetings from my brothers. "Who I spend time with is none of your business. I am a grown-up."

"Who is using my private plane to fly around the province. We've been through this once. I won't do it again."

"This is—" My cheeks are on fire. This isn't anything like my past. Tate isn't anything like Brian. But more importantly, this is so not how I wanted my parents to find out about…whatever it is I'm doing with Tate. If I ever wanted them to find out, which is probably no, not ever. "I'm sorry that I asked, then. I should have bought a ticket. I bet I still can. Did you know that Christmas Day is not a very busy travel day? Christmas Eve and Boxing Day have it beat. So yeah, I'll just—"

"Sit down, young lady."

Wow, from sweetheart to young lady in four sentences. That has to be a record, and I haven't even broken any laws.

To my immense shame, I sit down.

Way to be a fucking grown-up, Sasha.

"Boys, go help your mother with the pancakes."

"Crepes," my mother and I say at the same time.

My father doesn't blink.

They head around the island, and my dad moves to sit across from me, but he stops just as he pulls out the chair. "Come with me. We'll talk in my study."

I roll my eyes, but I follow him. That, right there, is my relationship with my father in a nutshell.

He sits in an armchair in front of his fireplace, so I flop out on the couch.

He steeples his hands together.

I wait.

This is his circus, he gets to direct it. I'm already composing an apology text to Tate in my head, because I'm going to have to hitchhike back to Ottawa.

"Last night," my father finally says slowly, as if he's picking and choosing his words carefully. "You made it clear to me that you will not be returning to Toronto any time soon."

Ever, but I maybe wasn't crystal clear on that point. "That's correct."

"And I was under the mistaken impression that it was because of your academic studies."

"It is."

"But your mother has since informed me that you are once again tangled up with an…athlete."

He says it like other fathers might say *drug dealer* or *homeless man*. I'm not sure my father would object to me dating a drug dealer if he was wildly successful. And assuming the homeless guy wouldn't have a significant social media following or any reason to be in the news, he'd probably be fine with that, too.

A man with no fixed address would be preferable to Tate.

That's the Brewster way.

I would have agreed with him a few months ago, but things have changed.

"I wouldn't say I'm tangled up with anyone," I counter. "I have a friend. His name is Tate. We have mutual friends, and once —*once*—I appeared on his Instagram page with him. It's a silly, simple story. I am not going to be publicly dating him or anything like that."

A pang pulls tight in my chest as I say that. That's not fair to Tate, but it's the reality of my life.

"We sorted all of that out once. It will be hard to do that again, and salvage your reputation." He frowns at me, as if I don't already know that.

"That was a long time ago," I say softly, trying not to get emotional. "And I was active in my own career rehabilitation, if you'll recall. I have no desire to be in the public eye."

"It's not good for your long term aspirations."

I don't know about that. Do people care if university professors or private investors have hockey player boyfriends? I know the shareholders of Brewster Industries don't like it, but—

Right.

I've been putting this off for too long.

"Dad," I say, standing up. I resist the urge to take a big swig of wine, lest he think I'm only saying this because I'm tipsy. "I don't ever want to be the CEO of Brewster Industries. I don't want to move back here, not in the near future, and not ever. I am grateful for every opportunity you and Mom have ever given me, but my future is my own."

He laughs.

I lay my heart out there, and he *laughs*.

"I'm serious."

"I'm sure you think you are, young—"

"No. I'm twenty-seven years old. I am not a young lady. I'm not even a lady. I'm screwing a hockey player." I wave my glass in the air. Damn, I might be a little tipsy. "And you know what? It's a secret. It's going to stay a secret, and that's kind of stupid, really, because there's no reason for it, except for the repressed, socially restrictive rules you've taught me. So… there. I'm serious, and we're done here. It's Christmas morning and we need to go pretend crepes are pancakes, so let's pretend this just didn't happen. You can call me tomorrow and tell me then how wrong I am."

He doesn't follow me, so instead of going straight to the kitchen, I detour upstairs to call Tate. He answers on the first ring. "Hey, what's up?"

"Can you talk right now?"

"For sure. Give me two secs—Okay, I'm alone now. What's wrong?"

My face crumples, but I don't cry. Not necessary. I twist my expression until it's more of a grimace, and I sigh. "I had another go with my father. I may have told him I'm screwing you."

"Wow. That's a level of sharing I didn't think happened in the Brewster house."

"It's not."

"Yikes."

"Yeah." I wince. "I may have crossed the line into total bitch."

"He probably deserved it."

"He definitely did. But I still regret how I handled it."

"Bitches get shit done and have healthy boundaries."

I close my eyes and drag in a deep breath. "Right. I know that."

"But you aren't a bitch, Sash. You're tough. You're strong. And you're amazing. I know you know that."

I laugh under my breath. "We all know there's nothing wrong with my ego."

"But all egos have soft spots."

And my father knows exactly where to poke. "Mm-hmm. So, anyway, I don't know if I'll have the plane to come home."

He laughs gently. "That's okay. Do you want me to come get you?"

"It's a four-hour drive, and it's snowing out."

"I'd do it in a heartbeat."

I rub my chest. "I know. No, I'll try to book a commercial flight, it's fine. I have to go and choke down crepes now."

"Update me as soon as you can."

"I will."

I take a few deep breaths, check my makeup in the mirror, and head back downstairs.

My father is waiting in the hallway for me. I give him a guarded look.

"That was quite the outburst," he says, rushing to continue before I can say anything snippy in response. "But I hear you. All except for the bit about the hockey player. I'm going to pretend you didn't say that."

"Okay."

"We only want what's best for you, Sasha."

And having me drunkenly flashing the media with my bright orange panties is not it. Having a famous boyfriend cop a feel at the same time was the icing on the inappropriate cake. "We have different ideas of what that is. But I think we agree on what isn't best for me."

He gives me a grim smile. Great. Now we're both remembering my orange panties. This is the worst Christmas ever.

## TATE

THE NEXT UPDATE I get from Sasha is a text saying she's leaving for the airport and all is "relatively fine." Whatever that means.

I give my parents one last tight squeeze and promise my mom I'll do my best to eat all the leftovers. "Whatever I don't get through, I'll put in the freezer."

"I can come back up in a few days…"

"Nah, it's fine." My parents live on a farm closer to Kingston, and I don't need my mom making an hour-plus drive to clean out my fridge.

"I guess you'll be happy to have the place to yourself for a day of peace and quiet." She pats me on the arm as my father holds out her coat.

I have zero plans for Sasha to be quiet. Or peaceful. "Yeah, for sure."

As soon as they leave, I have a shower and shave my balls, because nothing says Merry Christmas like smooth privates. Then I put her presents under the tree and put the fireplace channel on my television.

I've just heated up some apple cider on the stove when I hear her car pull into my driveway.

When I open the door, she's standing in front of me with a bag spilling over with wrapped presents in her arms and a tired, relieved smile on her face.

"I'll take those," I tell her as I grab the bag. "And kiss this." I taste her mouth, warm and soft, as she blindly shoves the door shut behind her.

"Merry Christmas," she murmurs against my lips.

"The merriest."

"I got you presents."

"We can unwrap them after I unwrap you." I haul her backwards, kissing her non-stop as I dump the bags on the couch, her coat on a chair, and settle her in my lap in another chair. "You're all dressed up," I say as I unbutton her blouse.

"It's a long story." She smooths her hand over my sweater before I weave my fingers into her hair and bring our mouths together again.

More kissing.

So good to have her in my arms again. It's a weird and wonderful feeling, to miss someone like this. The pure relief when they're back in your arms. It's not sappy. It's…pure. Basic.

Also, fucking hot. Her skin is warm and soft under her silk top, and her fancy dress pants cup her ass in a way that makes my dick pulse in anticipation.

Maybe for Christmas, I'll take her there.

She breaks away from my mouth and twists her head towards the kitchen. "Is that apple cider?"

I'm thinking how amazing anal sex would be, and she's hooked on my holiday festive touches.

Down boy, you'll wait your turn like a good cock.

"You want some?"

She grins and gives me a final, lip-smacking kiss. "Yes, please. It's cold out there."

"Come on."

She does up one button, but doesn't bother to fix her hair, and after I hand her a steaming mug of cider, I give her a long, lingering look of appreciation.

"What?"

"I like you all mussed up like this."

She smirks. "You can't wait to muss me up further, can you?"

"You don't even want to know what I'm thinking right now."

Her eyes flash dark. "Maybe I do."

I lean back against the counter. "I was thinking we should do something new today. Something…special."

"If you want me to tie you up, just say the word." She winks, and somehow makes it look innocent.

"Right back at you, tiger."

She purses her lips. "Mmm. Tempting."

I just grin. If she really wants to know, she can ask again. She doesn't. She sips her cider and watches me over the rim of her mug.

"I'm not telling you."

The corners of her eyes crinkle.

I laugh out loud. "Are you hungry?"

Her gaze drops to my dick.

Fuck. Me. "Finish your cider, and I'll give you your first present."

"Is it…" She takes one last delicate sip of cider, then sets her mug down. "Something hard?"

"I've missed you too, Sasha. Upstairs."

She spins around and runs, laughing as she climbs the stairs. "I don't know where your room is!"

"Then I'll probably catch you," I growl as I chase her. "Turn right."

She sprints into the master bedroom and leaps onto my bed. I catch her ankle in the air, and she tumbles sideways. I unzip her boot and toss it over my shoulder. She gets the other one off, then I'm on top of her.

I push her into the bed. Hold her down.

Hold her, period, my fingers wrapping around her wrists. Tight enough to lay a claim. It's Christmas Fucking Day and we've done our family duty. Now it's just us for the next twenty-four hours, and she's all mine.

Damn straight I'm holding on tight.

This is precious.

Sasha arches beneath me, rubbing her body against mine. "What were you thinking?" she whispers. "Tell me."

Precious, and dirty. "I'd rather show you."

Her eyes go glassy and unfocused as she looks up at me and nods. Zing. Like an electric jolt to my inner depraved jerk, her expression shifts me from emo to ego in a split-second.

From downstairs, the Christmas soundtrack filters up to us. The cheesy songs have ended, and we're into Johnny Reid now with some festive swagger.

I do exactly as I promised, and unwrap her. First her blouse, then her pants. I take my time teasing her skin around the edges of her push-up bra and minuscule panties, then those too are peeled away.

I roll her over and smack her pert, perfect bottom as I climb off the bed and discard my sweater, t-shirt, and jeans. The whole time, she watches me, her cheek pressed against my blanket, her body naked and stretched out across my bed.

I open the side drawer and grab a condom.

And lube.

Her eyes go wide, and I grin.

Except this is Sasha, and there's no upper hand to be had with her.

Without breaking the lock her gaze has on mine, she arches her back and, graceful as a wild cat, pushes up onto her knees.

My mouth drops open, and she grins.

Chuckling under my breath, I climb onto the bed. I lean over her and kiss her mouth before nipping at her ear. "Ready for more than a finger, tiger?"

"I can't wait," she breathes. "Merry Christmas."

That's the understatement of the year.

I take my time kissing and biting down her spine. By the time I get to her ass, she's rocking against me. I grab a good handful of her right cheek and bite her. The gasp followed by a desperate moan is music to my ears.

Maybe I've got a touch of sadism in me after all.

But then I ruin that theory by sucking and licking her flesh until she's warm and rosy all over, and that feels even better.

She tenses when I pop the bottle of lube open, but I warm the gel on my fingers before I circle it around her adorable little hole. I'm going to be so good to her.

"Show me how tight you can clench," I murmur, and she groans as she twists her head around to look at me.

"No."

I grin. "Come on. I love your ass."

"I know. But we're not talking about how tight I can—Ah!" I love that look of surprise on her face as I slide my finger in to the first knuckle. Her muscles flutter around the intrusion, and my cock lifts into the air, eager to feel the grip my finger is currently enjoying. "Jerk," she mutters, catching her breath.

"Show me again."

"Just do it."

"That is not how this is going to go down. What happened to the girl who pushed her ass in the air?" I rock my hand gently, nudging up against the second ring of muscles inside her body.

She sighs and presses up. Her breathing slides into an erotic groan as I penetrate her deeper, and I hold still, waiting for her body to adjust.

Then I add more lube.

As I ease a second finger into her ass, the sounds she makes are perfectly unholy. I love them.

I fuck her with my hand, slowly stretching her, until she's

mumbling for me to just do it already. I rip open the condom packet and roll the thin, lubed-up latex over my straining cock.

I murmur sweet nothings as I rub the thick, hard head of my dick against her entrance. This time, I don't need to tell her to tighten up—and when her body relaxes, as it inevitably must, I push in.

Just the tip, just enough to stretch her wide.

I settle my hands on her hips and hold on tight as she whines and twists and pushes back. When she sighs and drops her head, I ease in another inch.

Never in my life has my cock been gripped this tight.

"We were supposed to open presents first," I groan as I sink slowly into her amazing heat.

"Unnn..."

I ease back, pulling half of my cock out of her body before pushing in again. An easy start to her first ass fucking. *Another claim on her body.*

"I put on Christmas music." We can still hear it. Faint strains a surreal soundtrack to heavy breathing and slapping flesh.

"Cider..." she breathes. "So good."

"And this?"

"Ah..."

"Only okay?" I grin as she moans.

"So good too."

I slap her hip. "That's my girl. Fuck back against me. Take my dick in your ass."

"Tate!"

I laugh. "Too much?"

"Fuck me harder."

Deep inside her, my cock flexes at the glorious request. "Your wish is my command. Touch your clit. Get yourself off. If you come for me, I'll have a big load—"

She bursts out laughing, and holy shit, that feels good on my dick.

"You like that? I've got knock knock jokes, too." I bottom out inside her, and her fingers graze my nuts as she starts to stroke her pussy. "Ah, shit, Sasha. I can feel how wet you are. Come on, baby. Pinch your clit. Just like that. Oh, that's it. I can feel that. You like that, don't you? My cock buried in your ass, you rubbing your sweet little pussy, too."

She climaxes with a shattering scream, and I follow her into that bliss, my dirty words dying on my tongue as pure, hot pleasure bolts up my cock, pulling my balls with it.

Merry. Fucking. Christmas.

Some time later, after a slow, sudsy shower where I clean her up everywhere, especially where she's sensitive and sore, we get dressed and head downstairs.

I wear my favourite red flannel PJ pants. She wears the matching flannel top and a pair of my wool socks.

"Quite the change from what I wore this morning," she says, laughing as she looks down at herself.

"You've never been more beautiful to me," I promise. "Now let me feed you and we can finally exchange our presents."

"What are we having for dinner?"

I wrap my arms around her and gesture to the fridge in front of us. "Whatever your little heart desires."

There's a turkey breast, stuffing, cranberry sauce, roast potatoes, roast beef and gravy, four different containers of steamed vegetables, and my mother's famous aspic.

"Is that jello? With...vegetables in it?"

"And tomato juice, too. It's got some heat to it."

"That's vaguely terrifying." But it's the first container she pulls out of the fridge. "Is this what you had last night?"

"We had the beef last night. The turkey my mother would have cooked earlier this week. She brought me the breast, and probably kept the rest of the bird at home for them to eat when they got back."

"Tell me about your parents," she says as she opens the stuffing container and takes a taste with her fingers.

I catch her hand and lick the crumbs off. "They're pretty good people. Tell me about yours."

"They're pretty good people with some serious asterisks after that statement."

"Yours sound more interesting."

She wrinkles her nose and hands me the cranberry sauce. "Put this on the counter."

We plate up food, nuking the hot stuff before adding the aspic and cranberry sauce. Then we put everything back in the fridge and take our plates to my table.

In between slow, appreciative bites, Sasha tells me about her parents. How her father turned his father's modest tool-and-die shop into an international automotive supplier. How her mother loves Toronto society, and her husband, and her children, maybe in that order, but Sasha hopes not.

Then she falls silent.

I start to tell her about my parents. How my father moved here from Sweden as a teenager to play hockey, but then he fell in love with my mother, and chose her over a shaky career on the edges of the NHL. How they're my biggest cheerleaders, and—

"My parents aren't happy about you." She interjects it almost calmly, but there's a tremor in her voice.

I fall silent. She doesn't say anything, so I finally shrug. "Okay." I can handle some parental concern.

"They know me well, and my mother is an Instagram freak. She saw your post from New York and has been stewing on it ever since. She's convinced I'm going to fall into old, bad habits with you."

Only new bad habits here, and they're only bad in the most

prudish of terms. I frown. "Is this about your aversion to the media and publicly dating?"

She shifts nervously in her chair. "Yes. Maybe. Yes."

I wave my hand expansively. "I'm all ears. Or not. But it might be helpful for me to know what I'm dealing with. Is your father going to show up in Vancouver with a cheque to convince me to stay away from you?"

She laughs, then winces. "Good lord, I hope not."

"Come on. Let's figure out what dessert we want, then move this to the Christmas tree."

"You just want your presents."

I wink. "Guilty as charged."

I quickly wash our plates while Sasha makes a tray of dessert options, then we move into the living room.

She starts laughing at the fireplace on the television screen. "Was that playing when I arrived?"

I nuzzle her neck. "I did a good job of distracting you."

"You did, indeed. That's ridiculous."

I kneel in front of the tree and pull out her first present, which isn't wrapped. "Then you're going to hate this."

She grabs the white and silver toque with faux-fur trim and jams it on her head. "That's where you are wrong, sir. Mrs. Claus, at your service."

I grab my matching Santa hat and jam it on my head. "Then bring on the presents, Mrs. Claus."

The first gift she gives me is a tie in Lumberjacks colours, and cartoonish axe cufflinks. I love them.

I give her a travel survival kit, including a portable charger for her phone, an inflatable water bottle, and a privacy screen for her computer. "In case I send you porn at the wrong time," I say, and she crawls over and gives me a soft, sweet kiss.

"I've learned not to open your emails in public," she murmurs. "But now I don't need to be so careful, thank you."

"Just remember to turn your volume off."

"And we're back to not opening them." She winks and hands over a bigger box.

I rip into it and it takes me a minute to realize what I'm looking at. It's a clock, but as I read the package, I get that it's not just any old clock. It works with an app that tells the clock where specific people are.

"So you can see what time it is when you call Max in the middle of the night. Your parents, maybe." She smiles. "Or me."

There's an ocean of meaning in those two words. Or her. Like she's starting to understand that she's secretly become the most important person in my life.

Hell, yeah, I want to know what Sasha Time is, always.

"I'm speechless." My voice rubs raw as I reach for her. "This is so thoughtful."

"I know we're all on the same time zone, but if your parents travel, or—"

I silence her with a kiss, and there's nothing soft about it.

This is the perfect gift for a man a continent away from everyone he counts as family, and she deserves all the dirty kisses as thanks.

The next gifts we exchange are silly. I got her a BDSM handbook with cartoon illustrations, and she giggles as she flips through it. "I almost bought you an etiquette book, you know." She raises one elegant eyebrow. "Tips on how to have conversations in public, for example."

"But you didn't." I give her a charming grin. "What did you choose instead?"

She tosses a soft present my way. "Socks."

I open it up, and she's not lying. A half-dozen pairs of technical socks, all different brands. She's already gone back to the book, but without looking up, she tells me which were highest rated and why she got the others anyway.

There is nothing she can't research the hell out of it. I'm sure by the end of our few days together, she'll know that book inside and out, and have an itemized list of things for us to try.

I can't wait.

Which brings me to my last present for her. I grab the silver wrapped box from the back of the tree and hand it over.

She sets down the book and carefully peels off the wrapping paper. "Oh," she says, lifting the retro instant-film camera in the air. "Fun!"

"I know you've got some perfectly reasonable rules about public exposure." I point upstairs. "But I have a real fireplace in my room. And I know you like to watch. So…" I gesture at the camera. "If you wanted to take pictures of me, I'm game."

"Pictures?" Her mouth turns pink as the tip of her tongue sweeps along the crest of her lower lip. "Like…dirty pictures?"

"Like, I'll take myself in hand and make myself come for you if you want to take a money shot."

"Oh."

She inhales quickly, then holds her breath.

I wait.

She bites her lip, her teeth sinking into the flesh.

Fuck this. I'm no good at waiting. I drop my hand onto my bare belly and rub my fingers along the waistband of my flannel pants. My cock swells, lifting the fabric right below where my fingertips tease.

Sasha drops her gaze, her eyelids lidding heavily. Then she exhales roughly and shakes her head. "No."

"No?"

She grins. "Not yet. Dessert first. Then I need to figure out how to use the camera. *Then* you can touch yourself, perverted Santa."

2 9

---

S A S H A

I FINALLY GET DRESSED in something other than Tate's pyjamas on Boxing Day, in the early afternoon, because I have a wardrobe crisis that requires a trip to my apartment.

He drives us downtown while I text my friends.

**Sasha: I'm coming to the Rapscallion holiday party tonight.**
**Violet: Excellent!**
**Beth: Yay!**
**Sasha: … with Tate.**

There's a long pause while I watch dots appear on the screen, then disappear, then come back. Both of them are writing and revising their responses quite carefully, and that makes me laugh.

**Sasha: It's not a big deal.**
**Violet: Are you sure? It sounds like a big deal.**
**Beth: I want to know everything. Everything. All the details. Don't leave anything out.**
**Sasha: No details. But I'm not sure what to wear.**

**Violet: That's usually your area of expertise.**
**Sasha: The kink element has me flummoxed. I have...**

Two dresses, but I've already worn them both. Damn it, I may need to share some details after all. New tack.

**Sasha: What are you wearing?**
**Beth: I've got a Sugarplum Fairy costume.**
**Violet: Oh, I love that! Kinky ballerina! I'm wearing a ridiculously short mini skirt and a flowy top that doesn't really have a back. The mummy tummy is still a problem, so I'm focusing on my legs.**
**Sasha: I'm almost at my place, I'll text pictures of my options when I get there.**
**Beth: If you're texting, who's driving?**
**Violet: Good question, B!**
**Sasha: Never you mind.**

Beth sends a devil emoji in response, and Violet sends a big heart that showers more hearts on my screen.

"So Beth and Violet know about us," I say as Tate parks.

He takes my gloved hand and kisses my knuckles. "Good. Now I can hold you as much as I want tonight."

To my complete surprise, that doesn't make me nervous. I trust Tate more than I ever thought I would—or could. "Shall I model some outfits for you?"

"I already vote for the one that has the most access to your ass."

I shift in my seat. I'm still tender from yesterday. "Gentle access."

He leans in and brushes his lips against mine. "The gentlest."

After much consultation and debate, I decide on suede thigh-high boots and a green silk baby doll dress from the back of my closet. When I add the Christmas hat Tate got me, I'm a delightfully dirty elf.

"I just need pointy ears," I say to Tate as I fix his tie at his front door. He's wearing a fitted dark green suit I convinced him to buy this afternoon. And it's Lumberjack green, so he can wear it again to a game.

I don't know why I haven't taken him suit-shopping before. He needs to wear them constantly, and has money to spend. He's a treasure to my compulsive shopping-loving heart.

"Your ears are perfect." He traces my earlobe with the tip of his fingertip, and I shiver. Outside, a sweep of headlights cuts across the front of the house, lighting up the entranceway. "Our limo is here."

I also found an oversized silver-and-white knit wrap this afternoon, and Tate tucks it snugly around me before tugging on his own Christmas hat.

It's a lovely night, really—cold, but clear, and there's just enough light snow falling to be festive. Inside the limo, we find a bottle of Prosecco chilling on ice and two paper cups with hot apple cider tucked into cup holders.

Tate thinks of everything. I go straight for the cider. The bubbly can wait until the ride home.

He settles in beside me and we talk about what we're hoping to see and do tonight. Just before we arrive at Rapscallion, my phone vibrates three times in my purse.

"Sorry," I say, digging it out. "I should…"

But when I check my messages, I laugh, because it's not an emergency or a parental freak-out. It's just Mabel, hard at work late into the night on Boxing Day.

Of course.

**Mabel: I've figured out my pitch! All you need is a screwdriver.**

Then there's a picture of a screw driver and a smart phone, artfully arranged above a handwritten note scrawled in black marker.

**Can you screw? Then you're ready to get Weird.**

I show Tate, not that he's going to get the context, but I can't stop laughing.

"What's that?"

I wipe a tear from the corner of my eye. "Honestly, I'm not sure. But it's funny in a you-have-to-know-her kind of way. She's starting a business and I've invested in it. I think it's her attempt at a marketing tagline."

"For what?"

"It's a long story." I look out the window. The Rapscallion gates are just ahead, and cars line the winding road into the estate. "And we're here."

He nips at my ear. "I want the whole story, because I can screw. And I'm ready to get weird."

I tap back a quick note to Mabel letting her know I like it and will write more tomorrow. Then I tuck my phone away and give Tate my full attention. I'm totally ready to get weird, too. In a very different way than Mabel means.

---

Inside, we find a cocktail party in full swing on the main level. Lachlan and Beth are circling. He's all in black, tight t-shirt and jeans, and I bet Hugh is as well. She sparkles in chiffon and tulle, and I blow her a kiss.

Tate bumps into his friend Brandon, and I get a simple, but

accurate re-introduction. "Do you remember Sasha? She was at the party last year at Max's."

Then we move downstairs, where we find Hugh and Max playing with whips in the main space. There's less of a crowd down here, but still quite a few new faces.

New to me, anyway. Tate seems to know a lot of people. Some are apparently from the Ottawa kink scene—"Nice to see you again, man! Sorry to hear you got traded..."—and others are high-profile enough to probably have avoided that before, but wealthy enough to afford a membership to Rapscallion.

With each smooth handshake and murmured introduction, my curiosity grows.

At the first opportunity, Tate tugs me into the shadows and kisses me. "You have so many questions, don't you?"

"I do," I breathe, smiling as he moves his mouth down my neck. Making out in the corner seems to be our thing. I love it.

"Should I go and find out what public scenes are going to happen tonight?"

"Yes, please. I'll get us drinks. What would you like?"

"A beer would be amazing."

We share another quick, hungry kiss, then he heads towards the library and I go back to the main dungeon space, where a bar is set up under a twinkly-lights-and-handcuffs garland.

"What'll you have?"

"A lager and a glass of Riesling, please."

As the bartender pours our drinks, I scan the room. Violet is coming down the stairs, and I wave to her.

She joins me at the same time as a couple steps up to the bar. She greets them warmly, too.

"Sasha, this is Madeline, and her husband Henry. They just joined the club this afternoon."

"Nice to meet you."

I exchange a quick hug with Violet, then she flits off. I admire her legs in the minidress, and make a mental note to tell her later it was a great choice.

Then I turn my attention back to my new acquaintances. There are a lot of questions you can't ask at a dungeon. What do you do, where are you from…off-limits information.

I settle on, "This is your first time here."

Madeline beams. "It is. We've been exploring…things… privately, with a coach Porter found us. But having this open to new members relatively close to us was a gift. Just the perfect time."

And sometimes, even if you don't ask greedy questions, you get rewarded with plenty of information anyway. "A coach, eh? That sounds interesting."

Henry glances at Madeline and she tips her head sideways and smiles, giving him permission. Oh, fascinating. He leans in. "We're doing a scene tonight."

Even better. "You don't say…"

"There's something just so freeing about exploring these fantasies in a safe space," Madeline murmurs, her eyes tracking across the dungeon. The whole time, Henry's looking at her like she's just hung the moon for him.

I glance around for Tate. He's my guide in all of this. If he were here, he could have this conversation and I could just sit back and observe. He'd know what to say. "Right. I saw that in action in New York."

Saw it, freaked out a little, got majorly turned on…

"You should come and watch," Madeline offers. "Or participate, if you'd like."

What? No. Whoa. Hey, there, kinky couple, we've just met, and you're swell and all, but I'm— I take a deep breath before my thoughts turn judgemental. "Thank you," I hear myself saying. "I'll discuss it with my partner."

They both give me a super-warm look as our drinks are all set in front of us. I pick up my two glasses and zoom away as politely as I can.

I find Tate deep in conversation with Lachlan, who has come downstairs and is apparently a dungeon monitor for the evening.

I hand Tate his beer and greet Lachlan, who excuses himself.

Tate gives me a quick run down of what he's learned, and he finishes with, "And there's going to be a group scene in the library. A special request by the newest members, apparently. Something along the lines of..." He pauses and gives me a lopsided grin. "Well, a gang bang."

My eyes go wide. "The newest members?"

"Mmm."

"Madeline and Henry?"

"Yeah, actually."

"I just met them. They're kind of intense."

"I guess so."

"They invited us to watch." Or participate, but I'm leaving that out because nope.

"And what did you tell them?"

I bite my lip.

"Sasha..."

"I told them I'd discuss it with you."

"Interesting."

"It's really not."

"Why didn't you simply decline?" That's a fair question—I've been pretty clear that I'd rather observe things anonymously, from the back of the room.

But there's nothing simple about any of this.

When I don't answer, Tate leans in and brushes his lips against my ear. "Bet you a nickel it's because you want to see Madeline get railed by three guys at her husband's direction, and you don't really care who knows it."

"I wouldn't put it that way."

"Then how would you put it?"

"I find group dynamics fascinating."

He chuckles, low and hot and just for me. "Yeah. Fascinating. I have no doubt it will be."

*It will be.* Like it's a forgone conclusion that we're going to watch a gang bang. together.

## 30

## TATE

I DON'T WANT to push Sasha if this is somehow out of her comfort zone when Miscreant wasn't.

Maybe it's because we know people here.

I take a long, slow sip of my beer and let her process. There's nothing I like more than Sasha's face when she's thinking something through. The way her forehead furrows and her nose wiggles. The little flicks of her eyes, the tight pout of her mouth.

Thinking Sasha turns me on, but then again, all Sashas turn me on. Sarcastic, sexy, generous, shopping, and indignant, too.

And when she reaches a conclusion, and her eyes light up? Fucking hell, that's hot.

She nods. "Okay. Right. Obviously I want to watch."

I grin wolfishly. I can't help it. "Obviously."

"No need to brag, pervert Santa."

"I checked twice, and you're definitely on the Naughty is Nice list."

She blushes and her eyelashes dust her cheeks as she smiles. "Well, if I'm on a list…"

It takes a few hours for that scene to start. Before it does, we do a circuit of the dungeon. Sasha tries her hand at flogging my back, then I show her my rusty rope skills under Hugh's watchful eye.

By the time we've settled on a couch in the library, everyone is probably aware that we're together. And when I stretch my arm across the back of the sofa, Sasha settles in against my body, so she's made her peace with that—at least in this crowd.

Tomorrow we're flying to Vancouver, where we'll really be alone for a week, and the outside world won't matter.

After that? Who knows.

One thing at a time.

Right now, we've got an orgy to watch.

From the negotiations which happen in front of us, Henry's going to conduct the sex. But there's no doubt Madeline's in charge in their relationship.

She wanted this, and so she gets it. If Henry struggles with sharing his woman, and he clearly does, that's part of their dynamic.

She wants him to give her this. She wants him to suffer a bit, because she knows it brings him a sharp kind of pleasure he can't get any other way.

Or maybe she just likes to hurt him, and he likes it, too.

People are complicated.

Fucking, though, is damn simple. And the volunteers who have signed up are down for that—simple, straightforward, vigorous sex. It starts simply enough, with Henry introducing his wife to the other men. He encourages them to compliment her, and talks about what she likes—her nipples sucked, her clit teased, a feathery touch.

She wants to be worshipped, and that's what they give her. Beside me, Sasha fidgets and squirms, especially when one of the men gets between Madeline's legs.

I couldn't share Sasha like that. The bolt of possession hits me in a most unexpected place—my heart. Right in the middle of chest, the knowledge that I want her all to myself grows and throbs.

My fingers rub up and down her arm, and I squeeze her shoulder.

She licks her lips. Crosses her legs.

I think about her cunt, wet and swollen for me. Just for me. Mine.

My cock strains at my fitted suit pants. If anyone were to look over at me, with my legs spread and my slouched position on the couch, they'd see a clearly turned-on man.

They might think it's about the tableau in front of us. They'd be so fucking wrong.

As soon as the scene ends, I'm pulling Sasha through the house.

"So we're not going to say goodbye?" she teases me as I shove her wrap at her in the cloakroom that once had been a front sitting room.

I don't answer her. Instead I send a text to the driver to meet us out front, then I press her against the wall and kiss her as I work my hands up her skirt and rip off her panties.

"Okay, no goodbyes," she whispers, her chest heaving.

---

I don't fuck her in the limo. I want to, but I want other things, too.

I want her stretched out in front of the fireplace in my bedroom. I want her cries for my ears only, and I don't trust that privacy screen.

So I ply her with Prosecco instead, drinking it from her mouth until she laughs. Then I lick it off her breasts, making her sigh, and when those sounds threaten to break the erotic silence in the back of the limo, I take her mouth and I kiss her the rest of the way.

When we arrive at my house, we're both lust-drunk and wine-tipsy. I take the bottle and give the driver a five-hundred-dollar tip.

Inside, we kiss again at the door. Sloppy and happy. We make out on the stairs, shedding our clothes as we slowly climb.

And when I stretch her out in front of the fireplace, it's just as perfect as I imagined.

I get inside her and I stretch her out, my cock big and unyielding as it takes up space in her body. Claims her from the inside out.

In the back of my mind, there's a little thought that it might be time to talk about ditching condoms. I want to feel her pussy squeeze me, hot and bare and perfect.

I want to spill my seed inside her, and that drives me crazy. I deepen my strokes, my hips and thighs tightening up with need as she digs her heels into my ass. Fuck, she makes me frantic.

We roll, and I jackknife up, holding her on my lap as she rides me through the last, bucking thrusts. When she comes, I follow in a blinding, fireworks kind of orgasm that makes me say silent prayers to the sex gods.

After I deal with the condom, I grab the blanket off the bed, and we stretch out in front of the soft glow of the fireplace.

Sasha's the first to speak. She gives me a sated smile. "That was worth it, eh?"

I laugh. "Oh yeah."

She looks at me with the same curiosity I saw earlier, and I nod lazily. "You want to know more about all those people?"

"I want to know more about you." Her voice is soft and sweet, and she could ask me anything right now. I'm hers in every way, and she has no idea. "When was the first time you went to a club?"

I think back. I know this isn't exactly the story she's looking for, but this is the one that's most honest. "Early in my rookie year. One of the guys suggested we go look for some action at a club he knew in Las Vegas. I was expecting a regular kind of nightclub. Not even close. It wasn't really a kink club. Not in a Miscreant or Rapscallion sense. I'd say more…kink-adjacent. The only scenes, for want of a better description, were simulated on a stage while club goers danced, drank, and watched. So, maybe a cross between a strip club and a BDSM club? Somewhere for people to take a walk on the wild-ish side."

"There's a few places like that in Toronto, too. But they've got a weird reputation."

"Right. Yeah, this place probably had a bad rep, too. And it was only an okay night out. But what I saw spoke to me. I mean, I understood that what I was seeing wasn't real-world BDSM, though. So I started looking into it and was fascinated."

"How long did it take to find the real kink community?"

"Another year. I can't just go to any local munch, and I didn't know anyone who could get me into the private circles. I had to wait for another opportunity like that, and it came during a road trip out west. Alberta has a vibrant kink community, and there are some high-rollers in Calgary who are the real deal. I haven't looked back. It was like something clicked. I discovered a part of myself, you know?"

"Yeah, actually, I do," Sasha says, and her gaze shifts, going unfocused as she drifts into a memory.

"Max's party?"

She nods. "I mostly went as an excuse to get Beth there. And then…well, you know how that's unfolded for me."

I do, and what a fucking gift it's been to show her my favourite secret world. "There's something really special about early exploration. After my first real kink event, I needed to know everything. Experience everything. I became a total kink-geek."

Sasha reaches out and strokes my face. "That doesn't surprise me in the slightest. You're such a perfectionist." She's not wrong.

"Did you do like Doms I've read about—experience the receiving end of things as part of your training?"

God, that's digging deep. I nod. "That year, I realized I had a teammate who was deeply involved in the local kink community. He worked with me at first, then later, I was introduced to the woman who became my mentor. She encouraged me to experiment with every aspect of kink. I settled into hedonism as my main label, but I've got some brat in me, and a pretty good pain tolerance. I like to top in my personal relationships, but I can switch for a scene. So, even after I finished my training at the club, I volunteered to bottom for the occasional sadist who was looking to dish out more pain than his sub could handle."

"So, you have masochistic tendencies?" She pushes up, her eyes bright with mischief. Maybe she liked that flogger more than she let on.

"I think every athlete is a masochist to some degree. *No pain, no gain* has been the mantra for decades now. Even you have a masochistic streak when it comes to exercise."

She skips right past that to the juicy detail. "Never mind that. You *bottomed*? Tell me that bedtime story, Tate."

"Is your voyeurism fetish maybe not just confined to watching?"

She grins. "Maybe not."

Well, okay then. "Let's be clear, it was more of a service role."

"Crystal clear. Gimme the goods."

"Are you looking for a story that must have me as the whipping-boy?"

"Not necessarily."

"Here we go then. Once upon a time, in a city very far away from here, there was a Domly professional football player—let's call him Bull—who agreed to play with a sadist, Bob, and his sub, Jill. Bob was always careful never to dole out more than Jill could handle, but every once in a while, he needed to let off some steam. That's where Bull came in."

Sasha squirms a little, and that makes me grin.

"He took everything Bob threw at him—literally, with whips and floggers and everything in between. And he took it all for Jill. And a little bit for himself. Because not only did Bob take him right to the edge of his pain-threshold, whenever Bob gave Bull a reprieve, he ordered Jill to blow Bull, but not let him come. By the time Bob finished torturing Bull, he was dripping with pre-come—"

Sasha's hips rock against my thigh.

"Are you okay there?"

"Perfectly. Go on. Dripping with pre-come…"

I like the idea of her coming against my leg while I tell her a dirty story, but I don't want to tell her about fucking another woman. So I kiss her instead, until she comes apart in my arms.

"…And they fucked their way to very happy endings," I whisper before I pick her up and carry her to my bed, where I love her up one more time before I fall asleep with her snuggled into my side, her head on my chest.

## 31

## SASHA

THE DAY after the Rapscallion holiday party we fly to Vancouver. Before we leave, he closes up his Ottawa house. All the food in the fridge gets put in the freezer, except for the holiday cookies, which I rescue and take to my apartment. I'll be back in five days and ready to eat my feelings, I have no doubt.

Once I'm packed up, I head back to his place to pick him up, because I'll need my car at the airport when I return. It's a blustery day, but the plows have been out, and traffic is strangely cooperative.

"Shouldn't be any snow on the west coast," Tate says after we race from the parking garage to the departures terminal.

"I'm holding you to that."

He just grins.

We've already checked in, so we make our way through security, then head for the first-class lounge. On the way, we pass the departure gate. It's not busy yet, because there's still an hour before boarding, but there's a loud discussion happening at the counter. Tate slows his steps long enough to take in the scene—an irate passenger could delay the flight departure, and he has a game tomorrow.

He stops, and I follow his gaze. "What's going on?"

"I'm not sure." He frowns.

But the passenger isn't irate at all. If anything, they seem to be going out of their way to be patient, and it's the gate staff whose voice is raised.

Tate changes direction, and I follow.

Screw the first-class lounge. We can wait at the gate, and keep an eye on this conversation. It's two days after Christmas. Nobody needs to have their afternoon ruined.

I set my carry-on bag on a seat close enough for us to overhear their conversation.

"We don't make exceptions for carry-on sizes. You shouldn't have made it through security," the staff person says. He's dropped his attention to the computer now, no longer looking at the passenger. "If you'd like to check the bigger bag, we can do that. There's a charge, of course."

The passenger takes a deep breath. "How much?"

A loaded, painful question. Like there's a chance she may not be able to afford the hundred dollars, or whatever it is.

She doesn't get an answer. Instead, she gets a lot of clicking and sighing, and instead of sitting next to me, Tate prowls towards the counter.

I watch carefully, because he's probably best to handle this, but he doesn't need any drama, either.

The passenger gives him an apologetic smile. "Sorry."

"Are you on the flight to Vancouver?" He asks her. "We've got lots of time before boarding, don't worry."

The staff person snaps his hand out. "Boarding pass."

"Me?" Tate shakes his head. "I'm not looking to—"

"Boarding. Pass."

Whoa.

Tate visibly takes a deep breath and hands over his boarding pass. I get it—he doesn't want to get kicked off our flight by someone on a power trip. The staff person takes one look at the paper and rolls his eyes. "First-class lounge is down the hall."

"I'm aware. I only came over here to offer to pay for this woman's extra bags." Tate slides her an easy, don't-worry smile. "It's Christmas, after all."

That gets another sigh, and I can tell Tate is getting frustrated. He looks around, and his attention catches on someone else sitting on the other side of the desk. Someone with matching bags to the woman next to him; someone with big, worried eyes, and a too-frail body.

A young girl with a bald head.

"Is that your daughter?" he asks the woman.

She nods. "Her name is Amy. We're from Langley. We came out here for the holidays."

"Yeah, me too. I'm heading back to work, though." He glances around to me, a question in his eyes.

I nod. Fine by me.

"You know what, man?" Tate leans on the counter and clicks his fingers to get the gate guy's attention. "I'd like to switch seats with this woman and her daughter."

Damn straight. He's so getting laid when we get to his place in Vancouver.

I get up, my boarding pass ready to be traded in. "Hi," I say to the woman. "I'm Sasha."

"Bree."

"Did you have a nice Christmas?"

Bree nods, a stunned expression on her face.

"Me, too. And I get a few more days with my friend here, away from the snow, so I'm feeling pretty lucky. We'd be honoured if you'd take our seats, and I'm sure they can find room for your bags."

"My daughter needs more changes of clothes...just in case... And we have medicine, and special food, too."

Tate's face tightens up, and I can see him tearing the airline staff a new asshole if this doesn't get fixed now. But he's not going to throw his name around—which is sweet, for him to make this not about himself.

So maybe I can help.

I gently touch Bree's forearm. "Of course." I turn to the guy at the counter. "Is there an ombudsperson or passenger advocate we could get on the phone, maybe? Or can you pull up the compassionate guidelines for medical travel? I'd love to take a look at that, figure out what kind of exception could be made given the circumstances."

He blinks at me.

I smile blandly. "Now, would be great."

"I'm not sure—"

"That's clear. But I *am* sure, so either get someone on the phone, or switch our boarding passes. Understand?"

A vein pops to life in his forehead, and he clenches his jaw, but he nods. "I'll see what I can do."

"Thank you."

Tense seconds tick by as he clicks on the keyboard, then the printer whirs to life. He silently hands Tate a new boarding pass, then me.

Finally, he hands Bree two boarding passes without looking at her.

Tate clears his throat.

"Ah, the first-class lounge is that way," the guy says faintly.

Bree shakes her head. "We're fine here."

Tate gestures toward Amy. "Could we sit with you until boarding time?"

***

The gate guy gave Tate a middle seat, but I have an aisle seat, so we switch once we're on the plane.

His right leg spills into the tiny aisle, and his left knee is jammed into the seat in front of him. Economy seats can't be comfortable for oversized NHL players.

But he's grinning at me. "That was fun."

"You're a Christmas elf," I murmur as I cuddle against him.

"You carried the big stick there at the end."

"I have some experience navigating bureaucracies."

"It's hot." He snags my hand and tugs my fingers up so he can kiss my knuckles. "If I can move at the end of this flight, I'm totally giving you a reward fuck."

"Dare I ask what that might be?"

He grins wickedly. "Nope."

Another passenger takes the seat on the other side of me, but he breaks out headphones and falls asleep soon after take-off.

We both hop on Wi-Fi and check email. The university is closed this week, so I only have personal stuff to respond to, but I owe Mabel a marketing thought dump.

Tate offers a quiet running narrative as he checks in with his various teammates, and his friends who work for him on the back end in Ottawa.

"Two days after Christmas, and Rob is already sending me charity stuff to consider for next summer," he says with a fond smile.

"It'll be good to have you back in Ottawa for a while."

He slides a sideways glance at me. "Yeah."

My chest squeezes. Feelings. Bah. "Tell me about some of these charity ideas."

He lists a few of them. Pro-am golf tournaments, rent-an-arena free skate for the food bank, that kind of thing.

Good ideas, but they're all local.

"I'm surprised you haven't done something scaleable, like a calendar."

"That's a great idea."

I shrug. "It wasn't a suggestion, really. Just an observation."

That doesn't deter him. He leans in, lowering his voice. "But I think I'll do it naked."

He didn't just say naked on a crowded airplane. Yes, of course he did. I give him a shushing look that he ignores.

"Think it will sell? Maybe I can get some of my teammates to pose with me."

I swallow my tongue and try to think of a snappy response. For once, I'm stumped. All I can see is Andrushko tapping Tate on the ass with his hockey stick—and neither of them wearing so much as a jersey.

"Maybe you can all wear skate socks," I say after a painful few seconds of silence. I close my eyes and silently groan. Super weak come back, Sasha.

He chuckles in my ear. "Or just the pads." He drops his voice, practically purring now. He's really far too good at that distract-me-with-sex voice. It's unacceptable. "Strategically placed…pucks."

"Shhhh." Except… "Are you sure there are pucks big enough to cover up Andrushko?"

He laughs. "I'm jealous that you've give his junk that kind of thought." He's lying. He doesn't have a jealous bone in his body. The more complicated the orgy, the happier I'm sure he is.

I push the tease further. "He's a big guy."

"Not that big."

"Noted." I wink. "You and your dirty bestie will definitely sell a lot of calendars."

"My what?"

Ha. Now who has the advantage? I turn my face towards him and exaggerate my whisper. "Dirty. Bestie."

"No, that's not a thing."

"I think it is. He smacks your ass with your hockey stick every single game. You'll record that on video during the photo shoot. Bare ass, just a little jiggle—"

"Zero jiggle. Bite your beautiful tongue."

I give him a wicked smile. "That's going to go viral. Dirty besties. Totally a thing."

## 32

## TATE

The next morning, I wake up to sunshine streaming in the window, and sunshine in my arms as well.

My alarm quietly beeps at me, reminding me I want to head to the arena in an hour, but I'm in no rush to get up and do my usual routine because Sasha is in my bed.

In Vancouver.

This feels like a big deal. Bigger than her spending two nights with me in Ottawa.

"Morning," she says sleepily, and my heart bounces up and down like an eager puppy.

I kiss the soft skin behind her ear. "Nice way to wake up."

"Mmm." She stretches against me, and I fill my hands with her curves. She drained my body of all possible come last night, with her mouth and her hands and her pussy, and I should probably keep some energy for my morning skate, but damn, she gets my blood pumping.

"You feel good."

She arches against me, and we rub like that for a few minutes, slow and naughty. It's not going anywhere, it just feels good. And when she giggles and pushes me away, because she needs to pee and brush her teeth, I follow her. I give her privacy for the first task, but then I yank her into the shower with me.

Work is going to keep me away from her for two games over the next five days. Games, plus practice and press and team meetings.

Every other second is ours.

And not just for sex.

"What are you going to do today?" I ask her.

"I'll call around, see if I can find a spa." She takes my hand and slides my fingers over her fuzzy mound, with the short hairs there that she likes to wax away every so often.

I rub my fingers through her lips and around her clit, mentally reorganizing my morning to make room for an orgasm for her. I'll eat breakfast at the arena.

---

It's good to get back on the ice with the team. We're all jacked up about playing Chicago tonight. They're having a great season, leading their division, and we haven't played them yet.

The odds are not in our favour, either.

Coach keeps his notes short and to the point. "Get some rest this afternoon. And come back ready to fight. Now get out of here."

I walk out with Landvic, who apparently bought himself a Lamborghini for Christmas.

"What the fuck is that?" I ask, pointing at the bright yellow monstrosity.

"Shut the fuck up and get in your reliable Mom car."

I tap the key-fob, making my Land Rover beep. Mom car. What the fuck is that nonsense? "Leave my wheels alone."

"You opened the door."

"Get in your banana and screech out of here," I say, laughing.

I crank the raggaeton on the drive home and tell my SUV I'll never replace her with a flashy sports car.

When I get back, Sasha's strolling up the street.

"Perfect timing!" she calls out. "Did you have a good skate?"

"I did." I kiss the corner of her mouth. Her skin is all dewy and she smells faintly of flowers and grass. "How was the spa?"

"Amazing." We head inside, hand in hand. "Plus how sweet is it to be able to walk outside in a light jacket?"

"Pretty awesome."

"And during my massage, I figured out what was wrong with the chapter I'm working on in my thesis."

I open the door to my apartment. "Quality multi-tasking. I approve."

"How much time do we have before your game?"

I grin. "I need to leave in two hours. I was thinking we could have a nap."

"I like the sound of that," she purrs.

"Good. Oh, and I arranged for a ticket at the box office for the game for you."

Her brows pull tight. "You don't need to do that."

"Because you don't want to come to the game?"

"Because I won't use it." She moves closer and brushes a light kiss across my lips.

I frown. Sometimes I like how she pinches back against my efforts to be more couple-y. I like how she resists, because I fucking love the chase.

But something about this irritates me. "You could just say you don't want to come to the game."

"Should I say that?" She's not picking up on my annoyance, because her eyes dance.

"You are maddening."

"But freshly waxed, so you'll forgive me."

Always. I'll forgive her to the moon and back, and not just

because every last inch of her pussy is mine to bite and slap and lick and—

Sigh. "Completely forgiven. But I don't think I'm off-side for wanting my girlfriend to come and see me play."

"I watch all of your games. And I'm not your girlfriend."

"You aren't?"

"Not exactly."

That's news to my cock. "Huh."

"Freshly waxed, Tate. Focus on that."

So I do. I peel her clothes off and we have the most energetic nap in the history of naps.

But when her seat stays empty for the entire game—a match which we predictably lose, although only by a single goal—the irritation returns.

## 33

SASHA

The Pulpmill was almost sold out tonight, and it takes forever to navigate my way out of the arena. That was a hard loss, and I feel bad for Tate.

I know better than to worry about having distracted him, but after the miserable mood he was in after the loss in New York, I want to be there when he gets back.

Best laid plans.

For the second time today, he beats me home, and I'm getting out an Uber as he emerges from his underground parking spot.

He's scowling.

Shit.

And now I can't pretend I watched the game from his apartment, either.

He doesn't say anything as I approach. We go upstairs in silence, and the first thing he does is go to the fridge for a beer.

He doesn't offer me one, so I help myself to a glass of wine and drain half of it in the kitchen, trying to figure out what to do next.

I give him some space to brood, but I'm also a guest in his

apartment, and if we don't talk soon, this is going to get weird and awkward.

I top up my glass and head into the living room.

He's slouched on the couch, legs spread wide, beer untouched.

"I know you had a rough game—"

"I'm not pissed about the game, Sasha."

The way he says my name pulls me up short. "Okay."

He doesn't look at me. "Where were you?"

Oh. I sigh. "I was there."

"No you weren't."

"I was."

"I looked for you."

"I wasn't in that seat. I—I bought my own ticket up in the rafters."

He frowns, finally focusing his gaze on my face. Still pissed. "What?"

"I don't like the spotlight."

"Nobody would have paid you any attention."

I shrug. "And they pay me even less attention when I'm in the nosebleed seats."

He works his jaw back and forth as he looks at me. Less pissed, just tired now. "When? Have you done this before?"

"In New York."

He sighs, a rough, hard exhale. "Shit, Sash. Why didn't you tell me?"

"Because..." I trail off. Because I don't know. Because of complicated, weird history. "I always warned you I'm not an easy girl to date."

"That's bullshit."

"I'm sorry."

He holds out his arm and I go to him, setting down my glass. He kisses the top of my head. "It wasn't a bad loss tonight. We held our own against the best team in the league. It was fine."

Now I feel like crap. I really am sorry that I can't be what he wants, that I can't read him…in hindsight, I guess I see how he wanted me to come to the game tonight in a real way, he wasn't just being polite. "I'll come to the next game if you want."

"You don't need to."

"Wait, let me re-phrase. I'd love to sit closer to the ice for the next game."

He squeezes my shoulder. "I can find you a mid-level seat above the bench."

In every way that I'm a terrible girlfriend, Tate is a dream boyfriend. Compromise is his middle name. I crawl into his lap and lift his hand holding the beer bottle. "I don't deserve you. But you are the best."

***

"You. Are. The. Worst."

Tate just laughs at me and wiggles the rollerblades he bought me —a bonus Christmas present, apparently—in the air. "It'll be fun."

"I don't understand. I'm here for an entire week of hardcore kinky sex. Nobody said anything about getting road rash."

"I thought you were here to visit me, in all the fun west coast ways I could imagine." His voice rings with barely restrained laughter. "And I bought you matching protective gear."

I see that. I'm not impressed. So I go frosty. "I'm here for your tongue. And your cock. Not recreational fun."

Tate shifts closer. "You flew across the country because you can't get enough of my athletic prowess in and out of the—"

"I'm really just here for the orgasms, I promise."

"You say the sweetest things."

"So we should get naked."

"No."

"Tate…"

He grins wickedly. "It's sunny again, and Coach gave me the

day off, but I need to get in some active rest. I'd rather do it with you. Let's go rollerblading."

I look at the knee pads. They're cute.

He sets the blades down and moves closer, dropping his head to dust soft, coaxing kisses along my jaw. "Please, Sasha…"

And because he is the best, and the worst, we go rollerblading along the Seawall around Stanley Park.

The pathways are crowded, which makes sense since it's such a nice day, but we're in no hurry, so we take a leisurely pace. The blades Tate ordered me are amazing, I have to admit.

Plus the scenery along the way is breathtaking. The Vancouver skyline pokes up on our right, across an inlet, and the mountains beyond seem to stretch on forever. We wend our way along the path, dodging slower skaters and being passed by cyclists. Lions Gate Bridge comes into view, and it reminds me a little of the Golden Gate Bridge in San Francisco. I goggle at the sheer size of it as we pass underneath. The supports on the suspension bridge are massive.

The highlight of the Seawall for me, though, is Siwash Rock, which Tate points out. It's a tall rock sticking out of the water just a few feet from the seawall. And it has a tree growing out of the top, looking to me a bit like Sideshow Bob's hair from *The Simpsons*.

"You are a regular Vancouver tour guide now," I tell him when we return to his Land Rover.

"Wait until I impress you with my local sushi knowledge."

"Oh yeah?"

"We're going to this awesome place in Kits." He winks at me. "Kitsalano."

I stick my tongue out at him. "I figured it out."

Over lunch—which is awesome, and better than any sushi I've had in recent years—he tells me about adjusting to life on the west coast. It's not just abbreviated names for locations and a different climate. It's also living on his own, well and truly, for the first time...ever.

"I know what that's like." I find myself telling him all about my first year in Ottawa. How I resisted going home for the holidays, because I was worried I'd get homesick. "I never did, though."

He nods. "Right. It was different for me, I guess. I embraced the homesickness a bit too much in the beginning. But I've adjusted now. I'm really loving this city." He takes my hand and squeezes my fingers. "Although I'd like to see you more often."

The look on his face is way too serious. "Come on. Let's go home and have a nap."

Nap. Best euphemism ever.

---

Later that night, while we're vegged out on his couch flipping through the Netflix menu, Tate gives me a curious look.

"What?"

"Nothing."

I raise one eyebrow. Mm-hmm.

He grins. "Okay. I wasn't going to say anything, but...the team is throwing a New Year's Eve party for the players and staff."

I know exactly where this is headed, and I won't make him ask. "Yes."

"It's totally fine if you don't want to go, and if you would be willing to, we don't have to stay long. Just make an appearance, take a turn around the room, and shake a few hands—wait, what?"

"Yes. I'll go. But if we get to arrive late and leave early, I'll even be mildly enthusiastic."

"You'll come to my game tomorrow *and* be my date for New Year's Eve the next night?" Tate tangles his fingers with mine. "What did I do to get so lucky?"

"You understood me."

He laughs and tumbles on top of me. "I'm going to kiss you at midnight, and there will be fireworks, Sasha," he promises as he nibbles and kisses my neck.

"I'll hold you to that. And I expect you to win tomorrow, by the way."

He nods soberly. "Of course."

The next night, while I watch from a seat that he knows I'm sitting in, he does just that. And he scores a hat trick.

On the ice, and then again once we're back at his place.

34

## TATE

AFTER SASHA RETURNS TO OTTAWA, we head out on a road trip that doesn't start well. Simec is injured in Montreal, knocking him out of the next few games. Onetti joins our line, but he doesn't read Moore and I as well as Simec does, and we're scoreless until we get to Columbus. A win there bolsters us, and we take the next game against Washington—and I score two goals that night.

But the next game, in Minnesota, is another loss, and we find ourselves in the middle of January still clawing our way up the division standings as the decided underdogs.

There's a growing narrative in the media that something is wrong with the basic equation of our team. So far, we've done a good job in our dressing room of ignoring that, because it's not true. When we win, it feels right. We win when we click. And when we don't click, we don't win, which means we can fix this.

But we're running out of time.

Andrushko is named to the All Star team, which is a nice morale bump. And he deserves it—our defence has been on point as we've moved into winter. We're still losing games as often as we win them, but never by much. A goal, maybe two.

We arrive in Banff for a much-needed few days break between our games in Minnesota and Edmonton and the first thing I do is call Sasha.

The Christmas and New Year's week spoiled me. Going a month without seeing her is torture.

"I'm still at the university," she warns. Code for don't be inappropriate.

"I have to head out for dinner soon, anyway."

"It's good to hear your voice, though," she says softly. "Tell me something fun."

"We're going skiing tomorrow."

"Cool!"

"Yeah. Getting out on the slopes is a nice alternative to the usual workout, even though our insurance riders have a lot of constraints on where and how we can ski. And then we'll probably end up spending most of tomorrow afternoon in the chalet, chilling."

She laughs. "That sounds like a real hardship."

"I'd say you should fly out, but it's a team-only thing."

"I'm swamped anyway. My dissertation committee requires serious hand-holding, it's ridiculous. I thought they would be helping me, but it's the other way around. They can't pick a date to meet without twenty-seven emails back and forth that all end with, 'Can Sasha help figure this out?' No, Sasha bloody well can't, she's bloody well writing the last chapter of her analysis. Except of course I can, and I do, and each day that passes cements my desire to get the hell out of academia."

She takes a deep breath, and I tell her take another. "Just for good measure."

I get a delicate growl in my ear for that.

"When did you last eat?" I ask her.

"I had oatmeal for breakfast."

I look at my watch. "It's almost seven for you! Go find some food. Call Ellie, see if she wants delivery."

"That's a good idea. Okay, I'm going. Don't hurt yourself tomorrow."

"I won't. Gotta stay pretty for when I see you in two weeks."

"And don't have too much fun, either. Remember, I'm miserable here."

I chuckle. "Easiest promise to make, ever. I'm not going to have any fun at all. This is a work thing, no matter how they dress it up. A training day like any other."

***

Maybe not *quite* like any other training day, I think as I watch our physical trainers set up a team-building exercise on top of a mountain. The slopes are open for other skiers, too, and we've attracted some attention.

I'm always happy to pose for pictures with fans, so while we watch the defensive lines run through the exercise, I shake hands and say cheese until my cheeks hurt.

Then it's our turn. As a line, Moore, Onetti, and I need to cross-country ski a mini obstacle course—on a custom set of skis built for three people. Two skis, six toe clips.

And we aren't allowed to speak. We need to watch each other's body language, and at two exchange points, switch out the leader.

It's harder than it looks, and it looks fucking insane.

By the time we make it through—in the second-fastest time, bested only by Andrushko's line—we're drenched in sweat. But we're also working better, which is the point.

Full props to the trainers.

Coach huddles us up as a group to set up the next exercise, then we've got some waiting around time again.

Simec, true to form, has found a group of hot young things to bury himself in. He waves me over. I grab Onetti, because he deserves a reward for being a star team player, and go over to be polite.

Three hours later, when we get back to the chalet, my phone is blowing up because a picture of me surrounded by Victoria's Secret models has hit social media, and fans are loving it.

Fuck.

Fuck, fuck, fuckity fucking fuckers.

I abandon my beer and excuse myself. "I'll see you guys at dinner."

Sasha picks up on the first ring. "Hello."

"Hey." I wince.

"You had fun today."

"Not really."

"I told you not to do that," she says silkily. "I was kidding, of course. But did you have to have that much fun?"

"I swear it was zero fun."

"You went skiing with Victoria's Secret models."

I went skiing and there happened to be models on the slopes at the same time. I start to burn under the collar, because while I fucking miss her like crazy, that's only an important distinction if Sasha were my girlfriend. And two weeks ago, she made a hella big deal about the fact that she's not. "Jealous?"

"No."

"Liar."

"I'm not fucking you again until you get tested."

"But you will fuck me again. Which is good, because I'm not interested in sinking into any pussy that doesn't have a direct wire to your smart mouth. For real. It didn't even cross my mind. I only want you. I only have eyes for you."

"We haven't talked about being exclusive."

"We haven't talked about a lot of things, but they've happened anyway. We're exclusive. There's nobody else. I didn't even know they were models, and the second I got back to my phone and saw the picture, I called you."

She sighs. "I didn't like seeing it."

"I know. I'm sorry."

"I don't want to care about them."

I get that, too. "Nobody gets to make up the rules for us, but us. Outside drama doesn't touch us. Nothing touches us. This is sacred. You and me. Ignore everything else."

"I only have eyes for you, too," she whispers. "I only see you."

I like the sound of that. "Never worry that the feeling isn't mutual. And if you want me to get tested, I will."

She makes a humming sound. "Maybe."

"If I did, we could ditch the condoms." I want to be inside her. Bare. Skin on skin.

"That's an unnecessary risk."

"You're on the pill."

"I like the double protection."

"I'll pull out. Nothing wrong with spilling my come on your skin. That's hot, too."

She laughs despite herself. "You're so filthy."

"Is that a maybe?"

"That's a…I don't know. Yes. Maybe. Get tested, and we'll see."

Hot damn. "Okay. Consider it done. I'll email you the results as soon as I get them." But they'll be free of infection. I've never gone unwrapped, and I'm stoked that Sasha might be my first time for that.

"Tate…" Her voice goes small and soft, and I want to be on the other side of the country with her.

"What is it?"

"Do you have to go do something with the team?"

"Nah. Dinner's in a bit, but I'm all yours until then."

She's silent for a long stretch. Then she sighs. "I should tell you about my ex."

"If you want. But I don't need to know."

"Maybe I need to say it out loud. Get rid of it being a big deal in my head."

"Sure."

She tells me about some asshole named Brian. A pro basketball player who I vaguely know to be more flash than substance. "We weren't together that long, about three months, but in that time, my name kept popping up in gossip columns and photographers would look for me at events. It turned out, he was using me because the scandals kept his profile up. It was stupid and short-sighted, and by the end of our relationship, he was openly dating other people. The last scandal was him dumping me by way of a paparazzi video. I let him disrupt my first attempt at my MBA, and I had to start over the next year at another school. I know you aren't anything like him, but that's why I'm so cautious about having a public life. It doesn't take much for someone else to twist how you are seen."

"I will never do that to you."

"I know." But her voice is still small. I don't know that I've ever heard her like this.

"Not long until you visit again, right?"

"Yeah. I'll be in Vancouver in time for the All Star Break."

I want to stay on the phone all night. Screw dinner. Screw team building. I'm working on a team of two here.

"I should let you go."

"No."

She takes a deep breath. "Yes. And I have work to do. Always."

"Call me later."

"You call me."

"I will."

"Good." Now I can hear a smile in her voice. And she hangs up first, which is for the best. I probably would have kept going like that forever.

## 35

## SASHA

A WEEK LATER, I land in Seattle for my conference. Monday night, I go out for dinner with a couple of the Entrepreneurship faculty from the business school at U of W.

We talk about micro-lending lessons from developing nations until the restaurant is closing up around us, and I find myself very tempted by the unspoken suggestion—if I were interested, I could probably come back for a guest lecture.

Do some heavy lifting on a co-authored paper.

Visit again and meet more faculty.

Put my hat officially in the ring for a potential job.

In Seattle.

When I get back to the hotel, I've got a bunch of emails to catch up on. The owner of the lingerie store I've backed in downtown Ottawa had a boudoir photographer come in and do some networking. Might I be interested in meeting with her?

I don't know. Maybe.

Mabel's found a manufacturer in Quebec to put together her escape room kits, complete with a Weirdaker Games screwdriver.

I love that. I tell her to set one aside for me when I get back.

And then as I'm just about to clear my inbox down to zero unread messages, a new one pops in.

A thank you note for dinner.

I hit reply right away.

**Dr. Ali,**

**I'm the one who should be thanking you. Tonight's discussion helped clarify some of my thoughts on re-investment autonomy. I look forward to exploring that further via email, as you mentioned. There may be a paper in it for us.**

**All the best,**
**Sasha Brewster**

My phone rings as I hit send. I glance at the screen and smile. "Are you home?"

Tate yawns. "Yeah. We came home last night, actually. I've been asleep for most of the last twenty-four hours. I just woke up from another nap. Oh, shit, I didn't realize it was this late, I'm sorry."

"No, it's not so bad. I'm in Seattle, remember?"

"No way! Really? Did I know that?"

"I thought you did." I laugh. "Did I forget to tell you that? That's why I could come up for the All Star Break. I'm just down the road a few hours. I'll fly up at the end of the week."

"Excellent. Tell me about this conference."

"There aren't likely to be any Victoria's Secret models."

He snorts. "*Magic Mike 3* auditions?"

"More like *The Wolf of Wall Street*. I like my little corner of the biz world, but in general..." Damn. That's a good reminder before I get too excited about the U of W group. "Anyway, it's a lot of suits. You wear them better."

"Damn straight I do. I think it's your turn to tell me a bedtime story, don't you think?"

"Sure." I fumble my way through a sloppy blow job fantasy, and we both like it, but the real thing will be even better in a few days.

---

The next night, I watch his game while I eat takeout noodles in my hotel room.

They lose. Until I watched this season so closely, I didn't realize just how many games they wouldn't win.

That has to be a real mind fuck. Maybe I'll ask Tate about that once the season is over.

At the end of the game, I leave the TV on so I can listen to the commentators discuss the Lumberjacks' standing in the division. They're in fifth place, but only two points out of fourth, and apparently a few games can make all the difference. But they'll need to make that surge soon, or they'll end up too far out of the standings across the league for a chance at the wild card spot.

Which is more information than I ever thought I'd know about hockey stats.

I crawl into bed with my phone and read about the play-offs until my eyes are itchy and the words blur in front of me.

---

I present my poster on Wednesday morning, then sit in on Dr. Ali's presentation in the afternoon. I check my email on the break, and there's a message from Tate.

**From: Tate Nilsson**
**To: Sasha Brewster**
**Subject: For your reference: blood test results (NSFW)**

I know better than to open the email in public. I duck into an empty room and click on it.

Attached is a .pdf scan of his blood work results.

And embedded in the email is, as promised, a not-safe-for-work GIF image of wall sex.

The porn actor's butt is almost as nice as Tate's, and I bite my lip as I watch the little animation. Thrust, thrust, thrust…

Okay. Sold.

I close that and navigate to a new browser window. If there's a decent-priced flight out tonight, I'm leaving as soon as the sessions are done this afternoon.

And maybe I don't care how much the flight costs…

## 36

## TATE

**Sasha: Are you going out tonight? Might not be able to call until pretty late.**
**Tate: Nope. And I had a nap today, so I'll be up late. Call whenever.**

I'm watching game tape at a bit after midnight when the intercom buzzer sounds.

I roll my eyes, and it stops. Hopefully whoever it is doesn't bug too many other residents before they find the right one.

A minute later, though, I hear someone fumbling at the door, then a key slides into the lock.

I'm on my feet when it swings open.

But it's not a drunken neighbour's friend.

It's Sasha.

"Hey," she says on a breathy exhale, grinning at me. She drops her bag on the floor and holds up the spare key I gave her at New Year's. "Glad I kept this. You didn't answer the intercom."

"I never do." I cross the room in three quick strides and pick her up, spinning her around as she laughs. "My Wednesday just got a fuck-tonne better. What are you doing here?"

"I got your email."

Set aside absolutely everything else between us—jealousy, distance, fear, still learning how far we can trust each other—when I tell Sasha my blood test has come back clear of infection, she gets on an airplane so I can fuck her.

That means something.

Maybe it means something dirty, but it means *something*. I will fucking take it.

"You got my email."

"I did."

"And you came straight over."

"I was in the neighbourhood."

"You were—" I laugh as I twist us in the direction of my room. "You gorgeous little liar. You got on a plane for the D."

"Not if you're going to call it that."

"The bare, just-for-you, unwrapped C."

"Nobody calls it that."

"Rock hard, velvet B."

"B?"

"Boner. Cock. Dick. You want it. You want it bad. You—"

"I want you," she whispers as we stop in the doorway to my bedroom. "All the fucking time. What have you done to me, Tate Nilsson?"

I hook my fingers under the hem of her shirt, my pulse hammering away. "I don't know."

She gives me a tremulous smile as she lifts her arms, and I peel her shirt off. Unwrapping her has never felt quite like this. Like a gift.

I take my time with her jeans. The button first, my knuckles brushing her belly, then the zipper. She's wearing blue panties, and my dick aches to get inside them.

Bare flesh. Sasha in the raw.

I tug her closer and kiss her, soft pulls of my lips as I bring her hands to my waistband.

I want her to strip me bare as well.

*Please let me be a gift to you, too.*

Instead of shoving my sweats down my legs, she pulls the waistband back just enough to slip her hand inside. I shudder as her fingers wrap around my heavy cock, lifting off my body in its eagerness.

She strokes me as the scent of my sex rises between us. Clean skin, but beneath that a musky earthiness.

Nothing between us tonight.

My scent on her skin. Her scent on mine.

I play with her hair as she glides her palm up and down my length, as she cups my balls gently before dropping to her knees and swallowing the swollen, glistening head into her mouth.

"Ah…" I drop my chin, gaze glued on hers as she looks up at me. "You like the taste of me? Big cock in a little mouth."

She bobs her head and I tangle my fingers in the golden brown strands brushing her cheeks.

"Swallow me down. Take as much as you can. Fuck, yeah. That's going to be inside you soon. You're all mine, Sasha. And I'm all yours. Every last inch. Yours to do whatever you want with."

She opens wider and slides her tongue wide against the sensitive spot under the crown, then presses a delicate kiss right to the tip. "I want it all," she murmurs as she rises.

We tumble onto the bed and roll. I kiss her neck, her tits, the dip of her stomach and the rise of her mound. Then I slide my tongue between her pussy lips and taste the slippery sweetness that promises she's ready to take my cock inside her.

I push her legs up and out, revealing every inch of her plump, ripe sex. A fucking gift which I appreciate until she's on the edge of exploding.

When I surge back up her body, she lifts her hips to meet me, and we fit together perfectly.

Wet pussy, hard cock. The body knows what it wants, and my

body wants to be inside her like nothing else. My dick swells as she rocks him against her wet slit and up to her clit.

She gasps a ragged, perfect little cry every time her hips roll down and her hard nub makes contact with my erection.

Fuck, I could come like this. Grind against her and blow on her belly.

But I want more, so I set a firm grip on her hip and hold her still. "Shhh," I urge her as I get up on my knees. I rub the crown of my cock through her folds. The last thing I see before I notch us together is a bead of pre-come forming on the swollen tip.

I press into her, working that drop of my seed inside. She cries out and clutches at me. I thrust again, reeling from the tender, wet warmth of her. Big cock, tight pussy. Base, crude thoughts war with warmer, sweeter realizations as we begin to move together in unison.

It's sweet, slow, crazy emotional sex, and I never want it to end.

"You feel…" There are no words.

"I know." She tangles her fingers in my hair as she holds our heads together. Her breath is hot against my face, her eyes squeezed shut as her body works so hard with mine. Her tight nipples brush against my chest and I push up again, wanting her flesh in my palm. I cup a breast and tug on the peak with my fingers. There's a tightening inside her in response, and I do it again.

Her eyes fly open and she lets out a low keening sound.

Tension mounts deep inside me as I hold her gaze and thrust again. I think of her mouth, her ass, her sweet words and her perfect sass. I chase all the different Sashas twirling through my mind, and the very real one in my arms. I ride her hard until she explodes beneath me, then I thrust one last time as my own orgasm barrels in.

I pull out as the first jolt of come blasts out of me, and I stroke myself hard through the remaining spurts. My jizz paints the crease between her hip and her leg, and up onto her trembling belly.

As I brace myself above her, catching my breath, she reaches down and swipes her finger through the trail of come I've marked her with. Slowly, with cat-like grace, she brings it to her mouth and licks her fingertip clean.

Fuck. Me.

The head of my dick is aching and sensitive to the touch, but I keep stroking, because deep inside I feel the unmistakable resurgence of arousal.

"Do that again," I growl. "Lap up my come."

She arches beneath me and bites her lip, but she doesn't move her hands.

"Sasha."

"Make me," she whispers.

Oh, sweet mercy. My cock strains as I roll onto my side. I prop myself up on my elbow and with my free hand, I touch the wet smear of my release on her skin. Twenty years of sex, and I've never spilled on a woman's skin.

Twenty years, I've never wanted to. I learned early on that you wrap it up. Period, no exception, or you run the risk of having a kid at sixteen instead of being scouted for the NHL.

Easy call.

And then it was the constant threat of a paternity suit, although knock on wood, I've never had anyone try. No question, condoms have been my best friend.

But with Sasha, this isn't scary.

A new and unfamiliar tightness pulls inside my chest, and touching it isn't enough.

I crawl down the bed, kissing and sucking at her skin as I go. Her nipples, her ribs, her hip.

I settle between her legs and breathe in the familiar scent that's uniquely hers and wholly addictive.

There's a new layer now. Astringent and bold, a sharp counter to her sweet earthiness.

My come on her skin.

My mark.

My scent.

I never want her to wash it off. I can't tell her that. She'll make me wear a condom for the rest of my life.

For the—

My heart slams against my ribs and I press my mouth into the sweet softness of her inside thigh.

She's wearing my scent. She's mine. Forever.

I suck on her flesh. *I love you.* God, it's the wrong time to realize that.

*I want you forever.*

*I need you, too.*

Her fingers lace into my hair, tugging. "I'm messy," she whispers.

Damn fucking right. My mess. My woman.

I twist my head and cover her mound with my mouth. I'll clean her up. Every last inch.

Mine.

*I love you.*

What the fuck am I going to do with that stupidly-obvious brand new information?

Lick her up and bury my feelings for another day. That's what I'm going to do.

I sweep my tongue over her bare skin, and once she's all clean, I cover her with my body and make her messy all over again.

I can't tell her I love her, but I can imprint my scent deep in her body. We have another week together. I'll do this every day. She can fly home with my mark on her skin.

And when the season is over, we'll talk about what comes next.

She comes to my game the next night, the last before the All Star Break, and she sits closer to the VIP seats this time.

Afterwards, she meets me in the lounge where we meet our guests after games, and Andrushko makes a beeline for her.

"Tate's friend," he says, holding out his hand.

Sasha takes it and squeezes tight enough I can see her knuckles turning white. "Tate's teammate," she responds.

"You were just here at Christmas. And now again? Tate is a lucky friend."

"I was in Seattle for work. Popped up to see a game." She stretches the truth so casually, I almost believe it myself. "You made the All Star team, right? When do you leave?"

I smoothly interject and suggest we get going. "Late dinner," I say not apologetically at all to Andrushko.

He winks at me.

And as we move away, Sasha rolls her eyes. "Why is he so amused by me?"

"You're pretty. He thinks it's funny that you you push back."

"It's none of his business why I'm here."

I frown. "I think he's just making small talk." For someone who is so smart in so many ways, and can read strangers in crisis like a book, Sasha has a blind spot when it comes to professional athletes. Like she assumes the worst.

For good reason, I remind myself. She's been burned before.

"What do you want to do for dinner?"

She gives me a brilliant smile that sweeps everything else from my mind. "You're the local expert now. You pick."

We're in the middle of making breakfast on Saturday when

Sasha's phone rings. She looks at the screen, then excuses herself into my bedroom to take the call.

I slice the avocado and tomato while I wait for her to come back. The eggs will only take a few minutes, and I don't know how long this conversation will take, so I'll wait until she's done to start poaching.

We could do with another pot of coffee. I get that started, then pull the eggs out of the fridge.

I wonder how many she wants. I try to pick up any hint from the other room if she's wrapping up the conversation. A few words filter through the partially closed door. *Honoured* and *opportunity. West coast. Appeal.*

I frown and move closer to the door.

"I wasn't expecting such a direct conversation at this point," she continues. "Yes, it was a fascinating discussion. I agree. It would be great to work together. Thank you so much for reaching out to me. I'll give the position some serious consideration."

I stand there, in the middle of a living room that didn't feel lived in until she arrived, in a city that has always felt too damn far from home, but had started to feel like mine when I showed it to her. My thoughts are still reeling when she steps out of the bedroom.

She starts, like she's surprised to see me standing there. "All done. Sorry."

"Who was that?"

"Someone I met at the conference in Seattle. A professor at the University of Washington."

I wait for her to give me anything else.

She doesn't.

I nod. "Right."

She glances past me. "Oh, good, more coffee. Did you start the eggs?"

"No."

"I can do that."

"No." My neck is hot, and my back is tight. My throat feels raw.

She stops and gives me a curious look.

Fuck curiosity. Fuck secrets. Fuck love, because this is bull-shit. "When were you going to tell me that you could have a job on this side of the continent?"

Her eyes go wide. "I…I wouldn't say that—"

"When. Were. You. Going. To—"

"Never." She lifts her chin and gives me a fierce look. "Because I'm not going to take it. Were you eavesdropping?"

"I was going to ask you how many God damn eggs you wanted."

Her jaw flexes as she glares at me. "I don't think I want any right now."

"My appetite's feeling a bit off, too." I cross my arms over my body. "It didn't sound like you weren't interested."

"I was being polite to a professional colleague. And how much did you hear?"

"Not enough to understand what the hell is going on."

"It's none of your business!"

"I'm picking that up loud and clear. You don't trust me in the least, do you?"

Her eyes narrow. "Are you turning this into a thing?"

Yeah, I think I am. "You don't. You haven't trusted me with anything besides your body."

"That's not true."

"Then tell me about the job."

"No."

In the back of my mind, a little voice reminds me she's being stubborn because I'm pushing her.

I don't listen to it. "You love the west coast."

She throws her hands in the air. "There's more to a career move than liking the local sushi."

"Like what?"

"My life is in Ottawa." She says it like it's just the most obvious thing in the world.

Except it's not. I tap my chest, hard. "I'm here. University of Washington is what, three hours away? That's a day trip. We could be together every single weekend."

There's a long stretch of silence. So long it turns sharp. Painful.

Her answer doesn't change. And that's all I need to know. So much for just her and me. Turns out, it was always just her. I was disposable the whole time.

All I can hear is my own ragged breathing. She's frozen, staring at me in disbelief, like I'm asking her to go to prison for me or something.

I have to try again. I have to fix this. "Sasha, I love—"

"No." She snaps it out, cutting me off.

"I do."

"Stop." She stares at me, and I finally get it. This isn't what we agreed to. This isn't what she wanted.

She only wanted a single afternoon.

She wanted to keep our affair private.

She wanted to be a friend with benefits, not a girlfriend, no matter how intense our feelings.

I fell in love with a woman who never had any intention of loving me back.

"I should..." She trails off and twists around, looking around my apartment.

"Sash—"

"No." She shakes her head. "I can't. We always knew we had an end-date."

"*No.* That was..." A lifetime ago. "Things have changed between us."

"Maybe that was where we went wrong."

"I don't—"

She holds up her hand, and I fall silent.

I can only protest so much. "Fine. You want to put us on ice? Live on opposite sides of the country and just fuck occasionally? That's the worst plan ever, Sasha. I can't—" I can't think straight. I can't trust myself to say anything else, either. "I need some air."

I grab my keys and head out the door.

When I get back an hour later with two lattes, because I'm a dumb stupid fuck who doesn't know when to shut up, she's gone.

37

SASHA

I WAIT for Tate to come back. For him to hit the lobby and realize this is stupid. But when five minutes turn into ten, and he's still gone, other thoughts start to crowd into my head.

Like maybe we should reconsider what we're doing here.

He's right. We're not in the same place—not geographically, or emotionally. And he doesn't need my baggage.

I don't need the guilt for that, either.

I call him, but there's no answer. And really, there's nothing else to say right now. We both need some space.

I don't like the idea of going to a hotel to be melancholy, so I call the airline and see if I can change my flight home. I'm in luck, apparently.

It doesn't feel lucky.

It feels like I need a stiff drink from the first flight attendant I see.

When I land in Ottawa, I'm drunk. I turn on my phone, ignore the half-dozen texts from Tate—because he can go fuck himself and his stupid opinions about what I should do with my life—and manage to book an Uber.

I'll come back and get my car tomorrow. Right now, I need

my bed and a hot shower. I'm not picky about the order, which is good, because as soon as I hit the mattress, I'm zonked out.

In the morning, I have a brutal hangover headache. I roll over and go back to sleep.

That afternoon, I finally shower, then retrieve my car from the airport and go to the university, where I pour myself into work that doesn't require speaking to anyone.

Then I go back to bed.

The next day, I wake up with a panicked start because someone is entering my apartment. The door creaks open, and there are footsteps. I cast about my room for a weapon.

"Sasha?"

"Ellie?" I crawl out of bed and wrap my robe around my body. I poke my head out of my room. "What's wrong?"

She frowns at me. "I think that's my line. I called and texted a bunch of times."

Oh. "I turned the ringer off on my phone." Because Tate wouldn't stop calling.

I didn't use to take his calls. I can learn not to again, as much as it hurts right now.

"I'm sorry for the intrusion, but I have a shoe emergency." She blushes. "My feet have gotten bigger. We have a state dinner tonight, and I really didn't want to go to a store and be like, 'please, tell the world that the prime minister's wife's feet are getting fat'. Which I know is ridiculous, but—"

"Say no more. I'm on it. Okay, so I'm a full size bigger than you. How much of a size change are we talking? Can I measure you and maybe go and buy something? Let's start in my closet."

She follows me into my room as I shove my hair back into a bun and try to get my brain unscrambled.

"Do you have an outfit picked out? What colour shoe are you looking for?"

She scans my room, settling her gaze on my open suitcase. I

haven't unpacked, and everything is spilling out of it. "Are you on your way out to Vancouver?"

No. We can talk about shoes. We can't talk about Tate. I shake my head. "Outfit?"

"Sasha?" Ellie waddles around me, getting between me and the floor-to-ceiling shelf of shoes that I desperately want to save me from this conversation. No such luck. Hot tears prick my eyelids as she gives me a concerned look. "You're a mess. Your apartment is a disaster. What's wrong?"

I shrug helplessly.

"Are you sick?"

"Sure," I mumble. "Maybe I need soup."

"Are you pregnant?"

"What?" I jerk back. I can see how she would wonder that and I need to head that craziness off at the pass. "No. God, no. I protect against that like six different ways."

Well, only one way that last time... But the water everyone else is drinking is *not* tasty to me. Not tasty at all, but good for her and the prime minister. They'll have fabulously attractive and smart mini-people.

"Did you have a fight?"

I nod.

"Oh, that sucks. I'm sorry. What did he do?"

He made me fall in love with him. "It wasn't him. We just reached a breaking point."

"I don't know what to say. That's really sad. How are you feeling?"

"I'm miserable," I hug my knees to my chest. "And I don't know what to do about that."

"You should call Tate."

"I can't."

"Why?"

Because he's right. When it came down to it, I couldn't trust him with my secrets. With my fear. "I hurt his feelings."

"Did you try apologizing?"

"It wouldn't do any good."

"Why not?"

"Because nothing has changed. I'm not going to let my life be subsumed by a man's life."

"Did he ask you to do that?"

I wince. "No."

"Oh."

"But that's what would happen. I could see it happening. The urge to be closer to him. There's a faculty position opening up at a university in Seattle next year. It would be perfect for me."

"What a nefarious trap he's laid for you."

I ignore her sarcastic retort, because that's not the point. Of course Tate had nothing to do with it. The problem is that I wouldn't have been interested a year ago. "That was never in my plan. I've established myself here."

"You have more frequent flier miles than Gavin. Since when do you care about where your geographical base is?"

"I live my life on my own terms."

"And your terms are to be, in our own words, miserable?"

"I didn't want it to get complicated."

"That's love."

"I never said I loved him." My chest squeezes tight.

"You didn't need to."

I never said it. I never admitted it to myself, and I never told him.

*I love you so much it scares me.* Hot tears prick my eyelids and I squeeze them shut, refusing to let the fat, wet drops expose me as the fraud I am.

I want to live my life on my own terms, but I'm a weeping mess over the consequences of that choice.

And I still miss him.

"You should call Tate," Ellie says. "Right after you find me some shoes."

I can't call him. He has a game tomorrow. The last thing he needs is drama. "Shoes…black flats, maybe?"

She gives me a long, concerned look before nodding. "Sure."

I step around her and take a pair of silk slides off the shelf. "These have always been a touch tight on me. Try them."

"And then you'll call?"

I ignore the question. I don't have a good answer for her. Or for myself.

3 8

─────────

TATE

I SPEND three days wallowing in self-pity. I wear the same clothes to sleep in, work out in, even to blindly watch game tape that I don't absorb. When the break is over and I need to show up at The Pulpmill and do my job, I do it with a pissed-off, black cloud over my head that my teammates can clearly see a mile away.

Nobody talks to me unless it's about the game we're about to play.

I'm just fine with that.

I'd rather be left alone, to sink into the numbness and just do what I need to do. But I'm not alone. My thoughts make sure of that.

I don't want to think of Sasha as I step out onto the ice for the first time after our fight.

I'm minutes from face-off and I need to get my heart out of my head. We're coming off a three-game losing streak and two of those losses were on home ice. I can't afford to have my focus anywhere but here and now.

But she used to watch all my games. Would she be watching tonight?

Andrushko taps my ass, same as always, and that reminds me of our flight back from Ottawa at Christmas. How she paid attention to the tiny details, but she couldn't fucking see that I was falling in love with her. Fuck.

I bite against my mouth guard and promise myself if we win tonight, I can open the last bottle of that expensive bourbon I ordered.

I win the face-off and score within the first seven minutes. My entire game is fuelled by anger. I skate for the puck like I'm chasing the devil, and every shot on goal is an attack against a faceless enemy. Love and its sucker punches. I'll punch right back. And part of me hopes Sasha's watching. Notice this, woman. Notice how angry I am, and how I'm rising above it to conquer the world.

Two goals and an assist later, we've got the win and I'm stripping off my gear in the locker room. One down, thirty-two to go.

If I can't have the girl, I can fucking have the play-offs.

As soon as the press is gone from the dressing room—having gotten zero chances to ask me questions, because I wasn't making eye contact with any of them—Moore pulls me aside. "Are you okay, man?" he asks, his voice low.

No. "Sure."

"You just scored the game-winning goal."

"So?"

He raises an eyebrow. "So I'd expect you to be grinning from ear to ear with your head buried in your phone while you text with that friend of yours in Ottawa. But you're not. Something wrong on the home front?"

I want to lash out at him. Tell him to fuck off and mind his own business. He's too observant. I don't need to be reminded that there's no text from Sasha waiting for me on my phone. Yeah, I want to unload on him, but think better of it. Instead, I square my jaw and stare straight ahead. "It's complicated."

"It always is. I'll leave it for now," he says. "Just don't let shit bottle up too long."

I blow him off with a nod, and while he heads back to his stall, I finish getting changed.

When I get home, I grab a beer instead of the bourbon I really want, and nurse it while I watch the game.

It's well after three by the time I'm done my second beer and game analysis, but I'm in no hurry to go to bed. Coach gave us the next day off, so I click over from the PVR to the TV and flip through the channels, looking for highlights from the other games played tonight.

I wake up six hours later, smelling like beer and sweat and misery. I turn the TV off and head for the shower instead of my bed.

---

Two nights later, we beat Chicago. Then we play Tampa Bay, and I score a hat trick and we slaughter them six-to-one.

After each game, I turn on my phone when I get home and look through my messages. None of them are ever from Sasha. I'd thought maybe my hat trick might have elicited at least… something, and when it doesn't, I'm hit with a fresh surge of impotent anger.

Three wins in a row is worth a minor celebration, so when Simec and a few others head out to a pub to celebrate, I meet up with them. But I'm not feeling it, so I have one beer to at least give the pretence of being sociable, then I retreat home to another scintillating night of game tape and hockey highlights.

The team heads into a four-game road trip on a massive high. I find a perverse, painful joy in my suffering leading to my best play all year, and everyone else happily tolerates my new sullenness because they like what I'm doing on the ice.

I like it, too. I'm not so bent around the axle for Sasha that I can't appreciate what this new trend is doing for our chances. We've moved up a spot in the standings, and a wild card spot is now more within reach than before. We just need to keep up the momentum.

And I need to stop wondering if Sasha is watching me play.

## 39

## SASHA

THE VERDICT IS IN. I'm definitely some kind of masochist. There's no chapter in the BDSM book for watching my ex-boyfriend goon around on the ice like a killer with a taste of blood, but that's my preferred brand of torture.

I don't just watch the games. I devour the few seconds he gives the press, if they're lucky, afterwards. The clipped, pissed-off bite in his voice. The cold stare in his eyes. Every so often he flicks his attention right into the camera, and it slays me to the core.

Every game, I think about sending him a text message. *Good game. You're climbing the standings. Might make the play-offs yet.*

But sending him a congratulatory text is how we tumbled into an ill-fated relationship in the first place.

Or at least that's what I tell myself, over and over, until I wake up seventeen days after Tate walked out on me, and I decide I don't care if we're doomed.

I'm not done with Tate Nilsson. I'm not done with his cocky attitude, or his filthy tongue, or his over-the-top generosity.

I'm still upset about our fight, but more with myself than with him. Given his persistent and nosy nature, he'd been damn restrained throughout our relationship. He never tried to tell me what I should do with my career.

Maybe I should have told him about the position in Seattle.

My stomach twists.

Maybe…

I look at my phone. At the messages he sent me the day I left. At the radio silence since then.

No, a text message won't cut it.

I won't know where we stand unless I go to him. I don't need to pull up his game schedule. I know it by heart. He has a game at home on Valentine's Day, which is tempting, but I don't want to do a big public plea. He lives his life out there, but he wouldn't want a spectacle to detract from the team. And that night, they'll fly to San Jose for a game the next day.

I'll have to wait until they get back.

Three days.

I need to clear my schedule. And then I need to go see Mabel.

---

That afternoon, I pull into the gravel lot at the Weirdaker Games office.

The front door is open, but inside I find the first floor empty. "Mabel?"

From upstairs, I hear a muffled shout, then stomping shakes the light directly above me. I take the stairs quickly, following the sound, and find Mabel stuck on the other side of a door. Or at least, I find Mabel's voice.

"I'm sorry!" she says through the door. "It seems I've locked myself in here. If you're a potential client, that's probably good advertisement. If you're a thief, though, I'd prefer if you forgot that I'm locked in here—"

"It's Sasha," I say through laughter that hurts my sides. "How long are you going to be in there?"

"Oh! Hi! Not long if you can help me."

"Sure thing. What do you need me to do?" This is probably the weirdest conversation I've ever had through a door. But since I need her help in the biggest way, I'll do whatever it takes.

"There's a tablet in the next room, can you go and get it?"

There are actually a half-dozen tablets in the next room, but only one of the screens is lit up. I grab that, and by the time I'm back in front of the door, I think I get it—this is the administrator view of the game.

She's completed six of the eight puzzles, and she still has twelve minutes left—but I need her now.

I hit the red button in the corner to end the game sooner, and a shrill whistle sounds from the door handle.

Interesting.

The knob turns, and as the door opens, Mabel pokes her head around it and gives me a sheepish grin. "Hi."

I wave at her, secretly grateful for the amusing distraction. "Hi."

"This looks way less professional than it really is. I accidentally locked myself in there, and then…well, I thought, I might as well play the game to get out."

I hold up the tablet. "You were almost done. Sorry to spoil it."

"No, of course I don't mind! Happy to see you. But I wasn't expecting you today? Or anyone, really."

I laugh. "Obviously."

"Next time I'll lock the door."

"Nice side benefit of working out here…few thieves."

She blushes. "Right."

"Actually, I need a favour."

"Name it."

"What do you know about BDSM?"

Her eyes light up and a slow, curious smile curves across her face. "Only what I've read in books."

"How many books?"

"My ereader has seen some scandalous things."

Good enough. "I need to commission a kinky escape room. A really hard one. And I need to take it with me to Vancouver as soon as possible."

## 40

## TATE

ANOTHER WEEK GOES BY. We finish our road trip, getting back to Vancouver late—or early, depending on your point of view—so I don't have to be at the arena for practice the next day until eleven. The late start doesn't matter to me. I'm not sleeping well anyway, not that anyone would be able to tell from my performance.

Being dumped—or maybe having dumped someone by accident, I don't know—has been painfully good for my game.

Since I'm up, I head in early. Turns out, I'm not the only one.

Simec, Andrushko, Moore, and Leclerc are all in the lounge area. I grab coffee and an apple, but before I can join them, Coach walks in.

"Moore, Nilsson, a word."

We follow Coach to his office. He sits on the edge of his desk and waves for Moore to close the door, but he's got an easy smile on his face. "It's nothing serious. Figured I'd take advantage of you two being here early to have a quick, informal chat. It's time for me to start thinking about next season. We're still very much building our team, and I need to evaluate our strengths, weaknesses, wants versus needs, etc. We're still focused on snagging a wild card spot in the playoffs this year, and that's a good goal."

There's a but coming, I can tell.

He leans in. "Next year, I want a top three spot."

"We've got the raw talent," Moore says.

"For sure we do. But there's work to be done to get there. The others look up to you two. You're the ones who lead this team, that's why you have those letters on your jerseys. And part of leadership is evaluation and making tough calls. I want you both to spend the next couple months evaluating your team, then I'd like to meet with you and discuss your observations."

I nod. "Whatever you need."

"Yeah, me too," Moore says.

"And when we get to training camp, we're going to give you guys a day. Captain's Day. No coaches. Just teambuilding, driven by you."

I look at Moore, and his expression—surprised, honoured, pleased—hopefully is an echo of mine. "That's a novel concept, sir."

Coach laughs. "Make it look good for me, will you?"

Moore holds out his hand. "You know it."

"Great. Now get your asses out of here. I've got work to do before practice."

I shake his hand, too, then we head back to the dressing room.

"What do you make of that?" Moore asks.

I shrug. "Sounds like Coach is preparing us for the next stage of our careers."

"Agreed. And speaking of next stages…"

He lets the sentence hang. I know exactly what he's asking. "Not up for discussion, man."

"Just checking in."

"As my captain, or my friend?"

"Both. As your captain, I'm all for you to continue writhing in emotional pain, because you're a fucking rock star out on the ice when you're tortured. But as your friend—"

"Still not up for discussion."

Moore nods and switches to a safer subject. Leclerc's impending fatherhood and what we should get for the baby.

Two days later, on fucking Valentine's Day, we win at home against Florida, which bumps us up one more place in the standings.

I think of the sappy shit I'd have done for Sasha, and I get two assists and a very satisfying penalty.

The next night, we fly to San Jose for a single game. We lose, but they have home ice advantage and a hot goalie on a streak. Still, I worry that after a string of good games, maybe I've become a little too cocky. Or maybe something was missing. That's something I can think about when I get home and review the game. And it's what I expect the press to ask about when they crowd around me in the dressing room.

It's not.

I should have known a sea of microphones and recording devices being jammed up in my face meant something more interesting than a narrowly lost game.

"Have you seen the Facebook post?"

Ah, shit. I try to focus on who asked that, but go for a generic, to-everyone response. "I don't check my phone on the ice."

"Over Christmas, did you and your girlfriend swap your first-class seats with a teen with cancer and her mother?"

"Ah…" I frown. "Maybe if you guys give me some time—"

"Is it true?"

"Who's your girlfriend, Tate?"

"Who's Sasha?"

"Was it her idea to give up the seats?"

"Have you heard from this girl since Christmas? Have you visited her in the hospital?"

This is a fucking nightmare. I hold up my hands and wait for a chance to speak. "I'm happy to answer any questions you have about the game I played tonight, but at this point, that's all I can take questions on, since as I established, I don't check my phone on the ice, and I haven't seen the post in question."

Someone was clearly anticipating me saying that again, because a phone is shoved into my hand.

I rub my jaw as I quickly read it. It looks like Bree, Amy's mother, didn't know who I was at the time, but Amy's back in the hospital now—damn. I sigh and look up. "Jesus, guys, don't spring this on me. And don't drag a young woman into the spotlight like this, either. I, uh, will definitely be getting in touch with the family—privately—to let them know I'm tickled pink they're fans. And we'll probably do something else for them. Privately. Got it?"

I know it's the wrong answer when it comes to public relations. This could be a goldmine for winning over Vancouver fans and I suspect I may hear as much from the ownership later. But it's not just about me. At least they don't know who Sasha is. Fuck, now I'm going to need to call her.

Fuck.

"Come on, Tate."

When it's finally clear I'm not going to respond to questions about my personal life, a few reporters grudgingly ask the obligatory post-game questions before moving on.

I wait until I get on the bus to the airport before turning on my phone. As expected, notifications are insane. I ignore everything and go straight to Facebook and find the post.

It's a selfie of Bree and Amy in their first-class seats. I skim through what Bree's written, and other than referring to Sasha as my girlfriend, it's a pretty accurate and appreciative account of what transpired. Apparently they've been watching the games and recognized me the other day. The post has been shared thousands of times, and comments and likes are well into the tens-of-thousands.

Fuck me.

I'm happy for them, if it's what they want. If it makes Amy happy, that's fantastic.

I check my text messages. There are plenty from Rob, but none from Sasha. Even though she's cut communication with me, I would have thought she'd have had something to say about this.

It's only a matter of time before the press figure out exactly who she is, and what that will do to her, how it will make her feel, makes my gut clench.

I send her a text I know she won't respond to. But I can't just let her go. I can't stay silent. Not anymore.

**Tate: Just got blindsided with this after the game tonight. I know you may not like it, but...it's a sweet post. I'll do every-thing in my power to keep the focus off you. And it'll probably pass in a day or two.**

I attach the link to the post. Then, like the dam has burst, I text again, because I can't help myself.

**Tate: Also, I miss you. I don't care if that's misguided. I'm going to be home in a bit. If you read this, call me.**

## 41

## SASHA

WELL, Tate hasn't changed the lock on his apartment. That's a good sign. I let myself in, then set out establishing the scene.

A Weirdaker Games Do-It-Yourself Escape Room kit is pretty cool, if I do say so myself. I knew it would be, but actually using it in an as-real-as-can-be beta testing way pushes my admiration for Mabel to new levels.

The first thing I do is log in to the app and scan Tate's bedroom. On the screen of my phone, it's like I'm looking at the camera app—but there are some things on the screen which don't actually exist in his room.

Like a disassembled St. Andrew's Cross in the corner. That would be the puzzle that Mabel had the most fun designing.

I pivot toward the wall, where a row of floggers appears on the screen. They're all different shapes and sizes. As I move, I see other similar puzzles appear on every solid, blank wall space the camera captures.

The app also prompts me to make some choices. How long do I want the room to be locked, do I want to use a virtual final puzzle or do I have the deluxe kit with the real puzzle.

I look at the wrist-cuffs in the colourful box.

Mabel enjoyed buying those, too. I tell the app I've got the real props for the final puzzle.

Then I take a deep breath, because if there's any part of this that Tate's going to be seriously *what-the-fuck* about, it's the fact I'm taking a screwdriver to his bedroom door handle.

But once I commit to a plan, I'm in all the way.

Besides, this way he can't storm out again.

Win-win.

The instructions are easy to follow, and before long, I've got his door handle off and tucked away in the provided bag for all the bits and bobs.

I carefully install the trick door handle, which is linked to the app on my phone.

Then I lie down on his bed and think about all the ways I've been a total idiot.

---

I wake up with a jolt when I hear the front door open. Tate is back. I glance at the side clock. It's just after two in the morning.

My heart pounds as I listen to him move through the apartment. It sounds like he drops a bag on a chair, then opens the fridge.

Damn it, I didn't think this through. How do I get him in here?

I look at the books on his bedside table, then at the hardwood floor. I pick up a hardcover and drop it. It makes a delightfully loud clap, and I hear Tate mutter something that sounds like, "What the hell?"

I grab my phone, scurry to my spot behind the door, and wait for him to come and investigate.

It's not until he steps through the door and I shove it shut that it occurs to me he might not react well to a strange person luring him into his bedroom. In hindsight, that can be added to the list of ways I'm an idiot, but at least this one is motivated by affection.

He whirls around at the first movement of the door, his fist already flying, and I dodge out of the way. "It's me!"

"Sasha?" He gives me an incredulous look as he rocks back on his heels, his eyes wide.

If his heart is thumping as hard as mine is, I'm really sorry for the panic attack I almost caused. "Hi."

His mouth falls open, and he rubs his hand across his jaw. "I almost punched you."

"My fault."

"That's now how I'd feel if I— Jesus." He drops his hands to his side and stares at me, a muscle in his cheek twitching. "What the hell are you doing here?"

Right. I lift my phone and press the button to start the game. The door handle whistles and Tate jumps back.

"You're trapped in here with me for an hour." My voice shakes as I hand him my phone and explain. "There are puzzles on that app. So you can do those, if you want. It's a whole thing. An escape room thing. I invested in it, and this is my first time doing it, and I don't think it's really intended for hostage-taking, but that door is locked, so I'm happy."

"You're happy." He glares at the phone, then up at me. "You've locked yourself in with me inside my own room, told me to play puzzles instead of falling exhausted into my bed, and you're happy."

"Well, no."

"You're not happy."

"No, I didn't— Wait. Let me start again."

"Why are you here?"

Right, that's a good place to start. "I love you."

The muscle twitches in his cheek again. "Are you sure? Because three weeks ago you disappeared on me."

"I didn't know I loved you then."

"I did." His voice is as clipped and hard as it has been with the press, on TV. As it has been with people he doesn't really like that much.

My stomach drops to the floor. "You did?"

"Sure did. Could have told you, if you'd let me." He flicks his dark, unyielding gaze to the door. "You've locked yourself in here with me. Are you sure you're ready to hear what I have to say to you?"

"Yes." I swallow hard around the lump in my throat. Yes, I want to hear his objections. I deserve to hear his anger. And I'll take it all if I get a chance to tell him how I really feel. Not just love. It's so much more complicated than that.

He reaches out and tests the handle. Then he laughs harshly. "Wow." Instead of telling me how mad he is, though, he flips my phone in his hand and starts to prowl around the room. "How do I use this?"

"H-hold it up."

He looks at the screen as he points it at the wall. "Floggers?"

"It's a long story."

He raises one eyebrow. "We've got time, right? How long is that door locked?"

"An hour."

He taps at the screen. "Can you override it?"

"No. You'd have to take the door apart."

"You did that." He points at the handle. "Did you throw out my old one?"

I'm not answering that. "I can restore the room to rights when we're done."

"Done?" He stalks back to stand in front of me. "You think we're going to be done after an hour?"

"I don't know."

He reaches out and rubs his knuckles gently along my jaw. "Ah, tiger. We're just going to be getting started." He leans in and lowers his voice as his breath dusts against my ear. "And I'm never going to be done with you."

The air in my lungs whooshes out as I sway towards him. "For real?"

His fingers slide into my hair as he pulls me close. "For real. But I'm still mad at you."

"I know." I twist in his arms, desperate to taste his skin. My mouth runs over his stubbled jaw and up onto his cheek. He turns, too, and his lips catch mine.

He doesn't taste mad.

He tastes like home. "Oh, Tate," I whisper as I press into him. "I'm so sorry."

"It's done wonders for my game."

I laugh weakly as he kisses me again, his lips soft and his tongue insistent.

"This is it, though. No more hedging your bets. You came back to me, you need to keep me."

"I will."

"Because you're *my* tiger. You might like me to play the predator and chase you down, but I've always been your prey."

I gasp at that. No, it's not true. But when I pull back and search his face, I see the pain in his eyes. I hold all the power here. If I wanted to, I could rip his heart right from his chest with my claws. I've already made the first angry swipes, because I was cornered, because I felt threatened.

Tate has never been a threat to anything except *my* heart. And he's gently protected that at every turn.

"I'll think about the Seattle job," I tell him, my words jumbling up as they spill out in a rush. "Or I can commute. I was being stubborn, and that was silly. I do love Vancouver. I love you and—"

"Slow down," he murmurs. "I don't want you to take any job except the one you want."

"But—"

"We fell in love across a country. During road trips and short visits. Phone calls and texts. You don't need to be right in front of me to own my entire heart."

"But I—"

"Let me finish." He drags in a breath. "I know guys in the NHL get married and are happy, but I've always thought that if that happened to me, it would be when I was done playing professional hockey. Because I didn't want to ask someone to give me their entire life when I could only share part of mine. I had that all backwards, though. It turns out, when you fall in love, you give your everything, no matter where you are."

I nod. He's so right. These last three weeks have been awful, because my heart was smashed into a million pieces, into dust that scattered across the country as I fled.

"And then I fell for you. So hard, so fast, I didn't see it coming. And you kept insisting we weren't serious, we weren't official."

"That was stupid of me."

"Maybe it was self-preservation." He cups my face. "Or maybe you were scared."

I burst into tears. Fuck. "No maybe about it."

He leans in and softly kisses my wet cheeks. "I love you, Sasha."

Stupid, blubbery reactions. "I love you too," I whisper.

"Louder."

I grin and blink, my damp eyelashes sticking together as I look up at him. "I love you to the moon and back, Tate."

"That's better." He kisses my mouth now, hard and insistent. "We're going to be just fine. We're going to live together in Ottawa, and in Vancouver. And if you get a job somewhere else, be it Seattle or Boston or Halifax, we'll live there, too. We can have as many homes in as many cities as you want. They will all be ours, and we'll be together as much as we can. I'm not going to be playing hockey forever. When I retire, I'll be all yours, all the time."

"That sounds annoying."

"Incredibly so."

"I want that. Eventually. But as long as you're playing hockey, I'll happily meet you in New York, and Los Angeles, and Chicago…"

"All excellent shopping cities."

"I have my priorities." But I can't hold back a smile. "And you are, and always will be, my number one priority."

"I know."

"God, you are the cockiest, most egotistical—"

He covers my mouth with his and kisses away the bickering, but I'm sure we'll get back to it soon enough. I can't wait.

"And I'm sorry about the Facebook post," he murmurs against my neck as he slides his hands under my shirt. "I didn't know about it until after the game."

I freeze. "What Facebook post?"

He groans. "You didn't see my text?"

"No…" I cast about for my phone, but the app is still running, and— "What happened?"

"I texted you after the game. Bree and Amy posted about us on Facebook. They recognized me."

"Oh." My heart resumes beating normally. "Okay. That's not bad. Right?"

"It's gone viral. Media's picking it up as a feel-good story, and they want to know about you."

"Ah." I roll that over in my head. It doesn't feel as scary as I thought it would. "I fell asleep on your bed. I guess that's why I didn't see it."

He kisses my nose. "I like the sound of that. You in my bed. Missed that."

"Mmm. Have you responded? What did you say?"

"I growled something about it being none of the media's damn business."

"That's not like you."

"Maybe it is. Maybe for twelve years, I've been playing at being a certain kind of guy. But deep down, I'm a man who is fiercely protective of the woman he loves. Even if she's not speaking to him."

"Even if she's breaking into his apartment to lay a trap?"

He laughs at that. "You had a key."

"I like the idea of being a cat burglar."

"I like the idea of a skin-tight black outfit," he says huskily. That part of his personality hasn't changed a bit. Pervert Santa, now with extra growl and bite.

"Show me the post, you dirty man."

He pulls it up on his phone and hands it over. I read it, then whistle at the number of likes and comments. "That's getting a lot of love."

"Yeah."

"Is the team going to do something for them?"

"I don't know. I didn't talk to anyone in the front office about it."

"Why not?"

"Believe it or not, I haven't been the friendliest guy the last few weeks."

"I'm sorry."

"Nah, it's fine. I'm hardly the worst asshole in the league. And it's nobody's business who you are. I'll protect you always and forever, no matter what."

I believe him. "We should go and see Amy together."

"You'd do that?"

"In a heart beat."

"She might want to take a picture."

"She might." Maybe it's time for me to make some bigger sacrifices for Tate, too. "I wouldn't mind that."

He traces his fingertips over my cheeks. "I might want to take a picture, too."

"You have pictures of me."

"Yeah." His voice catches on a burr, like he's holding something back.

"What?"

"When we were in New York, and you had me post that selfie of us on Instagram. I had a different caption in my head." He keeps stroking my face, featherlight touches that make me go all wibbly-wobbly inside. "Never mind."

I kiss him. "Maybe—"

My phone beeps at us, reminding us we only have thirty minutes left to escape the room.

"Or what happens?" Tate growls as he grabs the phone, pointing it at the wall. "Did you rig explosives under the bed?"

I laugh. "No. We just fail the game and have to try again."

He hands the phone over. "Start it over again. I'm not letting you leave this room until morning, anyway."

"We don't need to do it."

"I'm a highly competitive man, Sasha. Set the game. Let's do this. I think I know how to solve the flogger puzzle already."

"How is that possible? You just glanced it."

"It's a logic sequence puzzle. Come on. We'll do this, then I'll do you, and then we can go out for coffee at dawn and sleep all day tomorrow."

I glance at the cuffs he hasn't yet noticed are attached to his headboard. He might be busy at dawn. "You're on."

# TATE

SASHA STAYS THROUGH THE WEEKEND. We go to visit Amy in the hospital on Friday, and Sasha promises her that when she's released, they'll come to a game together.

Bree apologizes for the over-the-top reactions to her post. "I never thought it would blow up like that."

I look around Amy's hospital room, stuffed to the gills with presents. "Is she enjoying the attention?"

Bree nods quickly, her eyes bright. "Yes."

"Then it's exactly as it should be." I squeeze her shoulder and promise to catch up soon.

Sasha comes to my Saturday night game against Boston, which we win, and every time the goal horn blows, she's on her feet cheering.

Coach gives us Sunday off. He tells us to make the most of it, because we're going to dig deep in the coming week.

He doesn't need to tell me twice. It's Chinese New Year, a much bigger deal in Vancouver than in Ottawa, and I find myself quite excited to show Sasha my—our—new home away from home.

We get up early and decide to go for dim sum before the

Chinatown Spring Festival Parade. It's already pretty busy by the time we get downtown—because it's a crisp, clear day with no sign of rain and of course, the rest of the city has the same plan.

After trying three restaurants, all jam-packed with people lined up waiting outside, we need a change of plan. "Okay, dim sum is a no-go. Ideas?"

"How about we go for a walk and grab coffee? Then we can come back for the parade, and go in search of brunch after that," Sasha suggests.

There's a greasy spoon in East Van I'd heard some of the guys rave about. "How does a diner sound?"

She grins. "Like an adventure."

We walk to Gastown, a neighbourhood I've explored a bit, and hit Starbucks. On the way we pass the statue of Gassy Jack.

After we order—a black coffee for me, a half-sweet hazelnut latte with no whip and extra foam for my complicated girlfriend—a table opens up in front of the window.

I hand her my drink. "How about you grab those seats while I wait for your latte?"

She kisses my cheek, then quickly snags the chairs, angling them so she can look outside and take it all in.

That's my Sasha. Ever the watcher.

A couple minutes later, the barista slides Sasha's latte across the counter, repeating the entire litany of changes she requested. I take it with a smile, then stop to grab napkins on my way to our table.

I hand Sasha her cup, and she takes a long sip.

"Gassy Jack. What kind of name is that to be stuck with through history?" She asks.

"Not a particularly flattering one, that's for sure."

"Where there's a question, there's Google," she says, pulling out her phone. Her thumbs move at warp speed, then she looks up at me. "Short version—he was a talker, and a bit of a storyteller. That's a little disappointing. I felt sure there would be a far more interesting answer than that."

"You'd think."

"Jesus," Sasha says, pointing out the window. "That clock looks like the top is on fire."

I turn to look, and smile. "That's just steam." I glance down at my watch. "It's about to do its thing."

"What thing?"

This is why I brought her to this Starbucks. "Just wait," I tell her.

A few minutes later, the steam clock whistles the entire Westminster chime.

"Ooh, that was adorable."

I swig the last of my coffee. "That also was our cue to head back over to Chinatown if we're going to watch the parade."

"I'm ready."

The walk back becomes increasingly crowded, turning what was a fifteen-minute walk into closer to thirty.

We walk part of the route, deciding on a spot a couple of blocks from the starting point. People are standing more than five deep in some places. I'm tall enough to see over most of the heads, but Sasha isn't. "How do you feel about shoulder rides?"

She looks up at me and grins.

I partially crouch, and Sasha steps onto my leg just above my knee, then scrambles her way onto my shoulders. I shift beneath her weight, getting her balanced, then squeeze her leg. "Comfy up there?"

"Best seat in the house, are you kidding me?"

Yeah, this was a great plan.

We hear the parade long before we can see it. Firecrackers exploding rapid fire and regular beating of drums.

A few minutes later, we see the festival banner, followed by the Vancouver Police Department's pipe band. Bagpipes in a Chinese New Year parade is a pretty Canadian thing, I bet.

Not long afterwards, we see the first lion dancers. I tap Sasha's knee and shout up to her. "Wow, look at these costumes."

"Stunning." Then she grins. "Hand me your phone!"

I pass it up to her, and she takes a few pictures of the parade, then glances around, nibbling on her lower lip.

After a few beats, she wiggles her finger. "Turn around."

Since we're at the back of the crowd, when I pivot, we can see ourselves reflected in the shop window.

She holds up the phone. "Say cheese."

She takes a photo of our reflection with the crowd and the parade in the background, then hands me my phone. "Done."

The rest of the parade is just as incredible as the start. The sense of community shows strong in the diversity of the groups taking part. This is Vancouver's multiculturalism at its finest, and I love every minute of it.

On the walk back to the car, Sasha points out that I look pretty happy with my new community, and I tell her what I was thinking during the parade.

"You should post that picture of us on Instagram," she says, squeezing my hand.

"Are you sure?"

She shrugs. "Yeah. It's a pretty awesome thing we just saw. And I'm honoured that you shared it with me. How do you say Happy New Years in Chinese?"

I look it up, and we make the post together. For someone who doesn't use social media, she's got big opinions about which filter to use.

After some good-natured teasing, we settle on the picture, slightly overexposed, with the caption, *Gung Hay Fat Choy! Best seat in #vancity.* That was Sasha's idea, and I love it. I take one last look at the picture—we look exactly as happy as we are—and I hit *share* before we get in the car.

Forty minutes later, we're standing in line outside that recommended greasy spoon in East Van.

Sasha points to the sign that advertises the all-day breakfast and grins. "Under three bucks for the full cholesterol meal deal? Are you a secret cheapskate?"

"Never let it be said I tried to impress you with a meal at a fancy, expensive restaurant." She laughs as I use her words against her, months later. "But I'm sure they have more than bacon and eggs on the menu. You can probably spend at least seven or eight dollars if you try hard enough."

"No, I'm getting the all day breakfast. I totally need to experience this." She pokes my chest. "And so do you."

When we get inside, the decor is along the lines of shabby-throw-it-at-the-wall-see-what-sticks. The furniture is scarred, but clean, and the walls are plastered in everything from movie and concert posters to graffiti.

The breakfast is surprisingly good, and plentiful. The service isn't exactly stellar, but the place is packed solid, and it doesn't let up. The minute one table empties, it's immediately filled.

I love how normal this all is. Spending a lazy Sunday with Sasha. Doing our thing, not worrying about whether I'm breaking relationship-on-the-down-low-rules. Kissing her wherever, and whenever I want, which is everywhere and often. Sasha taking selfies of us and posting them on my Instagram.

Normal, but rare and precious, too. As we head back to my place, I make a silent promise to never take this—or her—for granted.

## SASHA

In March, I break it to my advisor that I'm not going to be looking for a tenure-track position—in Ottawa, or Seattle, or anywhere else. "My heart is in small business investment," I tell her.

She understands.

That should give me confidence to have the same conversation with my father, but I put it off. Relations have been decidedly frosty since I stopped pretending that Tate and I aren't an official couple. That's only about my parents' stubborn attachment to being right—because in public, Tate and I are the perfect model of adorable romance.

In private, on the other hand… I blush to myself.

So I put off calling my dad, and bury myself in finishing my PhD so I can devote myself full-time to my version of a venture capital firm, for real women with amazing ideas.

I meet Tate in Chicago for his last game of the regular season against the Blackhawks, but we only have one night together. After the game, he flies on to St. Louis and I return to Ottawa.

"The end is in sight, though," I tell Ellie the next day as we slowly make our way to the university library. The thaw has finally come after a long winter, and I celebrated by buying us matching bright yellow rain boots.

Quite appropriate for an adorable duckling mama to waddle her way across campus in.

"Do you want to do another round of practice questions for your dissertation defence this afternoon?" she asks.

I don't defend until early May, but that's when she's due. And her own PhD is in a holding pattern while she takes her maternity leave, so really, her helping me is a good way to occupy her time.

Plus it's a nice trade for the gorgeous yellow boots.

"Sure. And we can order in some lunch, too. What do you feel like?"

"Uh..." She stops. Behind us, her security detail moves closer. "I..."

I turn to look at her. She's holding her belly, her eyes wide and panicked. "Ellie?"

"I think my water just broke."

I look down at her light-coloured maternity pants. A dark stain blooms across the tops of her thighs. "Oh, shit."

"Sasha!"

"Okay. Right. Ambulance? Gavin? Lachlan. I'll call Lachlan."

She rolls her eyes at me and turns toward her RCMP shadows. "Hey, this is exciting, guys. Okay, so I'm fine. Just...wet. Are you calling Lachlan? No ambulance. Oh, damn it. This is too early." Her voice wavers as she takes another step, then starts to hurry. "What car is closest?"

---

Gavin and Lachlan beat us to the hospital. They're waiting with a small army of men in black suits in the distance, a nurse, and a wheelchair as I pull up at the curb. Two RCMP officers spill out of my backseat like it's a clown car and they're about to do handstands. Gavin wrenches the passenger door open. "Come on," he says to his wife, giving her his arm. "I've got you."

"She's kicking up a storm," Ellie says. "I don't think she likes this."

"The first of many indignations I'm sure she'll tell us about." He kisses her gently. "It's going to be fine."

"You're not a doctor, you don't know that."

He doesn't blink at her panic. "Then let's go upstairs and talk to those that are. Sasha, see you up there."

Once I've parked, I text Tate and Violet to update them on the news. Beth already knows, and she's texting me a stream of instructions about Gavin.

**Tate: Are you okay? That sounds scary.**
**Sasha: I'm fine now. My heart is racing a mile a minute,**
**though.**

**Violet: What does she need? Max is at work, I'll send him up to**
**maternity.**

**Beth: Someone from the Privy Council office will be by soon**
**to set up a secure room in the hospital for Gavin to work out**
**of. I'll be there tomorrow, unless he needs me sooner, but**
**there's a lot of rearranging that needs to happen to his**
**schedule.**
**Beth: Grab him a sandwich from the cafeteria, he hasn't eaten**
**lunch yet.**
**Beth: Also, big hugs. You're going to be an aunt!**

I stop in the hospital corridor and blink away tears at the last text.

Who am, that I cry over babies and boyfriends? I barely recognize myself.

Right. I need to be helpful. Cafeteria first, then I'll find Max, get the medical scoop on a baby born early, and then update everyone once I know more.

I take a deep breath, but it doesn't do any good, so I race through the cafeteria, then I take the stairs to the maternity floor two at a time. I'm almost there when Max comes barrelling down the stairs in the opposite direction. It's really quite convenient today that Gavin's best friend is a paediatrician.

"Max!"

He stops and gives me a grin. "Hey. It's all good. They're in good hands."

"She was supposed to have the baby in May. This is early."

"Babies come at all different times. She's thirty-five weeks now, which is just a bit shy of what we'd call full-term, so they'll spend a couple of extra days here to make sure all is well, but don't worry. Baby and mom are both going to be fine. They're having an ultrasound right now if you want to get in there and see. I'll be back after my afternoon clinic."

"Okay."

He squeezes my hand as he keeps going back the way I came, and I dart through the door marked Labour & Delivery.

---

Seven hours later, Chandler Pia Montague Strong arrives into the world with a tiny, warbling little cry.

I burst into tears, again. I don't bother judging myself.

Ellie holds her for a very short minute, then a ghostly-looking neonatology team in head-to-toe green takes her to an intense-looking cart where they make her cry louder. That seems to please them, because they give her back to Ellie, and I draw my over-protective auntie claws back into my fingers.

Max and Violet squeeze in just before visiting hours end for a quick hello, and after hugging Ellie and Gavin and my new most favourite person in the entire world, Chandler, I walk out with them.

"She makes Noah look like a two-year-old," Violet exclaims. "So little."

"It won't be long before she's chasing him around." Max looks at me. "Noah's up on all fours now and trying desperately to crawl."

"Put candy in front of him and he'll get there in a flash. Wait, no, pretend I didn't say that. I want to be able to babysit Chandler."

Violet laughs. "Your secret is safe with us."

I wave goodbye to them and make my way to my car, where I just sit in the driver's seat and exhale a really good, solid breath for the first time since Ellie said her water broke.

**Tate: What are you doing now?**
**Sasha: Sitting in my car at the hospital.**

The phone rings two seconds later.

"Crazy day," he murmurs in my ear. And just like that, all the tension fades away.

"Yep."

"Tell me about the drive to the hospital again. Is there a giant mess on your passenger seat?"

"No, I had a towel in my gym bag. It's fine. She sat on that."

"Are you still thinking of meeting me in Edmonton? If you want to change that up, I'll totally understand."

"There is no way I'm missing your last game of the regular season. I'll be there. Just prepare yourself for a lot of baby pictures."

## TATE

We opened our season in Vancouver, but we're ending the regular season play as visitors in Edmonton. Across the league, games are being played today that may change the final standings going into the play-offs.

This game is no different.

It's Hockey Night in Canada. For more than twenty years, it's been the central part of my week. Saturday night in front of the television, and then doing my damnedest to skate in an NHL uniform.

And today may be the most important Saturday night in my entire life.

Above us, the game is almost sold out, and the arena is vibrating with energy.

The mood down here is more anticipatory than jittery. Andrushko's got his hands on Lanvic's iPod, but they can't agree on what to play, so the song keeps changing every thirty seconds.

The closer we get to puck drop, the tighter, more focused the chatter gets.

Then the dressing room goes silent when Coach walks in.

"We've got two things going for us tonight." He holds up his index finger. "One, Edmonton has a play-off spot." He sticks up a second finger. "And two, they've beaten us our last two times out. Chances are, they'll get cocky and a bit sloppy. Keep your eyes open, take every opportunity you see. Don't get fancy. Starting tonight: Nilsson, Moore, Simec, Andrushko, Lanvic, and Leclerc's in the keep. It's been a great season. Let's see how much longer we can make it last. Now get out there and play great hockey."

As I skate out onto the ice, the first thing I do is find Sasha in the stands. When Andrushko pats my ass with his stick, Sasha and I grin at each other. Somehow, it's become our thing.

"At least you're going to have a lot of extra time to correct your golf swing," Edmonton's centre, Gibson, mutters as he skates past me.

Seriously? That's the best this asshole's got? "Who are you playing for next season, again?" I shoot back. I've heard whispers that Edmonton is looking to unload him. And from the black look on his face, I do believe I've hit a sore spot. I'm going poke it hard every chance I get right up until the final horn.

Edmonton comes out strong in the first period, but we hold our own and we're scoreless going into the second.

The trash-talk flies fast and furious, but it seems the Edmonton players are a little sensitive tonight and halfway through the second, they make their first real mistake. Gibson misses a pass, it's snagged by Moore, and he scores on the breakaway.

We don't need a goal horn to blow up Rogers Place. There's enough noise that we know a good number of fans have flown in from Vancouver. He pumps his fist in the air as he skates back to centre ice, and Simec and I circle around him, letting Edmonton's offensive line hear us tell our captain how fucking hot he is to us right now.

I swear Moore blushes.

But Edmonton comes back hard and ties it up just before the end of the second period, the bastards.

Early in the third I make another crack at Gibson about the direction of his career, and he pops me one in the face. I grin at Sasha as I shake it off. He's the fucker in the penalty box. I don't care. And just like that, we've got a man advantage. Edmonton's penalty killers are among the best in the league, but they're no match for us tonight. Simec gets the powerplay goal and we're back in lead.

With just over a minute to go in the third period, Edmonton is still down by one. They pull their goalie to gain an extra attacker, and they manage to get one shot on our goal before Landvic gets the puck. He shoots it over to Simic who gets it up to me. I send it to Moore who fires it at the empty net with ten seconds left.

Two points for the win, and our position in the league standings is safely inside the four wild card spots. We've just clinched a spot in the play-offs. Take that, Roger fucking Brown.

And the night is still young.

I have two things I need to do tonight. Clinching the play-off spot was number one. Check.

Now I have to find Sasha.

We're in such a good place now. Her love is more than I ever thought I'd have, and she's the centre of my universe.

But I still haven't met her parents. And that's what I want to talk to her about.

Now's not the time, though. Now is the time to find her at the boards, give her a hard, happy kiss, and whisper that I love her before she blows me a final kiss and waves goodbye.

Then it's into the dressing room for a celebration, and all the time in the world for the press, because we're feeling pretty good tonight.

It's more than two hours after the game by the time I let myself into our hotel room. Sasha is waiting on the bed, deliciously naked.

Perfect.

I stop just short of the bed and put my hands in my pockets. I want nothing more than to strip off my clothes and bury myself deep inside her body, her soul.

And she knows it. She lifts an eyebrow. "I'm pretty sure you should be at least half-naked by now."

"I'll get there." I smile down at her. My tiger.

She sucks the tip of her index finger, then traces lazy circles around her nipple. "Are you sure? Because I'm pretty sure we should be naked, celebrating post-season play."

She's killing me. I strengthen my resolve. Because that's not all I'm hoping to celebrate tonight. I grab her robe and hold it out to her. "I promise to get naked as soon as we talk."

"I can talk naked."

"Humour me," I say, pushing her robe at her again.

She gives me the cutest little pout as she grudgingly takes it and puts it on. "Okay. Talk."

I squeeze my hand in my pocket. "I was thinking it's time for me to meet your parents." And to say that out loud, I totally needed Sasha to not be naked.

"Really? I don't see the urgency." She wrinkles her nose as she shifts her perch on the edge of the bed. "Definitely not until the post-season is over, anyway."

"I don't know. I think we can fit in a flight to Toronto." Here goes. My heart racing, I take Sasha's hand, lacing my fingers with hers as I kneel in front of her. "I would really like to tell them in person that I've asked you to marry me."

"You—" Her eyes go wide as I pull the ring box out of my pocket. "Wow."

"What I'm trying to say is, you are my best friend, and I love you. I want to spend the rest of my life with you, loving you, and even if you think it's going to be the most awkward morning in the history of brunches, I would really like to meet your parents. If you want them to be my in-laws, it would be great to show them I'm not the boogyman. Will you marry me?"

Putting her free hand behind my neck, she pulls me in and and kisses me hard on the mouth. "Yes," she whispers, holding me tight. "I'll marry you."

Best Hockey Night in Canada ever.

She pulls me into a long, smouldering kiss. And when we come up for air, she slides her robe off one shoulder. "You're done talking now, right?"

## 45

### SASHA

I'm in the room for a little more than an hour and a half. It feels crazy fast and painfully slow at the same time, and when I'm done, that's it.

I'm done.

My thesis has been submitted to the university.

I've completed a robust oral defence in front of the dissertation committee.

I'm. Done.

A PhD that I applied for on a lark, in an attempt to buy five more years before getting sucked into the family business, that taught me so much about myself and the world and women and business, is now one beat away from being complete.

The rest of my life stretches in front of me, and it feels very weird.

Also, wonderful.

I take a deep breath as I step out of the small lecture room we used for my defence. On the door is a paper sign.

**Closed Session**
**Please do not disturb**

I pace across the hall and wait in front of the window while the committee deliberates.

It takes ten minutes. Dr. Turnbull pushes the door open and gestures for me to re-enter.

"On behalf of the committee, I am pleased to inform you that we consider your thesis and the defence you have just presented to be of top quality. Congratulations, you have unanimously passed this oral exam."

There's some paperwork to sign, then handshakes all around.

When I step out of the room again, Tate is waiting at the end of the hall.

"You sneak," I whisper when I reach him. "Where have you been hiding?"

"Ellie introduced me to the graduate program coordinator. She's a fan."

"I'm aware." I take his hand and squeeze his fingers. "Hi."

"Hey."

"So…"

He raises his eyebrows. "Yes?"

"I passed."

"I never had any doubt you would."

I exhale and do the world's fastest happy dance before I settle down again. "Now, to dinner."

"Don't make that face. We're going to the best steakhouse in the city."

"Yes, but we won't be alone."

"Do I look worried about that?"

I shake my head. "I love you. But your optimism is entirely out of place in the Brewster family."

---

We're the first to arrive at the restaurant. My parents arrive next.

"Well," my father booms a little too loudly. "How did it go?"

"I got a gold star on my popsicle-stick art project," I say because I can't help myself.

Tate snorts and my mother sighs.

"It went well. I'll graduate next month."

"And then you're off to Iceland?" My dad says that like we're moving to a hippie commune.

"For a much-deserved vacation, yes we are. Midnight sun and all that." Naked hot springs, too, but I remember to keep that part to myself.

The door to restaurant swings open, and in walk Tate's parents. His mom gives me a reassuring smile. We've only met once, and she guessed that I was the person who ate most of her Christmas dinner leftovers.

I'm really not sure how tonight is going to go.

Introductions are made, then we're seated before the conversation can resume or turns sideways. Tate asks my father what he would like to drink—"How do you feel about sharing a bottle of wine, sir?"—and then we look at our menus.

So far, so good.

This is the third shared meal we've had with my parents.

The first was frosty and awkward, and went on far too long.

The second was deliberately short, a workday lunch in Toronto where my father could only drop by for thirty minutes.

Tonight, though, we've got hours ahead of us. And the Nilssons are such ardent Tate-fans, which I understand, but I'm worried my parents might bristle at.

It takes twelve minutes for my father to get to his favourite concern. "When do you go back to Vancouver again, Tate? Middle of the summer?"

"End of, sir."

"A lot of time to spend away from my daughter."

Oh, it's so tempting to point out that any time we do spend together is occupied by orgasms, so really, I'm not sure he should protest us being on opposite sides of the country.

But I don't.

I busy myself with squeezing my lemon into my water.

Tate squeezes my knee under the table. "It's almost three months apart over the year, that's right. But between travel that we can coincide—a week together in New York, the time she'd want to spend in Los Angeles anyway, and of course, any time she wants to be in Vancouver—it's more family time than you might think. And as you know..." He gestures towards his own parents. "Family is the most important thing to me." He looks at me. "And Sasha is my family."

"We'd love to see you set a wedding date," Tate's mom says. She turns to my mother. "Will you want to have the wedding in Toronto?"

Hey. My wedding, my location.

Tate squeezes my knee again.

My mom looks at me, then looks at my father, then lifts her wine glass. "That's up to Sasha, but I think she'd probably rather have it here."

Well, knock me over with a feather. "Probably, yes. It's easier to plan with a home base, too."

"On the other hand," my mother says. "Your apartment is awfully small. At home, we'd have more room for you and your bridesmaids to get ready."

I bite my lip. Totally walked into that trap. "Well..."

My father raises his eyebrow.

"The thing is..."

Tate clears his throat. "Sasha's giving up her apartment. We have a big house here that has more than enough room for everyone to get ready for any event, including a wedding."

"Tate's house is lovely," his mother says, trying to help.

"Not just my house anymore, Mom," he corrects her. "Sasha will put her stamp on it while I'm away, too."

The second spare room is going to be all about shoes. I

haven't told him that, though. "I'll move in July, once we're back from our trip."

"How…modern," my father says, and I give up on the lemon water. That's for people with patience.

I grab my wine glass and lift it in the air. "Yep. That's me. Unrepentantly twenty-first century. Sin and—"

"It's high time for a toast, don't you think?" Tate gives me a fully amused look that promises he'll be calling me a brat later. "To my fiancée. Soon-to-be Dr. Brewster, who will be buying all of us dinner tonight because she's building a business empire. Sasha, I am your biggest fan, and I can't wait to see what the next year brings for you."

"She's not buying dinner," my father thunders, and I start laughing.

"It's a joke, Dad," I say, but I'm looking at Tate. His eyes are twinkling.

*Love you,* I mouth.

*Love you more,* he mouths back. And as much as I do love him, with every inch of my being, I believe that he just might.

# EPILOGUE

## SASHA

*two years later*

I HADN'T PLANNED on coming to New York for this series, but I have news, and I want to tell Tate in person. Besides, I have shopping to do.

Tonight, I watch the Lumberjacks play the Rangers in the wives and girlfriends section with Zack Moore's wife, Alyson. The Moores split their time between Vancouver and a suburb outside of Philadelphia, so when the team plays on the east coast, she often travels out here, too. Tonight, their little one, Liam, is spending time with Zack's parents.

She's been a good friend, helping me navigate the realities of a long distance relationship and an empathetic ear when my frustrations get the better of me. It's nice to have someone to talk to who's been there. Ellie gets some of it, and she certainly has her privacy invaded way more than I do, but there are aspects to being a hockey wife that only another hockey wife understands.

When Tate comes out on the ice, he searches the stands, and the grin that stretches wide across his face when he finds me makes my belly flutter. I love that quick easy grin, reserved just for me.

The Lumberjacks rack up a big win for their first game in New York, Tate scoring two of their five goals. No hat trick for him tonight, but not for lack of trying. They got the win, and that's all that really counts when you're looking to make the play-offs again.

After the game, Alyson and I head back to the hotel together. "Feel like stopping at the bar for a drink before Zack and Tate get back?" she asks as we enter the lobby.

I consider, then decide against it. "Maybe another time?"

"Absolutely. I'm better off going to my room and getting comfy, anyway."

When we get to our floor, we say our goodnights.

I change into yoga pants and a soft t-shirt. Normally, I'd be naked, or sporting something sexually provocative, but I need at least the illusion of armour when I give Tate my news. Although the fact I'm dressed might give me away. Will he remember that he made me get dressed before he proposed?

As soon as I hear the sound of hockey players in the hallway, I turn off the television.

He walks through the door, shedding layers as he approaches me on the bed. Déjà vu wafts over me. How many times have we done this now? My life is not what I thought it would be. It's so much better.

"There's my babe. I'm so glad you're here. I missed you."

Wrapping me in his arms, he kisses me hungrily. I work at the buttons of his shirt and slide my hands along the hard, muscled planes of his chest. I love this man so much, I ache.

We come up for air, and he studies my face. His eyebrows knit slightly. "Is everything okay?"

"Of course." My heart beats fast, and my stomach is all jittery. I need to do this now before I pass out from nerves. "But I have news."

He shifts position so he's leaning back against the headboard, and pulls me into his lap. "Must be important for you to fly here last minute."

It's been a busy year for my company, and I haven't travelled with Tate as much as I did the year before that.

"It is." I climb off his lap and grab the small present I'd hidden under my pillow and hand it to him. I watch his face as he peels off the paper.

He pulls out the tiny knitted beaver hat. His face does the most amazing transformation as he holds it up and studies it.

"Pretty small," he says, his voice thick. "Holy shit, Sasha. Are you—"

"Yep. Took seven tests. I didn't believe the first six, but that last one convinced me." We weren't trying. We'd talked about it, though. After two years of just being the two of us, we talked about starting a family at the end of the season.

Now it looks like this baby might be born in the thick of it. Given his or her genetic material, I'd bet even money on Baby Nilsson being born on a Saturday night to a soundtrack of hockey anthems on the TV.

He grins. "Definitely important news. Hang on, you don't knit."

"No, but Ellie does. I told her three days ago and she knitted her little fingers off. But I swore her to secrecy, even from Gavin."

Tate laughs. "Since when do you think Ellie could keep a secret from her husband?"

"It could happen. There's a first time for everything." Ellie totally told Gavin. I knew she would, and we both know it was really okay.

"Ever the optimist." Slipping his hand behind my neck, he pulls us together and kisses me gently."One of the many things I love about you. Another is you're growing us a baby."

"You're happy?"

"Completely." He kisses me again, then pulls back a little. "It takes five to make a hockey team, you know."

"Hold on, Mr. My-Boys-Can-Swim, let's see how we do with this one before we start thinking about our own expansion team."

"Can we at least make it a hat trick?"

"You are incorrigible."

"Yes, and it's one of my more endearing qualities." Pushing me back onto the bed, he lifts my shirt and peppers my belly with tiny kisses. "It's hard to believe our baby is in here."

"Definitely there."

His head pops up. "How are you feeling? Are you sick?"

"Mostly tired."

"You can rest later. Right now, you are wearing too many clothes," he says, sliding his fingers under the waistband of my yoga pants and underwear. He peels them off, then kisses and nips his way up my legs, spreading them as he goes. I melt for him, my body going languid and warm as I watch his dark head dip between my thighs.

His warm breath teases my clit. "Tate," I gasp, lifting my hips in encouragement.

"Patience, tiger."

"Didn't anyone tell you, it's really mean to make a pregnant woman wait for her orgasm? In fact, it might be a rule. Yes, definitely a rule."

He chuckles against my inner thigh. "Rules were made to be bent. But the mother of my child can demand anything her gorgeous heart desires."

Thank you so much for reading Mr. Hat Trick! We hope you love Tate and Sasha as much as we do.

If this is the first time you've read one of our books, we have three more Frisky Beaver novels available! Visit our website at www.friskybeavers.com for all links.

Coming next year is the final novel in the Frisky Beavers series: Bull of the Woods.

**Jack:**
The last person I expect to see in an Ottawa dungeon is Addison Greer.

*Mine.*

She hasn't been that in four years, but I still remember how perfect it was between us.

**Addison:**
They call him the Bull of the Woods, because he made his first billion on lumber. Last I heard, he owned an NHL team in Vancouver, which is the main reason I avoid the west coast.

So when Jack Benton strolls back into my life at the point I finally decide to search for a new Master…

I'm not ready for him.

Not that I ever could be.

He was the only Dom to have my heart. And he broke it.

**Jack:**
I want a second chance.

And I always get what I want.

**THE RULES:**
* Itch-scratching only. No feelings allowed.
* No re-hashing the past.

Coming in 2018

~ Ainsley & Sadie

9 781926 527772